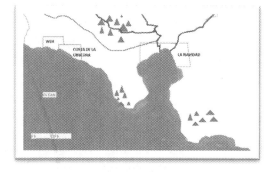

CORTESIA[1]

CORTESIA (Kor tay syah) is a small, extremely mountainous South American country. It is rich in mineral resources, and its land is among the most fertile in the world. Cortesia's population is approximately evenly mixed between Caucasians of Spanish descent and Indians. But, unlike in other Latin American countries, there has been very little mixing of the two racial groups. Cortesia (meaning "courtesy") was given this nickname that later became its official name by its Spanish Imperial Governor.

Cortesia is the least populous and, until recently, the most isolated country in South America. Because of the country's isolation, the

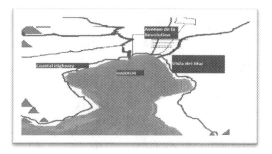

La Navidad

---

[1] Article written by Mariano Carrillo, Visiting Professor of History, Georgia State University

# FACTS IN BRIEF:

**Capital**: La Navidad

**Official Language:** Spanish

**Form of Government**: Republic (Oligarchical)

**Area:** 61,325 sq. mi. (155,490 km2); greatest distance—North-South = 136 mi. (219 km); East-West = 441 mi. (170km)

**Population:** Estimated 1989 population = 450,000. Distribution—62% rural, 38% urban. Density = 7.34 per square mile (289 km2). Estimated 1994 population = 600,000.

**Chief Products**: Agriculture—bananas, cocoa, coffee, corn, rice. Mining—antimony, bismuth, copper, gold, lead, tin, silver, zinc.

**National Anthem**: "Cortesia, La Carida" (Cortesia, the beloved)

**Money:** Basic unit—Libra

**Flag:** The flag of Cortesia features a silver background on to which there is a broad scarlet stripe running from the upper inner corner to the lower outer corner. Government offices and officials fly the flag with the State Seal in the upper and outer half of the flag. The silver stands for both the mineral richness of Cortesia and the strength of her people. The scarlet represents a willingness to shed blood for the Faith.

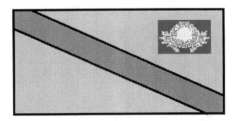

# THE
# INQUISITIVE
# YANQUI

BOB WILDMAN

ISBN: 978-1-4669-8984-9 (sc)
ISBN: 978-1-4669-8983-2 (e)

*Trafford rev. 04/18/2013*

 www.trafford.com

North America & international
toll-free: 1 888 232 4444 (USA & Canada)
phone: 250 383 6864 ♦ fax: 812 355 4082

# CHAPTER 1

# "IT'S A GOOD THING I TOOK SPANISH IN HIGH SCHOOL"

"**B**usiness or you in vacation, *Senor*?" the airport official asked.

"*Negocios, por favor, Senor*," Dave answered with a meek smile at the burly man behind the customs counter. His eyes strayed to the young, nervous soldier switching the machine gun from shoulder to shoulder in the corner. If the American was trying to hide being intimidated, he was doing a very poor job.

"What business?"

"I'm with Eastern Mining Industries, *Senor*. Here's my employee card." His hands trembled slightly as he removed the laminated paper from his wallet and handed it to the man in fatigues.

"How long you will be in our country?"

"I don't really know, actually. I'll just have to see how long it takes me to do what they want me to do."

"And what, please, do 'they' want you to do?"

"I look for mines . . . well, not actually holes in the ground, you might say. I'm not a geologist . . . I kind of look for them on paper . . ."

The uniformed man nodded his head in perplexity. "*Si*," he responded nonchalantly, as though this were the third or fourth arrival today who was in that line of work. "Is this address, 1605 Wilson Drive, White Plains, New York still *correcto?*"

"Yes, Sir."

"You realize, of course, *Senor*, that as an *extranjero*, a . . . foreigner, you will have to register at our Foreign Ministry."

"Understood," is all Dave could think to say as he yanked up his suitcase and walked toward the taxi stand.

The heat smacked him in the face as he got out from under the whirling fan that had cooled the surly guard. Dave was almost blinded by the tropical sun when he cleared the airport doors. Being in a foreign country always made him feel bigger than life, special as it were. He had grown up on James Bond books and movies, and the palm trees gently swaying in the wind put him in mind of his adopted soul brother, the suave British agent. "Dum'di-dum-dum . . . ," the James Bond theme rumbled through his head as his eyes searched for an available taxi. He straightened his black silk tie and adjusted the lapels on his brand new linen suit, bought especially for his arrival here in La Navidad. "Gee, I never did find one of those neat shirts with the rolled over cuffs like 007 wears," he thought sadly to himself.

"*La Catedral*," the driver announced as the taxi made its way past the city's central square. On the steps of the indicated rock pile Indians from the surrounding mountains had placed colorful blankets which became their shops for the vending of handmade goods. The clutter and seemingly random moving about of the people were very different from the apparent purposefulness of the inhabitants of US cities, he thought.

The hotel, thankfully, was located in the posh Vista del Mar section of the city, so there was a cooling breeze to greet him as Dave stepped from the two-decade old taxi. He wondered if the broken spots on the stucco walls were there for effect or from lack of upkeep. His childhood visits to Hollywood movie studios made him think that they were artificial. The place certainly looked picturesque behind the rows of bright, trembling flowers.

The tile-lined lobby was austere and spacious, palatial in fact. Dave laughed silently to himself. Had it not been for the plants and the skylight, it could almost have been a men's room in a train station! This effect was heightened by the sound of the fountain gurgling in the center of the huge space.

The desk clerk, as is customary, took his passport for "safe keeping" until his departure.

"Will Mrs. Robinson be joining you?"

"There is no Mrs. Robinson," Dave replied.

The clerk appeared not to understand whether or not a lady would appear later.

"*Soy soltero*," Dave explained.

The balding clerk seemed pleasantly surprised to be addressed in his own language by an American.

"It's a good thing I took Spanish in high school," Dave mumbled, mostly to himself.

"Ah, . . . in that case, one does not have to be alone here in La Navidad," the older man said with a knowing wink.

"That won't be necessary, but thank you for your concern," he answered, slightly embarrassed by the offer.

Eastern Mining's man in Cortesia threw his battered suitcase on the large bed as he entered the room. There'll be time to unpack later, he explained to himself in overcoming the compulsive need acquired in graduate school to take care of everything right away. He did, though, take pains to hang up his new white suit coat.

He had to settle for a good Mexican brandy called *El Presidente*. He sloshed some in a cocktail glass and walked out onto the balcony.

Dave watched the shadow of sunset move across the small adobe huts in the valley beneath him and up to the mansions overlooking La Navidad on the other side. It would be a pleasant evening for an after dinner stroll, he thought.

"*Senor?*"

Dave was startled, not knowing that someone had entered his room. The clerk from downstairs was standing by his bed.

"Will there be anything else?" He called out to the guest on the balcony.

"No . . . no thank you. I'm just fine."

# CHAPTER 2

## "WHERE COULD I GET A NEWSPAPER AROUND HERE?"

Not only did he not really mind shaving, but Dave had to admit that he kind of enjoyed it. It was refreshing and invigorating, a new beginning, sort of. The few times in his life he had worn a beard he had missed it. He carefully moped up the sink counter with a towel. Several women with whom he had "overnighted" had faulted him for leaving behind a "swampy mess," and he wanted to develop a better set of habits for future opportunities.

As he combed his hair, he was forced to notice that the proportion of gray was clearly and steadily increasing.

"Better than losing it," he consoled himself.

He selected a dark suit which he considered appropriate for calling at the Foreign Ministry. The red and black stripped tie, his favorite—his school colors, seemed to jump into his hands. A pocket handkerchief was inserted, and he was ready to go.

The Ministry was a massive Greek Revival building which would have made a good city hall for a large US town. But there weren't many city halls that were guarded by men with machine guns!

Not seeing the expected information booth, Dave approached the only unarmed individual he saw. He had to walk rapidly to catch up with the severely-cut woman's business suit which moved past him in the wearer's transit from one wing of the building to the other.

"*Perdoname, Senorita,*" he called ahead.

The trim figure turned smoothly on one of the short heels of her shiny black shoes.

"*Si, Senor.*"

"*Busco la oficina in que se puede . . . ,*" he began in explaining his need to register his presence and the nature of his work in Cortesia.

The woman turned her head inquiringly to one side as he spoke. A slight smile appeared on her lips which were lightly adorned with a pink gloss, the only cosmetic she appeared to be wearing. Her gigantic brown eyes widened noticeably through her heavy tortoise-shelled eyeglasses as she listened to his polite request for directions.

"Where are you from in the States?" she asked in letter-perfect English.

"New York, actually."

"I love that city. Somewhat bigger than La Navided, no?"

Dave nodded his agreement. He mumbled "*Gracias*" after she had carefully pointed him up the stairs to the office he sought.

Dave paused long enough to watch the tight bun into which the lady's black hair had been tied disappear down the hall to the right.

The visit to the office entailed nothing more than the completion of a three-page form, company name, immediate supervisors, that sort of thing. There wasn't even the usual interview with the officious functionary. As a matter of fact, the voluptuous dark-haired woman at the desk was totally disinterested in his attempts to make conversation with her.

Falling back on Plan Two, to try to find the lady who had earlier given him directions through the building, the American returned to the entrance hall and took the corridor to the right. The second time he had to explain to a guard who had challenged him that he was searching for the front door he gave up his quest and left the building.

The sun was so bright back out on the street that the back of his eyes literally ached. All the plain stucco house fronts Dave passed by affected him somehow, but he couldn't quite put his finger on what it meant to him.

A man in cut-off jeans approached him and held up to him a pair of sandals.

"*Barrato, Senor*, cheap."

"*No, gracias,*" he responded hurriedly. His wingtips did go better with his suit, after, all.

His mind returned to the emerging significance of the unadorned fronts of the middle-class houses of the city. He knew from having been in such homes that the plain entrance would lead the visitor into a lush, green central patio or atrium. This is the focus of the family's life. How different from the American system, he thought. We put our best furniture and paintings in the "front room." That way, people who come calling will be impressed with our affluence and culture. The family is left to huddle on the scarred, old pieces in the downstairs den. This, on reflection, certainly didn't make Dave feel superior.

This was Dave's third bar of the afternoon. He sure hoped that he found here what he was looking for. Three beers before sunset was a bit much.

As he took a sip of his not too cold beer, he heard what his ears had been searching for, English, loud English.

After allowing a few seconds to go by, Dave sauntered over to the booth in the corner. The three *gringos* were about half-way through their second pitcher of beer.

"You guys sound like home," he began.

"We're not Damn Yankees, like you," the small man in the checkered coat came back.

"Aw, we're all *Yanquis* here," another member of the group interjected in support of Dave's respectability.

"Well, if we're goin' to be slummin', hell, you might as well sit down."

The theme of the conversation was summarized and put forward by the gray-headed man Mark. "What in God's name are you doing in this bug-infested oven which is miles away from nowhere?"

For his own part, Dave explained about his paper prospecting.

"Most of us are in minerals in one way or another." The man speaking was the youngest and most athletic-looking of the group. "Jim and I are gold hunters. And Mark's a . . . What the hell are you, Mark? . . . A journalist, that's what the Ole Boy is, a writer."

"I'm a Soldier of Fortune," Gray-Hair retorted in mock indignation. "Really, though, I'm just a 'stringer,' as they say. I file a report whenever something comes down here in Hernandoland. Doesn't happen all that often, so I've taken to drinking and skirt-chasing . . . out of boredom."

"Such modesty," Sam quipped.

"He's got a lot to be modest about," Jim chimed in.

The three were actually most generous in sharing with Dave what they had learned about the hot spots in La Navidad.

Jim broke the hedonistic chain of conversation by asking, "What kinds of properties are you interested in?"

"All kinds, as a matter of fact. Eastern is a holding company for a number of mining outfits."

"Can't say that I've heard of it."

"New group. Anyhow, I won't know what I'm looking for until I find it. Uh, anyway, go on about the hot spots around here, please."

After a quite detailed and at times graphic response, Sam ordered another pitcher. As Sam and Jim fell upon it, Mark rose.

"I'm getting a bit hungry, fellows. Think I'll toddle off to eat."

There were a few comments about his being a "party pooper."

"Mind if I join you?" Dave asked as he sprang to his feet and threw a few *libras* on the table.

The chicken was outstanding at the small out-of-the way bar. They washed it down with a tumbler of white wine produced in the surrounding hills.

"It's a bit 'raw' yet," Dave commented, holding his glass up to the light. "But if they take a little care, I'd say they have a great future with their Chardonnay."

"Riesling," the older man corrected.

Dave was embarrassed. How could he confuse the greatest German grape with the grape that forms the basis for France's famous Chablis? 007 would never have made that gaffe, he admitted and lamented.

Hiding his chagrin, he addressed his older companion, "I'm amazed by your knowledge. You've really been around, as they say. Yes, you're the guy I've been wanting to talk to, a true Renaissance Man."

"Ahhh . . . ," Mark said with an overly dramatic wave of his hand and downcast eyes. "You see," I've always lived by my wits, so my work has been pretty much 'catch what catch can'. Bout ten years ago I landed a contract to do a piece on fine wines for *Preferred Living*. I got to tour, on an expense account, the great vineyards of Europe."

"Wow."

"My favorite was Bordeaux. In their classier chateaux, they plant rosebushes at the end of each row of vines. First rate, nothing but the best." The self-satisfied grin faded from his face, and Mark leaned toward Dave's stool. "Did you know," he whispered, "that a lot of the rich *vignerones* have themselves buried in their fields? Yeah, to fertilize the grapes. Now that's what I call throwing yourself into your work!"

Back on the street they had to dodge the children playing in their efforts to hold onto the fading day in the tropical sunset. Dave was impressed by how much better dressed the children were than their parents.

"I'll bet this is the kind of place where who you know has a lot to do with how much you can get accomplished," Dave offered while kicking a soccer ball back to the boys across the street.

"You, my boy, have a gift for understatement. Why, Hell, this is Hazzard County *en espanol.*"

Dave chuckled at the allusion to the corny comedy series of a few years back. It was even funnier coming from someone who was obviously from that part of the country.

"I've got some pretty good connections for an old drunk. Why, I could show you around. Might help you get some 'brownie points' with the Big Boys in the Big Apple," Mark intoned, raising his eyes mockingly toward the heavens.

Later in the evening, his newly purchased basket held tenderly under his arm, the American made his way carefully through the maze of flapping blankets being folded for the night. He strode past a trim Army major.

"*Buenos noches.*"

"Good evening, Sir," came the military man's reply.

Dave smiled at the officer, who was a man of about his own age. The Major stopped, obviously wishing to converse with Dave.

"You see," the uniformed man continued, "I went to military school in your country."

"Really, where?"

"Carolina Military College," he replied with a theatrically swollen chest.

"Oh, a friend of mine went there. The Junior West Point of the South."

"That's it! Arturo Rodriguez de la Castille, Signal Corps of the Republic of Cortesia, *a sus ordenes, Senor*."

After the completion of the introductions, Dave followed the surprisingly fair-skinned Latin on down the street.

"On your way home, Major?" he inquired nonchalantly.

"If only it were so," he said wistfully. "My family is in Costa de la Obscura, about three hundred fifty kilometers to the northwest."

Dave recognized the town's name as the location of Cortesia's military training center. Their elite officers were stationed there. He had already observed the scroll surrounded by an oak leaf cluster on de la Castille's epaulets, which denoted his assignment to Costa de la Obscura.

"Do you have a large family?" Dave inquired.

"Just Marta and the two little ones; a boy and a girl—an All American Family, you would say. But quite small by our standards. We like to travel, have fiestas, so . . ."

"I hope you'll get home soon."

"Oh, I'm only here for a few weeks . . . Uh, this, *mi amigo*, is where Father San Luis wrote the Declaration of Independence from *Espana*. He was our Thomas Jefferson, you might say. Or was it John Adams?"

"Jefferson, . . . I think." Dave was startled to see that the humble dwelling to which the Major had pointed was now equipped with a diaper-laden clothesline stretching from one of its windows to an electric pole on the street. He figured to himself that they must have cut the Park Service budget!

The two men really seemed to hit it off, so they exchanged business cards. They both made the grand gesture of penciling in the telephone numbers of their temporary residences and promising to assist each other in any way possible.

"Two blocks this way is an excellent café specializing in our grain-fed Cortesian beef," the officer stated, pointing across his chest with a brass-tipped swagger stick.

"*Gracias* . . . By the way, where could I get a newspaper around here?"

Dave parted from the Major and walked a block to the right where, as predicted, he found the newsstand. He picked up and paid for a copy of the "morning paper" which, he had been told, never hit the streets until mid-afternoon. Placing the paper under his left arm and transferring the basket he had purchased earlier to his right hand, he then returned to the street along which he and Major de la Castille had strolled, only this time going in the opposite direction.

He snapped his fingers as he walked away from the bed in his hotel room. He would need his glasses to go through the paper, and it was hard for him to get into the habit of taking them. He returned to the bed and lifted the black case from the left breast pocket of the suit coat he had just dumped there. Tossing the case back on the coat, he slumped into the love seat in front of the picture window with newspaper in hand.

The American opened the 24-page paper with a flapping motion. He began scanning the columns.

"Gorbachov on Way Out."

"Bush to Dump Quail."

Dave's eyes searched on.

"Foreign Ministry Announces Assignments." He brought the paper nearer for a detailed inspection of this article.

*Our beloved Minister of External Affairs, The*
*Count Guillermo de Diaz y Munoz, has caused to*
*be posted the international assignments of the most*
*recent graduates of Cortesia's Foreign Service*
*Corp School. These billets include duties for some*
*of the sons and daughters of the First Families of*
*our beloved Motherland.*

*Belgrade*
*Juan Antonio Hernandez y Perez*
*Havana*
*Roberto Guillermo Rodriguez y Portuando*
*Constantia Anna Piedra y de la Madrid*
*Antonio Rafael Mendoza y Alfonso*
*Paris*
*Guillermo Juan Diaz de la Castille*

Dave peeled the two pages containing this article off from the main body of the newspaper and placed them carefully to one side. The last page contained the *Noticias de Deportes.* The Sports Page, he sighed out loud to himself. The lead article was, "Cuba's National Soccer Team Scheduled for Exhibition Game in La Navidad." This page was added to his neat pile of newsprint.

The American stood up and stretched. It had taken him over an hour to go through the diminutive newspaper.

He grabbed the box the clerk had given him downstairs. He lined the bottom with the bulk of *La Luz de La Navidad* and placed the small basket on top. The set aside pages were cautiously wadded up and placed in the basket, and parts of other sections were pulled out and draped over this evening's purchase. A tremendous amount of butcher's paper was required in wrapping the box. Dave was once fired from his job as a Christmas gift-wrapper. Using a felt-tipped pen, he wrote on the box's front:

> Mrs. Cynthia I. Ainsworth
> 1025 Dulles Avenue
> Alexandria, Virginia 22301

Early the next morning everyone greeted Major de la Castille deferentially as he entered the War Ministry. Of course, all officers get saluted, Sired and snapped to attention for, but de la Castille was somehow a cut above the rest. He was an aristocrat who had turned his back on a life of self-indulgence, "a man with a mission who is on his way up," as the paper had called him after his success in commanding the defense against a recent border incursion.

It was 0700 hours exactly, the Major observed as he settled into the high-backed chair in the largely bare office.

Seeing none of the blue, urgent message sheets on the wooden expanse in front of him, he picked up the phone and dialed his personal access number plus the three letter code "USA."

"Major Blanco, Sir."

"de la Castille here," he began in very proper Spanish. *"En que puedo servile?"*

"I need you to check out a company and a man for me. The firm is Eastern Mining Industries, and the man is one . . ."

Two miles away, within the sound of the surf pounding against the rocks, the phone rang.

"Mark Stephens," identified the tremulous and breathless voice of the caller on the other end of the line.

"Good morning," Dave answered, immediately identifying in his own head the caller as—possible contact, claims connections, trying to hold on to fading youth, knowledgeable but needy.

"You know, Old Boy, I said I would show you around. Well, I'm on the list for a big 'Do' Friday evening. Black tie and all that. Want to go?"

"You bet!"

"The Military Attache' in Washington," announced the sergeant.

"de la Castille," he said crisply into the phone's mouthpiece.

"Eastern Mining Industries not only exists, but it's been most active of late. The company purchased two small West Virginia mines just yesterday. No one by the name of William Robinson is on their list of officers, but I called the number listed in their prospectus, and the lady who answered said that Mr. Robinson was away 'on assignment' and couldn't be contacted directly. She said that she could, though, get a message to him."

"*Gracias*. One can't be too careful."

"Of course not, Sir."

CHAPTER **3**

# "IT'S RIESLING, IF I'M NOT MISTAKEN"

"**M**oon River," Dave thought to himself. His part-time job at a local radio station during his high school days had made him an ideal candidate for "Name That Tune." Too bad the show had gone off the air before he had had a crack at it. It may, after all, have helped John Glenn get off the ground, both figuratively and literally. The band seemed to be alternating between North American and Latin tunes. He sang to himself the words to "*Cielito Lindo*" he had been taught by his Columbian girlfriend some years ago.

The scene he surveyed was comically elegant. The tuxedos and evening dresses were all pretty much standard issue. But many of the men and some of the ladies wore sashes with Cortesia's colors, scarlet and silver. Medals adorned the chests of some of the older men. There was a bit of bowing, and one of the elderly gentlemen even affected a monocle. "Gilbert and Sullivan have nothing on this place," he concluded.

Dave felt a tug at his elbow. "Quit gawking, it's not polite, Old Boy." Mark was somewhere between half and three-quarters lit. "Now, there's an old friend of Ole Mark's . . . ," he rambled on.

It took no small amount of agility to dodge the dancing couples he was drug past.

"His Excellency, The Minister of the Interior," Mark announced, motioning with his hand toward a slight mustached man in tails and a sash.

"*El gusto es mio*," the man said with more polite formality than friendliness.

"*Senor*, I read in yesterday's paper about your proposal for a series of wildlife preserves throughout Cortesia. The one up toward Costa de la Obscura seemed the most majestic, from all I could tell," Dave said to open the conversation.

"*Ah, si*. There are some exotic parrots there found nowhere else on Earth. Perhaps I could arrange a visit for you."

"I would be most honored, Sir."

"Good evening, Elena," Mark greeted the shapely brunette. The lady in question was wearing a twilight gray evening gown which left one shoulder discretely bare. Her deep brown eyes were hypnotically alluring as her long eyelashes moved up and down in front of them. Her hair bounced against her long neck as she turned her head to devote her attention to one man and then to the other. Largish lips were painted in deep red, while her use of rouge was restrained. The perfume was distinctive. Dave recognized it as expensive but could not, at the moment and with the Cognac he had consumed, recall its name.

"Oh, Mark," she began, "I was really fascinated by your story on the Native Peoples of Bolivia. Your summary of their creation stories was particularly interesting to me."

"Might ruffle a few feathers over on Holy Row."

"I seriously doubt that His Eminence has read your article or anything else recently, for that matter."

"It's true, it's true," Mark nodded in agreement, taking advantage of the opportunity to peer down the front of Elena's dress. "You're such a flatterer, my Dear Elena," he gushed.

"Not at all," she shot back. "I am an admirer."

"Elena here runs the Foreign Ministry," Mark stated conspiratorially to Dave after he had introduced him to the young lady as Bill Robinson of Eastern Mining. "So if there's any little country you want rubbed, she's the gal to see."

"I am merely an aide to the Minister," she said, tilting her head to one side and opening and shutting her enormous brown eyes rapidly. "I show out-of-town visitors the city. Glamorous work perhaps, but not exciting."

"I'm not exactly cabinet rank, but might I qualify for the program?" Dave inquired tentatively.

"But of course, *Senor*. As an overseas representative of a major corporation, you most certainly do. Monday, perhaps, would be good for me. Can you come to the Ministry? My office is 116. Shall we say mid-morning?"

"I'll be there with bells on."

After exchanging business cards, she continued, "I hope you approve of our country's wine," she said, shifting the conversation away from work and onto a more festive topic.

"It's Riesling, if I'm not mistaken."

"The boy's a regular connoisseur," Mark stated with paternal pride.

Room 116 was on the first floor on the right down a long side corridor in the Foreign Ministry. Absolutely no one stopped him or asked for any identification at all. Beautiful color paintings of scenes from around Cortesia adorned the office walls. There were waterfalls, ancient pyramids and coastal scenes, among others.

Seated at the desk was the business-suited lady in the dark-rimmed eyeglasses.

"I'm here to see Elena de la Madrid, please," he stated in a soft, polite voice.

Removing her glasses, she looked up at him and said, "I'm Elena, Mr. Robinson."

Dave was taken aback. "I didn't recognize you," he stammered.

"I didn't put it all together that you had been here last week until later myself," she admitted. "Ready for the Grand Tour?"

"Sure," he answered enthusiastically as she preceded him through the office door.

It was incredibly cool in the Cathedral. The walls were, at a minimum, five feet thick.

"Our old rulers, the Spanish Viceroys, were kind enough to construct for us all of our truly imposing buildings. There's this cathedral, the Royal, now National Palace and the Presidio. This cathedral is interesting in that while all of the other cathedrals in the world have had their Bishop's Chairs taken out, Cardinal Cortez refused to have his removed. He sits on his throne up there every Sunday that his failing health permits."

"Curious that cathedrals don't have 'cathedras' any more," Dave said with knowing irony.

"Are you Catholic?"

"Close, you might say. Episcopalian."

"Our back door neighbors."

He nodded in reluctant agreement that that description wasn't totally inaccurate.

The black Jaguar purred past the little adobe house Dave had been shown by Major de la Castille.

"Our shrines are neither so old or, it is a pity to say, so well preserved as yours," Elena said in continuing what had been both a knowledgeable and entertaining narrative. "You see, we were the last of the Latin American countries to break away from Spain. Accordingly, we're rather the most traditional, you might say. We still have a nobility. They don't actually rule us anymore, but they do have a place of special honor here in Cortesia. We go so far as to even stress the purity of our Spanish."

"I thought I detected a hint of Castillian."

"Thank you for noticing. So many of your countrymen return to the States telling everyone we lisp!"

They were still chuckling over the language thing as Elena pulled onto the Western Coastal Highway. She handled the car delicately and well. The road was little more than a ledge between a rocky cliff and a shear drop-off to the sea. She maneuvered the vehicle with seeming ease. There were no sudden twists of the steering wheel, no squealing of tires. It was like a Sunday drive, except that Dave had to acknowledge to himself that she had covered more road then he could have done under these conditions in the same amount to time.

Had it not been for the palm trees, the road could have been Highway One in northern California. Of course, there was also that pattern in the water of shades of blue and green that he had only seen before in the Caribbean. Somewhat confusing, perhaps, but Dave figured he could adjust!

That outcropping of rock would never, he thought, have been left there by a state highway department. It was postcard perfect, though. And the best part was that Elena missed hitting it!

Just beyond the finger of rock, the skillful driver took a sharp turn into what seemed to Dave, from outward appearances, to be a Western roadhouse. It was in the ubiquitous stucco and adorned with cactus on both sides of the walkway.

"The owner is a good friend of mine," Elena announced somewhat mysteriously.

They were greeted by a portly man with a checkered apron tucked into his pants.

"Dona Elena, como estas?" he greeted her with a broad smile.

"Well, don Ramon," she replied briefly, shifting the conversation to the northern language. "This is our new friend, William Robinson."

"Much gusto, don Guillermo," was the formal greeting from the proprietor of Ray's American Hideaway and Grill. "What brings you to our tropical paradise?"

"Mining."

"Rat-a-tat-tat," he said loudly, shaking his fleshy hands as though holding an air hammer.

"Not exactly," Dave said, half modestly and half mockingly.

Ramon shrugged, neither understanding nor really wishing to understand. He led them through his deserted watering hole to a choice table out on the balcony.

"Three-fifteen, that's after five in, how you say it, The Big Apple, no? How about a Margarita?"

Not protesting that, actually, the west coast of South America and the east coast of North America are in the same time zone, Dave shot back, "I'm ready!" He was not totally immune to the strain of the kind of work he was in.

As though to confirm their off-duty status, Elena's right hand delicately grasped the ear-piece of her black eyeglasses, removing them. Her left hand simultaneously went upward to remove the band around the bun in her raven hair, and it fell, Niagara-like, into a casual style.

Dave's eyes widened in appreciation of the metamorphosis.

Elena laughed softly. This was obviously a repeat performance.

"You appear to have an alter-ego," Dave said, trying to cover-up his all too obvious and not so "cool" impressed amazement at the transformation.

"Yes, I'm just not sure which is alter and which is ego . . . . Well, now that the work day is over, I'd really enjoy hearing more about you."

"Oh, I'm sure you're much more interesting."

"You'll be disappointed."

"Try me."

"*Pues* . . . , uh, let's see," she began in an uncertain voice the American had not so far heard from the confident and refined young lady. The drinks had just arrived, and she took a sip, clearly appreciating the cocktail's coolness. "I was born not so far from here. My father was Army Chief of Staff. He retired five years ago, and he and his new wife have moved to Alaska."

"Alaska?"

"Yes, it develops that during all those years Father detested the heat!"

He allowed his eyes to rest briefly on her parted lips, and then he gazed out to sea. The waves broke dramatically on the rocks. A rainbow had appeared in the cove off to the right. He was grateful for the salty breeze.

"I went to church schools, mostly," she continued, drawing Dave's attention back to an earlier life. "I once thought of becoming a nun!"

"That would have been a waste."

"That was only when I was a very young girl. I now realize that wearing black all the time would be so tedious!"

"I would think so. You impress me as a lady who likes a change now and then."

"How observant of you, kind *Senor*."

The charming young woman went on to tell of her childhood horseback riding and her father's pride in the dressage competitions she had won. She had been sent to a fashionable girl's school in New England and then on to a Spanish university.

Returning to Cortesia, she took post-graduate courses in international relations at the Royal University of Cortesia and passed the civil service exam to get the position with the Foreign Ministry. In taking this career route, she had passed up the safe and certain advantages in promotions to which her family connections would have entitled her.

"I enjoy studying other cultures. And I love to travel!"

"So do I," Dave allowed to slip out in a rare moment of self-revelation. "But, tell me, wouldn't you rather an overseas assignment than staying here . . . uh, at home, to you?"

"Oh, I've had several outside stations. But now I have something better. It's an unusual month when I don't spend a few days in another capital, usually one where 'the action is,' as the girls used to say at Mrs. Smith's."

"Do you go with your boss on his missions?"

"That's right. We just got back from Havana."

"Fascinating," Dave said as though just trying to keep the conversation going.

"Yes, it was actually, you know, to see how the people are faring under their . . . uh, new system."

"Well, I've spent years looking down into the ground instead of up, so I don't know much about politics."

"You have to, Bill, understand the historical context in which political events take place. Otherwise one can never appreciate how they're viewed by the people. You see, you might go to a country like England . . . Great Britain, I should say, and your reaction is, 'My, what a wonderful place . . .'"

"They can afford all those old castles."

"Yes," she responded tolerantly. Continuing, Elena said, "But things are so expensive there that people experience conditions as having gotten worse over the years. Their standard of living has declined."

"So . . . psychologically . . . they're worse off; so they're unhappy."

"Exactly. Well, you know, somewhat the reverse seems to be occurring with the Cubans. They don't have so much now, of course. But the poorer people, at least, can recall a time when things were so much worse for them."

"Gosh," Dave responded, "I thought things were great before Castro. I mean, a Cuban friend of mine said the country was so rich that even middle class families could afford servants." He paused and chuckled, obviously embarrassed by what he had said.

"Well," the lady continued, "that's just my point. There may, in actuality, be a smaller pie to go around, but it tends to be distributed more evenly now."

Dave then changed the topic of conversation to the seasons in Cortesia. It developed that there was little variation over the year owing to the country's closeness to the Equator. There was, though, more rain in what would be winter farther north.

It was a beautiful evening with a long twilight as Elena drove Dave to his hotel, the Hernando Cortez. He was made somewhat uncomfortable by the fact that their day together, while technically an official tour, had turned out to have some of the elements of a date. He didn't really know what the appropriate note to end it on might be. He contented himself with simply getting out of the car and giving her the slight bow he had seen Latin American men employ in salutes to the gentler sex.

"I enjoyed our conversation very much, *Sinorita.* Might we continue it over lunch some day?"

"But of course, Bill. Call me at my office at the Ministry."

The American fairly bounced up the steps to his room. He had found what he was looking for . . . he thought.

*Dear Mom and Dad,*

*This is a beautiful country. I had a chance to take a drive along the Coastal Highway southwest of the city today. You would have enjoyed it, particularly the colorful tropical flowers. Perhaps I'll be here long enough for you to come for a visit.*

*I made the trip in the company of a most delightful young lady named Elena de la Madrid. I have to admit that she really took me for the drive as part of her job at the Foreign Ministry, but she has consented to a social lunch with me at some time in the future. I'm sure you'd like her. She's done a lot of traveling and is a most interesting person.*

*This evening Elena was telling me about her recent trip to Havana. She has a different slant on what's taken place there than you usually hear. I hope to have an opportunity to talk with her more about this.*

*I hope that Uncle Albert has recovered fully from his vascular surgery.*

*I'll write again soon. I'll be at this hotel, which is very pleasant, for the foreseeable future, so you can write me directly here instead of having to go through the company.*

*Love,*
*Billy*

Dave carefully folded the letter and placed it in one of the expensively embossed hotel envelopes.

The message light was blinking when Dave returned to his room at mid-morning the next day. Upon calling the front desk, he was informed that Sir Humberto Portillo wished him to phone.

"Who?"

"Sir Humberto is our Minister of the Interior, *Senor*,"

"Of course, excuse me, please."

Getting in touch with the Minister was surprisingly quick and easy.

"Tomorrow, *Senor Robinson*, my staff and I shall be traveling to the . . . how you say . . . proposed wildlife preserve at Coast de la Obscura. Would you care to join us?"

"It would be a great honor, Your Excellency."

"You may then consider it arranged. Please meet us at the Government Gate at La Navidad International *a las nueve*, at nine o'clock in the morning."

"I'll be there, Excellency, *muchos gracias*."

"*De nada, Senor Robinson*."

"Things are looking up for Eastern Mining and, not just incidentally, for Ole Dave," he decided cheerfully.

He figured he might as well take advantage of being on a roll by going ahead and placing his next important call.

"*Elena de la Madrid, por favor*," he asked the switchboard operator at the Foreign Ministry.

"*Soy Elena*," came the strikingly informal answer through the phone.

They had a reasonably superficial conversation which focused on the recent cool weather and the Prime Minister's surgery. Both agreed that he had bounced back remarkably quickly for a man his age.

Friday at 12:30 was, it developed, a mutually convenient time for lunch.

The Leer jet was gray with scarlet trim, appropriately. As soon as all passengers were aboard, the sleek plane taxied to the head of the runway. No waiting. "How convenient," Dave thought.

They passed over miles of rain forest with no signs of civilization or even development.

"The Treasure of Cortesia," the Minister said to Dave, pointing out the window.

Dave smiled knowingly, although he wasn't sure exactly which of the many resources His Excellency was referring to.

Less than forty minutes from takeoff, the small posh jet was making its decent. The landing was perfect, not a single bounce. The Spartan wooden buildings and olive drab vehicles he could see out the window showed Dave clearly that they had touched down at a military installation. It could only be one place, he thought, allowing himself a moment of self-satisfaction.

The Minster preceded the group down the ramp of the plane. He was saluted by a young uniformed man.

Dave tried to be very subtle in his looking around as they were led into the Flight Control Building. His peripheral vision was able to catch a different flag flapping behind a barbed wire fence on the other side of the runway. It looked like the Puerto Rican flag, but the colors were reversed. Yes, he concluded, that's the flag of Cuba.

It was hard to believe, but it was true. He stood at that moment at the very heart of Cortesia's military complex.

He and the other members of the group sat in a drawing room which was richly appointed in what he recognized as a generally Victorian style. "Unusual military furnishings," he thought wryly to himself. They sipped deliciously rich coffee while the Minister was off for a courtesy call on his colleague, the Minister for War and Security.

About an hour later, the entire group was back on the tarmac for a brief helicopter ride into the nearby jungle. During the flight, Dave noticed that the instructions on the emergency handle were in the Cyrillic alphabet. The craft, quite obviously, was "from Russia with love."

They touched down in a clearing which showed signs of having been utilized as a heliport many times in the past. The party could hear the sounds of a waterfall growing ever louder as they moved along the well-worn path deeper into the jungle.

Dave had at times in his life flattered himself into thinking that he had seen everything. Nothing, though, had prepared him for the sight they beheld as the group arrived at the source of the gurgling and wishing sounds. He had to look again to make certain that it was really there. It was! A semi-formal garden! The flowers were not in perfect rows, nor were they rigidly divided into varieties. But they were certainly viewing the work of an expert landscape gardener.

Exotic birds in their beautiful plumage strutted nonchalantly along the garden paths. They pecked at the ground every so often. They, obviously, were provisioned, he thought. That's why they were so willing and eager to put themselves on display like this. Directly in front of the falls was a long table draped in a white cloth. Several men in chef's hats, the floppy type, hovered around the table. "I would have gone into the jungle sooner if I had known it was going to be like this," the American said under his breath, to the amusement of the staff aide standing beside him.

"Ladies and Gentlemen," the Minister began, obviously reveling in his role as Master of Ceremonies. "We welcome you to what will soon become our country's first wildlife preserve. We are pleased to have with us Dr. Alberto Suarez, who is an internationally known ornithologist and holds the San Luis Chair of Biology at our Royal University. The Doctor expressed to me on the plane coming up his concern that his presentation might be 'too dry.' I think he is being modest because he has a well-earned reputation for being both an excellent and entertaining speaker. But just in case, we are serving Margaritas during his lecture! Dr. Suarez . . ."

The group members sipped their drinks as the Professor droned on about the uniqueness of the wildlife in this part of the coast of northwestern Cortesia. It wasn't that Dave found the lecture uninteresting. In fact, the descriptions of some of the birds were fascinating. But old habits kept his mind working on several levels at once. "Why," he wondered, "were these paths so well traveled? Could there really be that many visitors to a soon-to-be national wildlife refuge?"

The professor was talking about a bird that kept her eggs inside her for an unusually long time after fertilization. The American was actually and truly interested to learn that this species had a remarkably low chick mortality rate. "Might this," Dr. Suarez asked rhetorically, "have been an early, failed attempt at live-bearing?" Dave thought he could hear some sounds off in the jungle. Straining his ears as much as he could without, hopefully, making it noticeable, he could still not make out exactly what they were. He was, though, left with the impression that they were metallic in nature.

A meal of Beef Bourguignon followed the scholarly but, thankfully, joke-punctuated lecture. The red wine that was so courteously served was even better than the Riesling he had sampled days before. "It made sense," Dave concluded, "that a warm county like this would excel with the reds."

On the way back to the clearing Dave spotted a smaller path off to the right. He shouldn't have been surprised at what he saw when he glanced furtively down it—camouflaged netting lying at the base of a tree in a bend of the footpath.

He was at something of a loss as to what to do next. He had already read all the plaques under the statues in the main hall in the Foreign Ministry.

"Sorry to keep you," came the increasingly familiar voice.

"Oh, quite all right. I know you're busy."

"Well, I didn't know I was going to be this busy. But, you see, our friends . . ."

Several men wearing fatigues stomped by. Dave inquired no further into the matter of Elena's tardiness.

Elena directed Dave to a seaside café, very Continental, down the hill from the Ministry. The seafood salad was lovely, and the Chardonnay complimented it nicely. Yes, it was Chardonnay this time. Commander Bond would have been proud of him! Apparently, one glass of wine with lunch was not inconsistent with being "on duty" for the lady.

# CHAPTER 4

# "EN QUE DIRECTION ES LA NAVIDAD?"

The little Fiat chugged up the steep mountain grade. It sure was a lot cooler here than down along the coast. But it was just as lush and green. On the seat beside him was a pile of maps showing directions to mining properties. He had visited five of the sites. Of course, he had also gotten lost a number of times.

As a matter of fact, he appeared to be "lost" just now. He was approaching a guard post, complete with a striped barricade which had been lowered across the road in front of him. He clearly had come to the Frontier.

The young soldier at the crossing seemed surprised to see him. "They probably don't get many European sports cars up here," he concluded to himself with some degree of amusement.

"*Buenos tardes, Senor. A donde va?*"

"It seems that I'm lost . . . it seems," he stammered.

"Lost . . . uh, ah *perdido*."

"Yes, *si, si, perdido*."

"Ah, I study English in school," the corporal said very slowly. "Where you go?"

Dave relaxed in the knowledge that he would not be facing an interrogation. "*En que direction es La Navidad?*"

The young man pointed back in the direction from which the American had just come. "*Alli, a la izquierda. Tres cientos y cincuenta kilometros.*"

Dave, as a matter of fact, had no difficulty whatever in finding the road to which the corporal had directed him. He saw it clearly as he had zoomed past it.

He came to a roadhouse several miles on down. There were chicks and pigs and other farm animals milling about in front of the stucco building.

A gray tabby cat walked down the bar and eyed him inquisitively as he seated himself on an end stool. When his beer arrived, the old cat walked away, seemingly disgusted by the fact that his new friend hadn't ordered anything with milk in it.

There were seven young men at the bar, all with crew cuts. Dave was surprised this time by his good fortune. He had to admit that he had seen no signs whatever of a military installation in the area.

He looked into his beer as though reminiscing about an old flame, but he was making great efforts to follow the young men's conversation. Their Spanish was quite correct, as was everyone's in this country. There was, though, something different about these youngsters' speech, but he couldn't quite put his finger on it. Then it came to him. One spoke of driving his "*maquina*" to the nearest town in an effort to meet young ladies. Dave knew of only one people who used the Spanish word for "machine" for contrivances ranging all the way from a sewing machine to an automobile. These young fellows were Cubans.

He sipped his beer and listened to them talk. This was not an easy task as it meant scanning and trying to keep up with four to six conversations, all without being able to look at the speakers. When one of the talkers fell into what seemed to be a protracted discussion of some topic related to matters other than military assignments, geography or politics, like sports, he would move on to the next group.

He did learn a few things. One of the boys had spent Christmas here. This seemed to make him something of a long-timer in that the others asked him questions about what it had been like. He didn't exactly describe it as a highlight of his life!

Another discussion centered on the escapades two of them had shared during their first leave while in some kind of training in Camaguey. Dave happened to know that was where the Cuban Artillery School was located.

He got back to his room at the local inn just as the sun was setting. He was thankful that it was cool enough that he didn't have to turn on the fan over the bed. The antique was perched up there so precariously that he feared that at any moment it would fall down on him. Actually turning the contraption on, he figured, would drive it through some part of his body with great force.

Dave was cheered by the fact that it was once again "El Persidente Time." In addition to the brandy, he extracted from his bag a big book map of Cortesia.

He located the bar he had visited. It was on Plate L. It was in Section D-6.

Another sip of brandy, and it was time for a letter to "Momma." Embedded in his scrawl were the following words:

> *Please give my regards to Larry. Sure hope he's enjoying his new job in Des Moines. Guess he's been there about six months by now, so I suppose he's got some idea of whether or not it's going to work out. I know that selling cars is a pretty tough way to make a living. Of course, I don't know how strong the competition is.*

Dawn's early light found Dave back at the roadhouse, not for a beer this time, but rather to travel up the road about a quarter of a mile farther away from the Frontier. There were some mining properties down there, and the Cortesia representative had decided that it was very much in Eastern's interests that they be looked at closely.

He was thankful that he had brought along a sweater. It got cool in the tropics if you got up early enough where it was high enough.

Plat in hand, he walked the perimeter of the designated property. He occasionally stooped down to get a handful of soil. He allowed it to slip through his fingers as he pretended to examine it minutely. He found this to be an amusing affectation. After all, all dirt looked pretty much the same to Dave Wilkinson.

He glanced around the area frequently. But he made a concerted effort to spend at least as much time looking at the property as he did around it.

Visually exploring the surrounding area, he spotted some kind of building about a hundred yards beyond the boundary of the field. He could sure have used a pair of binoculars, but that would have been a bit obvious. His questions about the structure were soon answered, however, and with only the naked eye. Several two-legged, feathered creatures strutted out the door. It was a large hen house!

There was another "potential mine" about a mile farther down the road. It received a similar dose of the North American's attention.

Running beside this site was a chain-linked fence topped with barbed wire. Dave thought it a bit elaborate for your average substance farmer! He decided that this land was of great interest to his firm.

Returning to the car, he got out a number of plastic bags and a small spade. He dug a little hole in each corner of the property and put a cup or so of soil in a baggie from each dig. During this process his attention was diverted by a clicking sound. Looking through the massive fence, he saw two soldiers walking the inside perimeter. The sound he had heard was their canteens jostling on their hips.

Dave looked up, smiled and waved at the young men. His presence would definitely be noted, and he might as well demonstrate his lack of concern about this fact. The two khaki-clad men appeared somewhat disconcerted by the unexpected and informal greeting. Instinctively, they moved their hands up toward the shoulder straps by which they carried their machine guns, but, to Dave's relief, the monstrous weapons did not move from their heavenly-pointed positions on the youths' backs.

He realized, strange though it may seem, that the wisest course for him to take was to remain right where he was. No sense annoying them by making them look for him! He could always dig a few more holes. But there must be some point at which that would be overdone. He just didn't know what that point was!

As he milled around, hopefully looking busy, he engaged in one of his most frequent activities, trying to extrapolate from what he had observed. In other words, given what he knew, of what other things could he be reasonably certain? Let's see . . . the substantial nature of the fence and the two man patrol suggested to him that the installation was of some importance and significance. The fact that the perimeter guards found it necessary to carry canteens appeared to make it likely, he reasoned, that they had a substantial area to cover. So the place, whatever it was, must be pretty big. Yeah, whatever it was. He didn't know what they were doing there. But beyond that . . .

The entirely flappable Dave was not the least bit surprised by the sound of a jeep barreling up the road toward his position. "Mining," he said to himself. "Get your mind back on mining".

The driver brought the vehicle to a smooth halt. He took his hands off the wheel, keeping his eyes all the while trained directly on Dave. The passenger stepped briskly out of the jeep.

"A full colonel, not too shabby a welcoming party," Dave concluded.

"You know, Officer . . ." Dave stammered, "I'm not trespassing . . ."

"Colonel," the man corrected.

"So sorry . . . This is public land. Well, yes, someone has the mineral rights . . . A *Senor* . . ." He pulled papers from his shirt pocket and fumbled with them. "A *Senor Miranda*. But anyone can come here, I think, Sir."

"I'm sure they can," the man in the tailored uniform said, simultaneously relaxing and adopting a condescending tone. "We here in Cortesia merely wish to insure that our . . . guests are comfortable. No problems with the automobile, I hope?"

"No, Colonel, no. I'm looking for mining properties . . . Oh, no, no. My vehicle is operating perfectly, thank you."

"Could I trouble you for some identification, *Senor*?"

Dave pulled out the copy of his registration from the Foreign Ministry and his New York driver's license.

The Colonel made something of a show of comparing the names on the two documents. Similar attention was directed to insuring that the face on the license was, in fact, attached to the man in front of him. Satisfied on both counts, the Army officer continued his interrogation in a more informal vein.

"You mentioned mineral rights. Are you, how they say, a heologist?"

It seemed to take Dave a second or two to figure out yet again what a "heologist" was, but he did succeed in overcoming that little language barrier.

The Colonel took the time of his subject's hesitation tapping his swagger stick against his thigh and surveying with upturned eyebrows the little pits in the ground which had appeared.

"No, not by training, I'm not. I'm a paper-pusher . . . uh, an administrator. I work for geologists. You see, Sir, I'm sending them some dirt to play with, to analyze. Samples."

"And what do you hope the heologists will discover in these samples?"

"Precious metals, mostly," Dave responded quickly. "But every now and then they get excited by something less glamorous, like zinc or molybdenum."

"Ah," the Colonel said with a faint smile. Clicking his heals together, he continued, "Have a pleasant, and may I say, *Senor*, profitable visit with us."

"Thank you, Colonel."

Dave resumed walking around with his eyes directed at the ground. After the sound of the jeep had faded away, he decided that it was now safe for him to depart also. His stomach was reminding him that he had been out since quite early in the morning and could do with some lunch.

He spread out one of the maps he had picked up at the Interior Ministry prior to leaving the Capital out on the table of the little restaurant. The place wasn't impressive looking, but the aromas from the kitchen were enticing.

Putting his finger on the site he had just visited, he noticed something very interesting. A number of nearby properties had been crossed off. As properties don't just disappear, the Xs must indicate that these parcels of land were now unavailable. Why? Interestingly, while there were a number of such crosses scattered throughout the map, there was a solid bank of them just to the east of where he had dug his little holes this morning. Quite a coincidence that the mineral rights to all of these properties had been snatched up all at once, wasn't it?

He folded the map carefully and put it to one side as his beef taco was brought to the table. The young lady who placed the dish in front of him expressed the hope that he would enjoy it. With that, she turned and walked back to the kitchen. As he watched her black hair bounce against her shoulders, he was intrigued by the red highlights it contained.

Dave most certainly did enjoy both the taco and the rice that came with it. They were delicious. He reflected on how different they were from what passes as tacos in U.S. fast food restaurants, those hard shells in which have been laid hamburger and American cheese. He, in contrast, was biting into pieces of lean beef covered in sauce and onions, all encased in a soft, doughy tortilla.

He contemplated his next stop as he finished his lunch. He would, he decided, go to an available property as directly across from "No Man's Land" as he could locate. He calculated that it would take him no little time to get there as he would have to travel across no less than four dirt roads to get to the other side of whatever it was.

The property Dave had selected was precisely as he had envisioned it—a simple clearing in the jungle. And there was, to the west this time, the bobbed wire-topped fence. He didn't tarry this trip. Two meetings with a security patrol in one day, while explainable on the basis of "business," might be a bit much.

Back at the inn, well before sunset this time, the fan swayed menacingly above his bed. But it had to be on or he would have suffocated. Referring back to his maps, the base was, at a minimum by his calculations, twenty mile long and ten miles wide. That didn't help in determining what it was. You could put about anything in an area that size, he concluded, resigned to the fact that there was a lot more work to do here. This was not an appealing conclusion in view of the obvious lack of entertainment in the immediate vicinity. There was, though, the gal at the restaurant. But she was a bit young for him. But she might have an older sister or even a mother! That must be a sign of aging in any "business," including his own, he decided, looking at a young woman and wondering what her mother looks like!

"Oh, well," he thought, "it's a good time to 'write home.'"

CHAPTER **5**

# "THE BREEZE AND I"

The little outdoor café had become Dave and Elena's favorite meeting place. The food was excellent, the view of the harbor was magnificent, and the cooling breeze was glorious.

He found himself humming the Spanish song whose words were translated as "The Breeze and I" as he waited for Elena. They had been seeing a lot of each other since his return from the countryside.

Dave stood up as she approached his table by the trellis. He returned her smile, wondering how she could look so fresh after having worked all day.

"Find any paper mines today?" she asked as she placed her briefcase on the vacant chair.

"I'm not sure," he replied as he shifted somewhat uncomfortably in his chair. "There are some promising sites, but I'm having a bit of trouble running down whether or not someone's already picked up the mineral rights." Dave had a moment to think as she scanned down the menu. It was strange. He usually enjoyed telling people about his "job." In fact, he took no small measure of professional pride in his ability to convince people that he really was what he said he was. It was more than just professional pride, he actually knew. It was fun! It was exhilarating! But, somehow, it didn't feel right with this young lady. Hard to figure?

"Well, how was your day?" he began after she had had time to peruse the menu.

"We had quite a number of foreign guests today. You know, the treaty."

"Oh?" Dave had been taught to make noncommittal utterances, like "Hmmm" and "Oh." Open-ended questions also encouraged people to talk, sometimes more than they may have intended. By contrast, asking people directly about what he actually wanted to know usually resulted in them clamming up.

Elena's eyes widened. Despite his caution, had he gone too far in expressing interest?

Deciding it was wise to change the subject, he looked beyond the frame of the umbrella that adorned the table and said, "Lovely breeze, isn't it?"

She relaxed visibly. "Yes, we always have this in late afternoon. My brother is with the Weather Service. He tells me . . . now, I hope I get this right . . . that as the land heats up during the day the air over the city rises. Then the cooling ocean air rushes in to take its place. The temperature has been known to drop as much as twenty degrees in a few minutes."

The waitress appeared at their tableside and politely inquired as to what they would like to order. As she wrote down their responses, she kept her eyes on Dave. She smiled and winked at him as she completed the process.

"I think you have an admirer," Elena commented after the younger woman had gotten out of earshot.

"I beg your pardon?"

"The waitress," Elena explained with a hesitant laugh.

"The waitress? Why, I'll bet I'm old enough to be her father."

"Yes, perhaps, but you do look younger than you in fact are." She paused, considering her words. "Besides, she," stressing the word "she," "uh . . . doesn't seem the type to allow a handsome man to slip by just because of a few calendar pages."

"I'd say it's more like a few stacks of calendars," Dave said, making an effort to laugh the matter off.

Elena was uncharacteristically quiet as they walked toward her apartment. This concerned him, but he decided it was best to give her some "space." He sure hoped he hadn't put his foot in his mouth back at the restaurant. He didn't want to scare her off.

He savored the tropical smell of the air. Must be some plant blooming, but he was never sure about that kind of thing.

At last, the silence made him too uncomfortable.

"Is something wrong?" he inquired.

"Oh, no," she answered, smiling at him sweetly.

Her reply was neither a lie nor completely honest. Dave would, perhaps, have been relieved to learn that Elena was not, after all, concerned about his interest in the treaty. The young lady was, in actuality, in the throes of a conflict of cultures.

Elena had been brought up in a very traditional and strict Spanish home. She had never, never actually been alone with a boy until her first trip to the United States. Always during her formative years there had been a chaperone present when she dated. This was relaxed to where it could be a brother or sister; but alone on a date, never.

On the other hand, she took great pride in the beginning modernization of her country. She was particularly pleased about the opportunities women now had. Her mother, every bit as bright as she, could never have had the life she had experienced. No, she was stuck at home with the children and servants. "I've sure had a lot more fun", she concluded silently to herself.

All that didn't make her a Woman's Libber, though. She wasn't rude to men who opened doors for her, and her idea of a perfect man included the manners of an old-fashioned gentleman. And Bill certainly fit that description. He always stood up when she entered the room, and he always helped her with her chair. She really valued little things like that.

But all of her thinking about the place of women in the Latin America of the 1990s didn't actually help much with the immediate issue with which she was grappling. Should she invite Bill up to her apartment? She had never done that before, and this must be, what, their tenth or eleventh outing? She used the term "outing" because she wasn't sure at what point their meetings and visits had become "dates." But that most certainly had happened.

It had all taken place quite gradually, she recalled as they walked along. Of course, as the gentleman he was, Bill would extend his arm to her as they crossed a street or walked across a stretch of uneven ground when she was in heels. Then he took to putting his arm around her waist in such circumstances. As time went on, it seemed that his arm remained around her longer and longer after the "threat to her safety" had passed.

And the goodnight hug. That started after their third or fourth supper together. It took a long time. Bill certainly hadn't conformed to the popular image of American men as being "fast movers." Elena didn't know whether to be impressed or offended, actually. In any case, a little peck on the cheek had come to be included in their hugs. Last night had been the first time their lips had met.

Despite herself, Elena couldn't help pondering the question of why the relationship was progressing so slowly. It couldn't be, she figured, that Bill didn't find her attractive. Her problem with men over the years had been quite the opposite of that, to say the least. Besides, he didn't have to keep asking her out, did he?

Perhaps he doesn't think I find him attractive, she speculated tentatively. But how could that be? Bill would have to know that he's attractive. He's thin with broad shoulders, regular features with a nice smile. Of course, maybe he doesn't know that, or maybe he thinks I don't see it. Sometimes really attractive people don't. But Bill doesn't seem to be self-conscious. Even so, perhaps she should in some way communicate to him that she found him to be a very handsome man. Of course, she had sort of done that back at the restaurant. Sort of? She had been afraid at the time that she had gone too far.

"Well, here we are," Dave announced.

Elena was brought back suddenly and rudely from her reverie. She had been so deep in thought that she had been unaware of how far they had come.

"Oh, oh," she said, looking up the steps to her apartment.

He put his hand on her shoulder and kissed her cheek softly.

"Lunch tomorrow, right?"

"Right," she replied. She had never come to a decision about inviting him in. It didn't matter now, she decided. She turned and watched him walk away down the street.

Mark was well into his third drink by the time Dave got to the bar.

"How are you, Mark?"

"Never better, my boy, never better."

"What's the big news these days?"

"Not much, at least on the surface."

"On the surface?" Dave asked, probing for more information. At the same time he got the bartender's attention and ordered drinks for Mark and himself.

Mark took a long sip, more accurately a gulp.

"Oh, all the suits in the government will tell you that things are peachy. But I wasn't born yesterday, and something tells me something's up. Some kind of a rift, I'm pretty sure."

"A rift? About what?"

"Well, that I don't know, actually. I just know that Diaz in the Foreign Ministry, Caballo in the War Office and your friend in Interior are spending a lot of time huddling these days."

"Yeah, Sir Humberto paid a visit to Caballo when we went up to Coast de la Obscura."

"Those guys are thick as thieves. Thick as thieves."

Whatever else one might say, Dave concluded, you had to admit that Cortesia was a friendly country. After all, here he was, a *gringo*, sitting on a deck chair by the home pool of the Foreign Minister. Sipping his champagne at that!

Drops of water sprayed him as Elena dived back in. That girl couldn't seem to keep out of the water. And the men, of whatever age and rank, couldn't keep their eyes off her. She was stunning! He too went somewhat gaga-eyed when she had walked out of the house. Inside she had shed her suit and glasses. The swimsuit she had donned had been simple to the point of being modest, a plain black one-piece. But the way the girl filled it out! He had never seen anyone in a Nevada chorus line who had anything on her. Mother Nature had sure been kind to Elena, a small waist, ample in other places. Her appearance certainly wasn't the result of dieting. She had a healthy appetite, that's for sure. He now knew that she loved to swim. He couldn't help wondering to how many areas her obvious zest for life extended.

Not to be dubbed an "Old Foggy," he dived in after her. She had made it to the shallow end of the Olympic-sized swimming pool by the time he caught up with her. He reached out and tapped her on the foot as it flicked up in front of him. He hoped that wasn't a breach of some local rule of etiquette. They both stood up and faced each other, laughing.

Then she did something that really took Dave by surprise. Elena reached out and stroked and smoothed the hair on his chest. As she did this, her laugh faded to a faint smile. Noticing, after some delay, the stares of the others, Elena giggled and splashed water in Dave's face. Their little interlude together had turned into a game. In a way, it was reassuring to him that he hadn't gotten too old for that kind of thing.

Later in the evening, there was a black tie dinner. They had spent a lot of time at the Minister's changing, Dave reflected. It was a good thing that he occupied a largish mansion.

He appreciated the hostess' kindness in making Elena his dinner partner. She had resumed her dark red lipstick, and the candlelight reflected brilliantly off her dangling earrings.

The Minister rose, oversized champagne glass in hand.

"*Senoras y Senores*," he began, "we are honored to have with us this evening the distinguished Ambassador from our Sister Republic of Cuba, The Right Honorable Antonio Santos de Camaguey. *Senor Doctor Santos de Camaguey* is an internationally known economist and the former Minister of Economic Development of Cuba. We are most honored, *Senor*, that your government has elected to send to us such a distinguished and capable representative as yourself. It is our earnest prayer that your time here in Cortesia is proving to be both happy and professionally rewarding." Raising his glass, the Minister announced in a deep, resonant voice, "It is my honor to offer a toast to The People of Cuba."

Everyone in the room rose and sang out, "The People of Cuba."

The Ambassador stood up. He was a tall, thin man whose graceful movements announced that he was very much at ease both in his tuxedo and in this quite formal setting. Dave tried to imagine Santos de Camaguey crawling through a jungle in fatigues, but without much success. He must have been recruited directly from the Halls of Ivy, he concluded.

"*Mis amigos*," he said, holding out his arms as if to embrace everyone in the room. "During the year it has been my privilege to be in your beautiful and warm country, my heart and soul have been touched to a depth to which my poor words could never do justice."

Santos de Camaguey smiled benevolently. "The only time in history I can compare it to is the 'Orgy of Sacrifice' during the French Revolution. As you will remember, my dear friends, on that grand occasion noblemen came forward and lay the emblems of their hereditary and unearned status at the feet of the Champions of the People. The spirit I have seen here in Cortesia is so wonderfully and refreshingly reminiscent of that.

"Your country has a grand tradition of nobility. Quite frankly, I came expecting you to disparage our Dictatorship of the Proletariat. Instead, you have expressed warm and encouraging interest in what we are doing for the welfare and improvement of the People of Cuba. Many of you, many of Noble Birth, have expressed a desire to do similar good for your own people. It has been my honor to escort some of you in seeing our Works for the People. So many here have come to me saying that they too would so much rather serve their own People than the interests of exploiting capitalists."

Dave squirmed a bit in his chair. Usually in Latin America the term "capitalist exploiter" followed "*norteamericano.*" He looked around. Gratefully, no one was staring at him. Strange, he thought, the Ambassador's speech, which contained words that would have shocked even a luke-warm Republican, seemed to have been well-received. And he too, a *yanqui*, had been most courteously dealt with here in Cortesia. He wondered how both could be true at the same time.

Dave leaned back in the comfortable seat, surprisingly well-stuffed for a sports car, as Elena maneuvered through the city's narrow streets. He was tired. A lot of this was swimming and champagne, but some was also the fleeting experience he had had of being deep in "enemy territory." He should have gotten used to this by now, but he really hadn't.

"The Cuban Ambassador is a pretty impressive guy," he said noncommittally.

"Yes, I guess so," Elena replied, her mind apparently on other things.

"Elena, there's something I don't understand." He had learned that there are times in his line of work when things get so complex that you had to just come out and ask a direct question. "The Ambassador spoke of 'capitalist exploiters.' Well, my country has been called that. People seemed to approve of what Santos de . . . whatever . . . said."

"Camaguey."

". . . Camaguey. And, yet," he waved his arms, "everyone has been real friendly to me."

"Oh," she said, glancing briefly at him from the road, "we know that every American can't be held responsible for all that's happened."

Interesting, he thought to himself. There is resentment about what "America," broadly defined, has done, but each individual American isn't held accountable. He was especially pleased that "capitalist exploitation" hadn't hurt his relationship with the dark-haired lady in the driver's seat.

"We're here," Elena announced. To Dave's mild surprise and great happiness, they were not at his hotel!

Dave put his brandy snifter down and carefully picked up the silver-framed picture on the mantel. In the photograph, Elena, who looked about ten, stood holding the reins of a very spirited-appearing horse. On the other side of the horse's head stood a gray-haired gentleman wearing a tweed sports coat. The man's posture left no doubt that he was a career military officer.

"My favorite photo of the two most important males in my life . . . at least at that time, Daddy and Maximillian."

Dave turned and compared the photograph, over two decades old at this point, to the woman before him. Elena was still in her black velvet dress, but she had removed her shoes. Her feet were tucked under her as she leaned against the back of the sofa. She had certainly filled out, but her face still had the same angelic smile. It was a very romantic situation, but the feelings engulfing Dave were more those of tenderness and admiration for Elena.

He walked across the room wordlessly and slowly seated himself at her side. He placed the picture on the marble-topped coffee table in front of the couch. Their eyes had never left each others' faces throughout.

He reached out and stroked Elena's hair. She allowed her head to move gently toward his hand until her cheek nestled in the palm of Dave's hand. She smiled playfully and then closed her huge brown eyes. Dave leaned slowly forward and allowed his cheek to move up and down on Elena's, finally resting it softly there. His lungs expanded with the smell of her perfume. Her breathing became deeper. She moaned contentedly as she placed her right hand behind his back and pulled his chest onto her breasts. There was the sound of rustling clothing as her head sunk deeper into the sofa's corner and she extended her legs down the thick cushions.

Dave watched her black hair fan out along the folds of the couch. His heart raced. It was like a dream, like something happening to someone else.

Elena opened her eyes. The playful expression faded into one of seriousness and longing. She put both hands on his shoulders. Her stare was penetrating hypnotic.

"I do hope you want to kiss me," came the words through her full lips.

"Yes . . . yes I do," was the chocked reply.

Dave kept his eyes closed. If it had been a dream, he was in no hurry to wake up. "Good," he thought, "Elena's perfume was still in the air." He snuggled closer to her bare back and went back to sleep.

Light flooded the room as Dave felt her stirring next to him. Another tropical day had begun. He could feel one of her ample breasts come to rest on his chest as she turned toward him. She ran her fingers through his hair.

"Good morning, Bill."

"Mmmmmmm," was his only response. He squirmed a bit to settle further into the comfortable bed. He pulled the single sheet under which they had been sleeping up to his neck.

"Do you want to get up, *mi cielito lindo*?"

"No, I'm dreaming."

"What are you dreaming of?"

Dave widened his eyes in mock surprise. "Oh, it's not a dream!"

"You're sweet," she said, kissing his forehead. "Well, now I have to get up."

Elena swung her long legs over the side of the tall bed and walked casually across to the wardrobe. Dave watched her and thought to himself that he may have been dreaming after all.

Elena put on a gray satin gown and turned toward Dave as she tied it across the waist.

"Do you have to go to work?"

"My boss is 3000 miles away."

"Lucky boy," she laughed. "Then you can stay in bed, if you wish."

"No, not this boy. I'm going to wow you with my coffee making."

"Wow?"

"Impress."

"Good. That's not, how you say, my strong suit. Everyone says I make it so strong the spoon stands up in it. But, in my defense, that's how I was taught to prepare it."

Dave got out of bed and walked to the chair by the balcony on which he had placed his clothes. It took some effort to be as unselfconscious as Elena had apparently been. He put on his shorts, pants and a shirt, the sleeves of which he rolled up. Then it was off to the kitchen and the percolator.

Sipping the coffee, which wasn't actually half bad, he watched her dress.

As she left, she kissed him lightly on the lips. "See you at lunch," she said cheerfully.

She was gone. Only the scent, the place and the feeling of a dream fulfilled remained. She left so casually, so matter-of-factly. It was like they had been married for years.

While making the bed he thought of how wonderfully his life had changed.

# CHAPTER 6

# "WHAT AM I GOING TO TELL MOTHER?"

B ack in his hotel room, Dave showered and shaved. Still in his robe, he decided to write "home." But what should he say? "What am I going to tell Mother?" he mused.

The Manual acknowledged that the contacts agents had with sources of information would at times resemble "personal relationships of a friendship, business, or, rarely, romantic nature." He smiled. Given that he had spent the night with her, he guessed that he would have to classify his relationship with Elena as of the "romantic type"! But, as the bible went on, these relationships are "established and maintained for the sole purpose of information gathering. They are never to be allowed to become personally meaningful or important to the agent." It was this last clause that was giving Dave some trouble. He hadn't actually directly asked Elena anything about her work for over a week. He had to admit that he was ahead on the romance and behind on the information gathering!

Well, he decided, he would have to report at least an outline of the relationship. Of course, they already knew of his contact with her. He might, though, soft-peddle what was going on a bit—not lie, just soft-peddle. That way the bean counters in Washington wouldn't be all bent out of shape that he hadn't collected more information from his "local un-recruited source." That might work for a while, but he realized that he would have to start reporting more things as having been learned from Elena.

Dave wrote a very cautious letter to "Mother." It sounded more like an account of a visit to a convent than what had, in fact, transpired.

Elena was already at the café and seated when Dave arrived shortly before one o'clock. Anxiety seized him as he approached the table. Perhaps, he feared, Elena had regrets about what had happened last night. She had, after all, been drinking. She gave him a gentle, protective, almost motherly smile as he sat down. Oh, oh, was he being given his walking papers?

When he picked up his napkin, something fell out on the table—a key. He looked at Elena wide-eyed.

"You know, you really must come back."

"Oh, I will," he stammered, a bit in shock. "Last night meant . . . a very great deal to me . . . Uh . . . I really enjoyed hearing about your childhood. I had always thought that parochial school was quite strict, but it seems you girls were able to enjoy yourselves."

Her face reddened slightly. "I am, to tell you the truth, a bit embarrassed to think of some of our pranks."

"I thought they were cute."

"But you are not fair, *Senor*. You make me talk about myself all the time. Listen to how I chatter on, I think that's the idiom, no, when I talk with you. I'm putting you on warning, however, that I'm resolved to find out everything, everything about you."

"I'm afraid you'll be disappointed."

A sea gull landed on the railing beside the table. He began squawking. It sounded for all the world like the big bird was laughing at everyone in the café. Elena was about to offer their new-found friend a morsel from her seafood platter when a waiter came over and shooed the gull away before she could get the food to him. Dave was grateful for the comic relief at that particular moment.

Dave fairly skipped down the cobblestone street toward the harbor. Things couldn't be going better, he concluded. Cortesia was fast becoming an open book to him. This was a nice job, went his thinking. He was enjoying himself. No, it was more than just a sense of contentment. In many ways, it was like being on vacation. But then, on the other hand, he felt quite comfortable, even at home, here. People had been kinder to him over the past month than ever before in his forty or so years. His breathing stopped suddenly. He was startled. He wasn't supposed to be thinking this way, he suddenly realized.

But that rather down thought passed, or perhaps was excluded from his consciousness. It was, after all, a glorious day. Dave walked on, enjoying the increasing coolness as he drew close to the water.

The harbor of La Navidad was clearly divided into three sections, pleasure, commercial and military. He began his stroll by what was decidedly the largest of the three, the pleasure craft. The collection of yachts was breathtaking. He allowed himself to glance out of the corner of his eye at the people sunbathing on the decks of the gleaming white vessels. The festive atmosphere and the drum-punctuated music contrasted sharply and intriguingly with the severe walls of the Old Spanish Fort next to which the parties were moored.

The fishing fleet must have been out as there were only a few boats in the commercial sector.

He couldn't actually enter the military part of the La Navidad harbor, but he had a relatively unobstructed view through the metal fence. He was even more discrete in the use of his peripheral vision than he had been earlier in eying the bikini-clad ladies on the yachts. The mine layer and the mine sweeper were there, of course. This appeared to be their home port. The number of Coastal Patrol boats had swollen from the usual four to seven. Two light cruisers had joined the little flotilla flying the scarlet-stripped flag of Cortesia. He was reasonably certain that he had seen these two ships among the twenty at anchor at Costa de la Obscura as they were taking off from there several weeks ago. Another and larger ship, one that Dave had never seen before, was moored at the far end of the dock. It had no smokestacks, indicating that it was nuclear powered. And it was adorned with an impressive array of antennas and microwave dishes. One of its main functions, obviously, was communications, almost certainly related to surveillance. The flag the vessel was flying had some blue in it. That's about all he could tell from that distance. Of course, he would, for the sake of certainty, later train his binoculars on the ship from a nearby hill. But there was no doubt in his mind that he was seeing through the slight mist the Cuban flag.

Dave nodded deferentially to the Marine, machine gun in hand, who guarded the entrance to the military sector. He sauntered on up the road back toward town. He would, he concluded to himself, have to write Mom about all this. She took such interest in goings on at the harbor!

He had been standing on the front steps of the Interior Ministry for about fifteen minutes when the black Jaguar approached and came smoothly to a halt. He slid in beside Elena. He took a deep breath of her perfume and kissed her cheek.

"Sorry, I'm a bit late, Dear," she said with that warm smile of hers. "I had a little shopping to do."

She carried a box and a shopping bag with the word "*farmacia*" printed on it up the stairs to her flat. She declined Dave's offer to carry them for her, pointing out that he was already laden with a briefcase.

"You could, please, open the door for me?" she said as they got to the second floor.

He pulled out the key from his pants pocket. The lady noted that the old-fashioned, oversized key she had given him at lunch had already taken its place among the symbols of the other rooms to which the American had access. It took about fifteen seconds of struggling with the unfamiliar lock, but the heavy door finally swung inward, and the couple walked through the portal.

The atmosphere in the front room was almost exhilarating. Probably, he thought, this was because of all the oxygen produced by the multitude of green plants arranged in large planters around the room's floor. It was hard to believe that just twenty-four hours ago he had never even been here. These rooms now seemed so familiar and comfortable to him. He even experienced a sense akin to nostalgia here, like when you go back to your home town after a long absence. Something very meaningful and significant had happened in this place, he understood deep within himself.

Her heels clicked on the tile floor as she walked in her yellow suit to the rod iron loveseat beneath the mini-atrium which had been installed in the roof. She plopped the box on the loveseat and placed the bag carefully beside it. Opening the box, Elena withdrew a white terry cloth robe. She held it up to Dave and turned her head to one side as she gauged his reaction.

"I want you to be comfortable here, you know. Some of the items from the pharmacy are for you, razor, shaving soap, tooth brush, that manner of thing. I wasn't sure exactly what . . ."

"I am very comfortable here," he said between kisses. "I am also grateful."

She smiled contentedly.

On the couch with drinks, Elena opened a topic which he knew was inevitable.

"I warned you, *Senor*, that I would find out everything about you. Well, that starts now, please."

"Oh, why waste a potentially wonderful evening on such a dull topic?"

"Hmmm," she said, writing on an imaginary notepad, obviously un-dissuaded by his self-depreciatory comment. "You were born in what city?"

"Columbus, Ohio, Inspector."

"Date of birth?"

"September 22, 1948."

"Parents?"

"Robert and Sandra."

Softening, Elena tossed her heavy glasses on down the couch and put her hands on Dave's shoulders. "Tell me about your parents, Bill."

Dave shuddered slightly, involuntarily. Being addressed by that name here, with her, shook him.

"Are you alright?" she asked.

'Yes, yes . . . just getting comfortable."

He was grateful that she couldn't see his face. He was visibly shocked at what he had done. His birth date and parents' names were correct. Correct for David Wilkinson that is. They would not, though, jibe with the forms he had filed out at the Ministry, which were, undoubtedly, still on file just one floor above Elena's office. How had this happened? How had he allowed it to happen?

This had been the very first time in his career that his cover identity had been in any way breached. Of course, he consoled himself, Elena might not, probably wouldn't, pull his file. But if Elena was anything, she was certainly bright and inquisitive. He shuddered as he recalled the incident when he had reviewed the file of an appealing female graduate student. She might just do that to me, he feared. Boy, would she be surprised to find out that he had listed his birthplace as Syracuse, New York. Gee, what a blooper! But there was nothing he could do about it now.

"I'm not sure you're alright."

He was startled to discover that he had been starring off into space.

"Oh, no, I'm fine," he said, shaking his head in an effort to clear it.

"You know," she said, "one thing that troubles me is that maybe I'm pushing you. Perhaps you don't want as much closeness as I do?"

"No, no, that's not it at all. Gosh, I couldn't love you more . . ."

Elena opened her big brown eyes even wider and appreciatively.

This was certainly his day for being a chatterbox! He had never told Elena that he loved her. Why, he hadn't even told himself, although in all honesty he knew that he did. Dave's work had brought him into quite a number of relationships with women. But there was something different about Elena. What was it?

She kissed his lips strongly. "I love you, too," she whispered. "I do truly love you."

He felt a sense of joy with her that he had never before experienced. It sure felt good to be in her arms, warm and safe, soft yet secure. He had to admit it; he really had a case on this lady.

His hand fell from her shoulder and ran along the firm outline of her breast.

Unable to make any sense of the matter and being so comfortable anyway, Dave allowed all of the "why" and "how" questions to slip from his thinking for the time being.

"You're a very elegant lady," were the last words he said to Elena as he left her apartment that evening.

# CHAPTER 7

# "IT'S A GLORIOUS DAY, *SENOR*"

A s he lounged in his room mid-Saturday morning, the waiter brought up a carafe of coffee and Dave's mail. He recognized the even handwriting of the boss' secretary Penny. He called her "Moneypenny," of course, in honor of M's secretary in the James Bond movies. His hands trembled a bit as he reached immediately for the letter from "home." These communications didn't always contain good news. On more than one occasion, he had been pretty severely chastised in them.

*Dear Son,*

*We're real happy to learn from your letters that things are going well for you down there in Cortesia. I'm sure the heat is tough to deal with, but your Dad has checked the weather reports and says it's no worse than what we get here in July*

*and August. And you've always survived that,*
*William, so I guess . . .*
     *We're doing OK here. Things are as per usual.*
*Your Aunt Gracie had another bout with her*
*arthritis, but she's getting around a lot better now.*

He was pleased to learn that Mother, the real one he meant, was doing better. Of course, he didn't have to read these letters in fear that something truly tragic had occurred at home. The "Office" would have contacted him by phone in, say, the event of a death in his family, and they would have gotten him back long before any such letter could have arrived. This was not, after all, a time of total warfare.

     *It's good that you've come into the company of*
*such a nice young lady. Your father and I are very*
*anxious to hear much, much more about her.*

Dave chuckled to himself. He certainly didn't need his Captain Crunch Decoder Ring to read this letter! That, he thought, was a not so gentle slap on the wrist. And, yes, he would definitely have to tell them more about Elena.

He tipped the waiter and took a sip of the hot black coffee the young man had just poured him. The letter went on . . .

     *Mrs. Sanders from Church told me her*
*daughter is leading a student group through Latin*
*America. La Navidad is on their itinerary, but Mrs.*
*Sanders wasn't exactly sure when the group would*
*be there. I gave her the address and phone number*
*of your hotel, so Janet should be looking you*

*up, your being so far from home and all. You've
always enjoyed her company so.*

Well, it wasn't enough for Moneypenny to stick in the
knife; she had to twist it too! The "enjoyment" issue aside, this
was certainly going to further complicate his life for a while.

*We pray for your safe return.*

*Love,*
*Mom & Dad*

Well, he thought, not a disaster, but not exactly good
news. He would have to get his act together. This, he figured,
would be a good time to summarize for himself what he had
learned to date. He rose from the desk in the corner of the
airy, sunlit room and walked to the antique dresser. Inserting
the key into the old-fashioned lock, he carefully and quietly
turned it. He removed some of the notes he had made during
his time in Cortesia.

Back at the gleaming wood desk, he poured himself
another cup of coffee and removed a single piece of hotel
stationary from the left hand drawer. He began writing:

There is a great presence of Cubans here in Cortesia:

1.  What appears to be a permanent installation at Costa
    de la Obscura, the military headquarters
2.  There are many young Cubans at an installation in the
    Santa Maria Mountains:

A. This is a "mystery base." No mention is ever made of it in the newspaper, radio or TV.

B. The Cuban soldiers appear to be artillery. In fact, the base may actually be totally operated by Cubans. The only Cortesians I saw in the area were security officers.

C. Cuban warships appear with dramatic frequency in Cortesia's harbors.

D. There is a heavy presence of Cuban military officers in Cortesian government offices, particularly the Ministries of War and Foreign Affairs.

E. The Cuban Ambassador is of unusually high rank and polish for a country this size. And he's spouting a populist/pinkish line. And he's exceedingly well received here in the Land of Knights and Ladies.

Questions

1. Why would this nobility-oriented country have such a close relationship with the scraggly beard of Fidel?
2. . . . .

Well, he couldn't really think of another question. That was the question. Why would this nation of frustrated Royalists put up with the presence of such an uncouth group of ruffians that a slob like Castro would dispatch?

Dave sat back in his chair and reviewed his list. He got up and walked with it into the bathroom. He tore the sheet of paper into four pieces. He took one quadrant of what had been his "think sheet" and tore it into an uncounted number of smaller pieces. He picked up these giblets and threw them into the toilet. They floated like so many little ships in a flotilla of the mind. The other three quadrants were given similar treatment. He flushed the toilet by pulling the metal cord suspended from the ceiling. He watched them disappear down the tube, with his head turning in synch with the swirling water. If they're 1) monitoring my sewage and 2) able to make anything of that, he concluded, they deserve to catch me!

Back outside on the cobblestones, the sun reflected brightly off the adobe houses along the narrow streets. The American found himself, yet again, grateful for the sea's cooling breeze.

He walked past the statue of General Perez. The General had led the Cortesians against the Spanish in the War of Independence. In actuality, though, all that had remained of the Spanish "forces" during the "War" was a group of clerks in the Tax Collector's Office. Naturally, the General had soundly defeated them! As a matter of fact, the Spanish "forces," armed with little more than quill pens, raised the white flag over what is now the National Palace at the mere sight of Perez' well-attired but essentially untrained "Army." Dave always chuckled at the sight of the rearing horse on which the General was seated. He had been told that the way the horse's statue stood indicated the warrior's fate in battle. He had been informed in college that one foot off the ground meant that the soldier had been wounded in combat. Both hooves in the air, as in this sculpture, indicated that the person had been killed in battle. Perez, in actuality, had died at the hands of a jealous husband!

Walking, he had found, always helped him figure things out. This was probably because it calmed him down. He just seemed to be able to see things more clearly when out on a stroll. Of course, it didn't really seem to be helping him that much this time. He just couldn't figure out why these people who made such pretenses to nobility would allow revolutionary Cubans to operate on such a wide-ranging basis in their beloved Motherland.

Without really thinking about it, Dave found himself walking in the direction of Elena's apartment. As he noticed this behavior in himself, he toyed with the idea of simply putting this question to her. But would that be wise? Would she be offended? She was, after all, a member of a prominent Cortesian family, a titled one at that he had discovered only when her younger sister's engagement had been announced. And she had chosen to go into government service. Might such a question tip his hand and scare the young lady off?

He had come to no definite decision on the matter when he arrived at the old ivy-covered building in which his "un-recruited local source" . . . and lover resided. Approaching her door, he could hear a man talking inside. His heart sank. Might there be someone else? He was tempted to walk away unobserved. But no, if that were the case, he needed to know. Besides, that would actually help him in his increasingly futile efforts to keep their relationship one of "business," at least in the sense of the peculiar "business" which he was in.

He noted that his breathing had become labored as he knocked on the heavy door.

After what seemed an eternity, in which he could hear several people chatting and laughing, the door swung open.

In addition to her heavy black eyeglasses, she was wearing faded blue jeans and a large denim shirt, unbuttoned and tied in the front. She had on neither shoes nor makeup. Dave found himself slightly embarrassed, as though he shouldn't be seeing her like this. This reaction on his part was more than just a little difficult for even him to understand in that, after all, he had seen her completely undressed.

Elena's wide eyes, Dave had come to know, indicated that she too was surprised and uncertain. But she quickly regained her composure, and the familiar warm smile returned to her now pale lips.

"Oh, Bill, what a pleasant surprise. Come in, come in. I want you to meet some friends of mine."

The furniture in the large room had been rearranged to form an irregular circle. Six people occupied the chairs. They ranged in years from about Elena's age to the late 40s. They were all dressed in the casual "sixtyish" attire Elena was wearing. She introduced the three men and the three women to him in turn, and they greeted him in excellent English.

"Gosh, I really didn't mean to intrude."

"Nonsense, Old man," the oldest male said soothingly. "We were just chatting."

After an awkward pause, the man with the graying hair continued, "As a matter of fact, we were just leaving."

Taking Roberto's lead, some apparently taken by surprise, the others clambered to their feet.

Dave gave Elena a quizzical look as the group made its exit through the door. She winked at him as she closed the door behind them.

She walked to the middle of the room where he stood. She placed her hands lovingly on his upper arms. "Fellow students in a study group," she explained briefly.

"A study group?"

"*Si, mi amor*, we took some post-graduate courses together at the University, and we continue to meet. Is something wrong?"

"Wrong . . . oh, no, no. It's just that I heard a man's voice from outside, and I couldn't help wor . . . wondering . . . ?"

"*Ah, que mono*," she said, smiling broadly. She leaned forward to kiss his cheek. As she did, the temple of her glasses grazed his chin. "I'm sorry," she purred. "I sometimes forget they're there. But no, no, it's totally academic—economics, that sort of thing. But it's sweet of you . . ."

Great cover for his curiosity, he thought. Of course, he had to admit that it was a pretty easy and believable, certainly to himself, technique to use!

"Well, come, come, sit with me. We can surely think of something less academic."

The couple crossed the room and sat down on the couch, the very same overstuffed sofa on which their openly romantic relationship had begun just last month. Elena put both of her hands in Dave's and allowed her head to fall back onto one of the cushions.

"I've missed you today, Bill," she finally said softly.

He winced a bit inside.

"You know," she continued," we have lunch together most days, so I've usually seen you long before now. I've been, how it is said, deprived."

"I've missed you too." That could, he figured, have been the understatement of the year!

She looked straight into his eyes. "You know, I've been thinking about something you said last night."

"Ah, what was that?" Dave was again going through an intriguing interplay of emotions. On the one hand, it felt so good to have her show such interest in him. On the other hand, though, his guard shot up. He didn't want to commit any more "bloopers." In sum, the experience could best be described as exhilarating. And in the face of it all, he was making an effort to seem casual!

"Well, as we walked along the harbor last night, you pointed to a small blue craft and made the comment that it reminded you so of your grandfather's boat. You were telling me about your summers as a *nino* on the lake, but then we ran into the Major and . . ."

"Yes, yes, when did we say we'd meet him and his wife for dinner?"

"Seven-thirty," she replied off-handedly, not to be put off from her chain of thought. "But I was disappointed that you didn't continue to tell me about those summers. They sounded lovely."

"Ah, yes, they were that. As a matter of fact, after Granddad retired I'd practically spend the whole summer up there. You almost couldn't get me back to the city. Gee, it was so nice and cool up there—a wonderful breeze most of the time. And the fishing was fantastic . . ."

Several hours later, Dave stepped out of the ancient building into the fading sunlight of the day. He was on his way back to his room to change for supper with the de la Castilles.

"It's a glorious day, *Senor,*" an elderly gentleman in an impeccably pressed white linen suit said in greeting.

"*De veras, Senor, de veras*," he replied in absolute agreement, as his springing steps carried him rapidly on down the sidewalk.

Dave got out of the black car and walked around to the driver's side to open the door for the young lady. She stepped out and took a moment to smooth a few wrinkles out of her black cocktail dress. She removed her eyeglasses and turned to place them carefully on the dashboard.

"Do I look alright?" she inquired.

He thought for a moment about how to answer what is typically a routine question, but at that moment had caused to well up within him a host of feelings which concerned more than just her truly stunning appearance.

"You're a very elegant lady."

The restaurant, La Playa de Oro, is the most famous of all in La Navidad. Its specialty is paella, a seafood in rice dish much esteemed by Spanish gourmets and travel writers who come from all over the world to savor it. It has a great wine list and handsome, polite waiters. It has a spectacular view of the protected and gentle bay just south of the city. In fact, you could walk out the back of La Playa and directly onto the white sand beach. The only thing it doesn't have is walls! It was constructed in the form of the roof of a gigantic grass hut suspended on poles. While it may not have passed U.S. health codes, this arrangement cleared the way for a deliciously cooling breeze as you enjoyed your fresh and local seafood.

Heads turned as Elena and Dave approached the Maitre D's station. They did make a strikingly good looking couple.

Dave had to look carefully to spot Major de la Castile at the corner table on the ocean side. He had never before seen him in anything but his uniform.

The Major stood and bowed deeply to Elena as the couple approached. While shaking hands with Dave he displayed the informality and comfort he had in past weeks come to feel with the American.

"You know, William," he began with an expansive wave of his arm, "It didn't bother us so much when you *yanquis* came and put all our fruit in the holds of your giant ships. And it mattered not at all to us when you dug the gold out of our hills and put it in your Fort Knox. But now you Colonialists-Imperialists have gone a bit too far. You have come for a treasure such as our Elena. Tsk, tsk." The tall thin man wagged his finger in mock disapproval at the averaged-statured American.

The lady in question laughed heartedly. "How gallant of you to say that, Arturo."

Seated at the right and smiling at the proceedings was another woman, attractive even though somewhat overweight. de la Castille quickly shifted gears and said to the seated lady, "Marta, you know Elena, of course. And this is our new friend, of whom I have been telling you, Bill Robinson."

Marta looked up at Elena and Bill. "*Hola, Elena*," she said. "*Much gusto*," was her greeting to Dave.

Mata had black hair, almost. Dave was intrigued again by the red highlights.

Dave and Elena seated themselves after de la Castille bowed again.

The waiter brought the menus. Elena opened hers and stared blankly into it. Dave knew that she actually couldn't read the first word on it without her glasses. He wondered why she took them off on such occasions. She was obviously very uncomfortable without them. And Dave thought she looked quite "chic" in them. Besides, he had come to enjoy the little ritual of taking them off her face preparatory to kissing her.

"I'll have the paella, of course," Elena announced to Dave, handing him the oversized menu.

The two men sipped cognac as the ladies toyed with their glasses of Chablis.

The sight of the sea seemed to jog de la Castille's memory, and the cognac probably loosened his tongue.

"*Mis amigos*," he began, "this lovely evening on the beach puts me in mind of the months I passed at your Naval Training Station near San Diego. There are, as you know, beaches very much like this one in Southern California."

"But none so pleasant as this one," Dave interjected.

"Oh, I don't know. In any case, Marta and I passed many pleasant evenings in your Southern California."

"It seems," Dave went on by way of spurring on the conversation, "that your traveling has been quite international."

"Indeed so, *Senor*. We may be a small country, by your standards, but our military is, as you say 'state of the art.' All of us on the General Staff are the graduates of the War Colleges of no less than five countries. I myself have attended seven."

"How impressive. Might I ask which?"

"Well, there is no harm in my telling you about France, Great Britain, Canada and your own country."

Sensing a hint of resistance, Dave shifted gears.

"Ah, Canada. Isn't Ottawa a lovely little replica of London?"

"I could not agree more. But, in actuality, their Command College is situated in Quebec. Montreal is, as you know, a bit of a mess . . ."

"Yes, I wouldn't drive a cab there for a million bucks a year!"

"*Tienes razon*, Bill. A cautious person such as yourself would not last more than a day at it. But Quebec City is, as you say, a jewel. It is, I believe, the only walled city in North America."

"I believe you're correct, Arturo. Of course, you have a magnificent walled city right here in Cortesia. From the photographs I've seen, La Ciudad de Los Reyes has always struck me as a Quebec City in Spanish."

"Oh, yes", Elena said, making her first contribution to the conversation. "We are very proud of our 'Los Reyes.' It was the first Royal Capital established by the Spanish here in the New World. Fifteen ninety-one is, I think, the date on the Palace's cornerstone. Everything has been preserved within the walls exactly as it was when the last Royal Governor of Cortesia was recalled to Spain. Not even automobiles are allowed to pass through the gates."

"It's like going back in time," Marta commented.

"Particularly during '*Adios a Nuestro Gobernador*'," Elena continued.

"You know," Dave said, "I've heard of that, but I'm afraid I don't know exactly what it is."

"It is," the voluptuous brunette went on, "the annual reenactment of the ceremonious leave-taking of the last Spanish Royal Governor of our country. His name was Juan Jorge de Seville y Barcelona, Viceroy and Knight *de Guerra*."

Dave watched in fascination as his lover spoke, holding the attention of the little group. If beautiful women weren't supposed to be bright and articulate, then Elena certainly hadn't read that book!

"You know, the term 'Royal Governor' sounds so repressive. But, in actuality, Sir Juan was a most enlightened man. Our people never had a better friend than that *caballero*. He believed early on that people should govern themselves. He actually worked behind the scenes for our independence. Regrettably the Spanish bureaucrats here in La Navidad didn't see things in that manner. No, no, they were more concerned with their jobs and their pensions. Some had their 'hand in the till,' as it is put in American newspapers."

"Yes, Sir," Dave said to himself, "she's got it all. This is going to be one of those assignments that's going to be tough to end."

Dave chimed into the conversation, "As they say in the American newspapers. You've got that right. We've sure got them up there."

"Oh, we know," said de la Castille. "We've seen them here, my friend, with the mines, the fruit companies and your Embassy."

Elena looked at Dave, and, turning her head slightly, she gave him a regretful glance. Her look seemed to say that what the Major had said was true but that it saddened her that it was so.

Recovering her momentarily lost composure, she continued, "But coming back to our country, the clerks were in due course forced to abandon their offices. Being cowards, they didn't put up much of a fight, really. But then it was time for our Beloved Knight to depart from us.

"So the Governor's leave-taking was a time of great emotion . . . ambivalence, I think you would say . . . for our people. On the one hand we were overjoyed to be rid of Spanish rule, which, in general, had been both oppressive and exploitive. But we were at the same time losing a dear friend. The real pity and major problem was that, in all candor, we had no one even close to his stature with whom to replace him. Father San Luis, being a priest, could have nothing to do with holding public office, *claro*. And General Perez, though he thought himself great, was only so in the size of his belt!"

"A legend in his own mind," Dave threw in.

"One might say, indeed one might say," the Major chuckled, obviously amused at the contemporary American sarcasm.

"You two . . . gentlemen do not seem to be taking your history very seriously this evening," Elena scolded in playful irritation at the frivolous comments of the two middle-aged men. "In any case, *muchachos*, it was with no small amount of regret that the people came to say their goodbyes. This was before the day of air travel, and we knew that we would see him, who had given so much and received so little, no more. The people threw flowers before his and Lady de Seville Y Barcelona's carriage all along the hundred or so kilometers of the journey down to the harbor here and their waiting ship for their return home to *Espana*.

"So you see, Bill, what a momentous and heart-touching day the Governor's leave-taking was. And so in celebration of it each year, on June 15th, our President dresses in the Spanish-cut suit and laced cuff shirt that the Knight preferred and leaves the Governor's Palace to the cheers of those assembled and is driven away in a carriage. The flag of Spain is pulled down . . . with dignity . . . and our own flag is raised. Moments later, the carriage, now without the Royal . . . paraphernalia, *correcto?* . . . returns and the President, now in a modern suit of business, steps out and reads our Declaration of Independence. The Prime Minister then reads the Preamble to our Constitution, and the Chief Justice reads the Bill of Rights. It's a most impressive ceremony. I plan," she continued while looking across the table at Major and *La Senora de la Castille*, "to take our *norteamericano amigo* here to it next week."

"*Excelante*," Marta replied enthusiastically.

The meals arrived at the table. Elena dived into the paella with her characteristic gusto. Dave had followed her lead in ordering, and he found the dish to be indeed memorable. He was intrigued by how the chef had managed the preparation in such a way that while you could taste each of the many kinds of seafood, the whole achieved a delicious and harmonious integration.

With the exception of a few comments such as "*que rico!*" in appreciation for an obvious culinary achievement, the two couples fell largely silent as they began their meals. The company, the paella complimented by the French Chablis and the cooling breeze which swept through the open-air restaurant all contributed to what would remain in their memories an "enchanted evening."

The earlier discussion of both history and Cortesia's old walled city had drawn Arturo's mind to a recent visit he had made to La Cuidad de Los Reyes.

"We had a conference in Los Reyes last year," he began.

Dave had deduced by careful observation that when Arturo said "we" in a business context he was referring to his fellow support officers on the General Staff.

"We spent an entire weekend in analyzing your Persian Gulf War. We found some rather striking historical parallels.

"On cursory examination, the Iraqi strategy at the beginning of the war appeared quite antiquated and naïve. The lines of oil-filled trenches and bunkers in Southern Kuwait put one in mind of World War I. It put one in mind, actually, of the Maginot Line, which was built after that war to prevent Germany from re-invading France. But, as any student of history will tell you, the Maginot Line was a total failure. Hitler merely rolled into Belgium and then down into France. And, quite predictably, the Allied strategy in the Gulf was exactly the same as Hitler's. The bulk of Allied forces were deployed not against the bunkers but were, rather, sent west of Kuwait and to the north into Iraq, and they then came down into Kuwait on the other side of the fortifications.

"But we came to the conclusion that Saddam's strategy was not so hopelessly naïve as it may have seemed to the Allied High Command. This is because, basically, you see, he did not position his best troops on the Maginot Line as the French had done a half century earlier. No, no, he kept his elite forces, the Republican Guard, some miles north of the ditches, at the likely point at which the American flanking movement would enter Kuwait.

"But at that particular point, the Iraqis, from a theoretical perspective, called into play yet another grand lesson of history. This relates to extending, or should I say overextending, your lines of communication and supply. Twice this classic blunder was committed in invasions of

Russia. This was done by Napoleon, and then the same mistake was made by Hitler. If you look at the map, you will see that by penetrating into Iraq in this fashion, the Allies created a line of march of about seventy to seventy-five miles through enemy territory. And I emphasize that it was through enemy territory, right through, in fact, the homeland of the Iraqis soldiers.

"What that means is that the chain of supply of the Western Forces was vulnerable to interdiction through many, many miles of the home territory of the soldiers they were fighting. Theoretically, it should have taken a force of about as many troops as had been deployed by the Iraqis to hold and maintain that vital corridor. This would have left few, an inadequate number in fact, for the actual invasion of Kuwait. This would have been an almost impossible burden. You must remember that in absolute numbers, the Allies and the Iraqis were about equal. So, again theoretically, only an inadequate number of American and British troops would have attempted the penetration into Kuwait to face the forces Saddam would have posted at those borders.

"But, of course, something went wrong for Saddam. Everyone thinks it was his plan, his strategy. But that actually was not so. We came to the conclusion that his strategy was quite sound. In fact, he could have cut off the main body of the Allied troops by cutting through their supply lines through his own territory.

"So, what was Saddam's mistake? He committed another classic military blunder. He neglected to adequately supply his own troops. So his troops were hungry, and, of course, morale was low. It's quite remarkable how often throughout history commanders have neglected such matters. People tend to think war is all fighting and firepower. But war is conducted by people, and people have to be taken care of. One would think that that lesson would have been learned, but . . . but I'm boring you ladies . . ."

"Not at all, Arturo," was Elena's gracious reply.

Dave wasn't sure that he had agreed completely with the Major's analysis of the War in the Gulf, but he was most decidedly impressed with the sophistication of the thinking that had gone into it. Apparently, Cortesia was more than just a Banana Republic when it came to its military establishment.

His thoughts turned to the delights of the promised upcoming trip with Elena as he began his dessert.

# CHAPTER 8

# "I USED TO COME HERE OFTEN WHEN I WAS A LITTLE GIRL"

At lunch on Monday, Dave asked Elena about their upcoming trip, which she had announced Saturday evening.

"Oh, I need to go home to check on a few things, and since the *estancia* is so close to Los Reyes, I thought we could go there, too. We can be there for the *Adios*, you see."

"Home? I'm afraid I don't understand. I thought you were from here, the City."

"Oh, *si,* Papa worked here, of course. And I went to school here. But our, how you say, family home is *una estancia,* sort of a combination farm and ranch, about a hundred kilometers to the north.

"My grandfather ran it as a working plantation until his death. Then Father became the *Patron*, at least technically. But as Army Chief of Staff, he had but little time for agriculture.

"What has happened is that our former workers still live there. They raise cattle and till the soil. But they do so to feed their own families. And when they sell something they keep the money. Our family gets nothing from the *estancia*, though legally we still own the land. The workers maintain the family home, and they treat us as honored guests when we come to visit, as you will see."

"When do we go?"

"I've arranged to take a long weekend. We go up Friday morning and spend the whole weekend on the estancia. The celebration at Los Reyes is on Monday morning, of course. So we can attend that on our way back to the City."

"Sounds great to me!" This, he thought to himself, would be his first truly extended time alone with Elena, and he couldn't imagine a more appealing way to spend a long, leisurely weekend.

Dave was at the wheel of the black Jaguar this time. He had now learned his way around the winding and narrow roads well enough to help Elena with the driving.

Entering or leaving the City via any route other than La Gran Avenida de la Revolucion took one through the barrios, squalid neighborhoods of adobe cottages. They were obviously without running water or other modern utilities. Sanitation was clearly a problem in these areas.

A pained expression came over Elena's typically smiling face.

"My poor people," she sighed. "You see how they are forced to live. It is not a lack of industriousness on their part, Bill. The men work, and the women take in laundry and sell their hand-made goods in the Close of the Cathedral. It is that the wages are so low."

"Why? Why is that?" Dave asked, both because the answer might contain important information, but also out of genuine concern.

Elena opened her mouth as though to speak. But a perplexed look came over her face, and she hesitated. Momentarily, her expression softened. "Oh, let's not go into all that now. It's such a lovely day. We'll just 'commune with Nature,' as it is said." She winked at the driver, restoring at least for the moment the occasion to what it was, a lovers' outing.

It didn't take long to clear all signs of urbanization. Soon they were out on the road. One really couldn't say "open road," as Highway 20 was a small, two-lane affair tunneled through a tropical forest. The resulting green wall that surrounded them made periodic encroachments onto the thoroughfare, despite the best efforts of the Cortesian Corps of Engineers. Dave swerved to skirt around a branch that jutted out. It had obviously grown very rapidly since the last trimming the roadside had been given. The sports car's top had been removed for the trip, so they were able to appreciate the coolness and airy, invigorating atmosphere seeping out of the jungle's undergrowth. This meant, though, that they had to almost shout at each other to be heard over the chirping and chattering of the local residents.

Dave was luxuriating in that sense of calmness, contentment and joy he had come to feel in Elena's presence.

The romanticism was rather rudely interrupted for Dave on the far side of a hairpin turn in the road. A group of men who were clad in khaki stood casually on one side of the highway. Their machine guns gleamed in the sunlight admitted into the clearing.

"Soldiers," Elena said in an attempt to be reassuring, sensing her companion's uneasiness.

That information didn't completely take Dave off his guard. The knowledge that they were approaching government soldiers was, after all, less than reassuring when you were a spy!

He began gradually, so it wouldn't be noticeable, the relaxation exercises his therapist in college had taught him when he had suffered a spell of test anxiety. Besides, he reasoned, there wasn't the faintest sign on his person of the real line of work he was in. It was, as a matter of fact, "company policy" that no such indications of one's true affiliation ever, ever be carried. If he should be killed in a road crash, the only way an agent in his branch had ever met his death on an assignment (at least so far), they could go over his entire body in minute detail and find absolutely nothing. What they would find would be identification that would check out completely with any and all law enforcement/ investigatory agencies in the States. The carrying of revolvers, decoding devices and suicide pills—how ridiculous—was something for the movies. Besides, all you really needed to collect information was paper, a pen and a camera. And his camera was just a stock 35mm model, expensive, but less so than many legitimate tourists bring with them. And, on the pessimistic side, if they figure out who you really are—and want to get you—one guy couldn't possibly carry enough armature to blast his way out of a country.

It suddenly occurred to him as he slowed to a halt that if they were on to him, they would have collared him back in the Capital where they had backup, etc. He was nothing if not a guy who could see the bright side!

All in all, he was feeling pretty comfortable by the time the officer neared the car. "*Buenas dias*," was his perfunctory greeting.

"Good morning, officer," Dave replied, mixing politeness with what he judged to be the expected amount of respect. He could, though, have spared himself a goodly portion of his act. The young man's eyes were focusing beyond him entirely.

The voluptuous figure turned her knees slightly toward the man in khaki. Her tan dress parted unintentionally but none the less suggestively. The soldier's eyes were then drawn up to the red scarf around her long neck. To say that Elena was striking would have been a gross understatement. She removed her sunglasses and squinted into the sun at the blurry figure in front of her.

"*Estamos en vacaciones, Capitan*," she explained.

"*Ah, Senorita de la Madrid.*"

"*Si, soy yo.*"

There was a very definite lessening of the tension associated with the occasion.

The young man shifted his weapon to the other shoulder and informed the couple that a band of bandits was operating in the mountains through which they would be driving. He grandly announced that he would provide them with a military escort through the inhospitable terrain. So off they went through the tortuous mountain passes behind a jeep with sliver and scarlet stripes on its side. "This is the way all spies should travel," Dave thought to himself.

The gravel road widened slightly after they had descended the other side of the small mountain. It led them into a tiny village. The military vehicle slowed respectfully to allow the chickens and pigs to cross the street at their own pace.

At the center of the collection of adobe cottages, the officer in the Jeep stood up and saluted the sports car. The military vehicle then made a U-turn in the middle of the street and moved quickly in a cloud of dust back up the mountain. It was obviously considered that Dave and Elena were safe on their own at this point.

Elena instructed Dave to pull the car into a vacant lot between two of the simple buildings. The couple entered the café through swinging doors, very much like in the Old West, Dave conjectured. Elena removed her sunglasses as they walked into the long, dark, cavernous room within. It took some time for Dave's eyes to adjust to the darkness. He could finally just make out the outline of a long bar off to the left. Of course, there was a huge set of horns mounted above its counter. A slight figure moved rapidly from behind the shadowy enclosure and toward Elena and him.

The thin gray-haired man approached Elena and put his hands gently on her shoulders. He kissed her cheek lightly but with feigned intensity.

"Ah," he said as he stepped back, clasping his hand to his breast. "You have come back to Pedro. I always knew you would, *claro*. But who is this little boy . . . this *nino* . . . you have brought with you?"

"This, don Pedro, is William . . . Bill Robinson of an American mining firm."

Dave was treated to a vigorous *abrazo* by the older man.

"Welcome, welcome," the tavern owned effused. "Please, you two, sit down. Pedro will bring you some of his wine, no?"

He led them, his arm gently around Elena's waist, to a table in the corner of the large room. Scurrying into the back room, he left the couple alone.

"Wine?" Hearing the tremendous resulting echo, Dave checked himself and lowered his voice. "Wine," he resumed, "it's only nine-thirty in the morning, Honey."

"Oh, Bill, don't be so rigid. This is, to tell the truth, a little fault of yours. don Pedro is so very proud of his wine. You know, he actually founded the modern wine industry here in Cortesia. Yes, it is true. He went away many, many years, a half century ago, up to California to get cuttings of grape vines."

"Sort of Cortesia's Count Harazathy," Dave interjected.

"Count . . . who?"

"Harazathy. He went to Europe to get vines for California."

"Oh yes, yes then. don Pedro is our Count Harazathy. But our local connoisseurs, like the Major, say that his wines are better than those of Europe, as a matter of fact. The reason for this extraordinary statement has something to do with a disease that attacked the vines many years ago . . ."

"*Phylloxera*?" Dave commented questioningly.

"Yes, yes, I think that was just the name Arturo used. In any case, they had to do something in Europe and North America which don Pedro doesn't find it necessary to do here. And it's said that whatever he doesn't have to do makes his wines much better."

Dave's eyes widened. "I'll bet he doesn't graft his *vinifera* vines onto American rootstalks."

"*Que*?"

It was not without some pride that Dave undertook the task of informing the bright, aristocratic young lady about a typically upper-class topic, wines. At such times, he was pleased that he had made wines one of his hobbies over the years.

"You see, Dear, the North American continent is covered with grape vines, particularly in the Northeast, New England and the upper South. In fact the Norsemen called it 'Vineland.' So when Europeans came to America, they expected to enjoy an abundance of wine made from the native grapes. They were, though, disappointed. It turned out that the wine made from these native grapes had a sharp, pungent taste. We've come to call it 'foxy.' Now a lot of people from that part of the States have actually come to like and appreciate that taste, as you experience in the wines from the Finger Lakes region of New York State. But the true lover of European wines doesn't.

"It developed that the North American vines were of an entirely different type from those of Europe. We now know that the European vines are *vitis vinifera*, whereas the native American variety is *vitis labrusca*. Well, the Colonial gentry longed for the Old World wines. So no less a person than Thomas Jefferson attempted to get *vitis vinifera* vines to grow in Virginia. He failed. The European vines died. I've seen the plot at Monticello where he tried to grow them: it's just a barren square of soil. Everybody, Ole Tom included, thought that what had gone wrong was that the climate in North America was simply too severe. The winters were too cold.

"That was the accepted theory for many, many years. During the latter part of the last century, though, something happened which dramatically changed everybody's mind about what had happened to Jefferson's vines. Toward the end of the 1800s, some botanists in Europe, for some reason, decided that they wanted to study the American vines. Maybe they wanted to try to find out what made them tough enough to withstand the New York winters. But what they actually succeeded in doing was to bring upon themselves the worst disaster in the history of winemaking.

"You see, it turned out that creeping among those American root stocks were some little bugs, a plant louse called *phylloxera*. It didn't affect the American vines. They had developed a resistance to it. But when the *vinifera* grapes were introduced into this hemisphere, the little buggers attacked them, and since they had no resistance, the bugs won. Well, from the imported American root stocks, *phylloxera* spread all over Europe. It came close to wiping out their historic and ancient wine industry, as a matter of fact.

"The solution they came to was of sort of the 'if you can't lick 'um, join 'um' type. They grafted the European vines onto American root stocks. This step virtually saved the wine industry. But it started a controversy that has raged down to the present day. We might just shed some light on the argument right here in Cortesia. You see, most wine buffs maintain, perhaps self-servingly in the case of the European *vignerons*, that the use of American root stocks hasn't affected in any way the taste or quality of the wines. Others, though, argue that the pre-*phylloxera* wines were vastly superior to the ones we have today, more refined and delicate, you know, without the brash American influence of our root stocks.

"Of course, we wine buffs have gone round and round on that one with no way to be sure one way or the other. There aren't many people around who are old enough to have actually tasted a pre-*phylloxera* wine to comment! But there's been speculation, hope I guess, that there might be some isolated corner of the world in which they truly haven't found it necessary to resort to the use of American roots. And if I'm right about what your don Pedro has been up to, Cortesia could just be that place. We might, in fact, learn something truly fascinating."

Elena looked at Dave with her head tilted slightly to one side. She was, Dave knew, processing what he had said to her. Oh, how he wished he were as attentive a listener as she, particularly in view of the type of work he was in!

The approach of the youthful steps of the ancient innkeeper interrupted the couple's staring into each others' eyes. don Pedro carried a bottle of wine wrapped in a towel and two tulip-shaped glasses.

"don Pedro," Dave interjected as he began to pour, "please join us."

The old man's eyes widened. "You do not wish to be alone with our Elena?" Turning to the young lady, he commented wryly, "This *muchacho* is even younger than I thought!"

The American chuckled. "It's hardly that," he said, "it's just that we've been discussing your wines, and something of great interest has come up which I would, please, like to ask you about."

"*Claro*," don Pedro answered softly as he pulled a chair over from the next table.

Dave slid a wineglass in front of Pedro. The innkeeper started to rise to get another glass, but Dave gently put his hand on the older man's forearm to stop him.

"Elena and I can share a glass," he said by way of explanation.

"Ahhh," don Pedro exhaled with raised eyebrows, but his expression quickly settled into a warm and accepting smile.

"don Pedro, I was going to ask you a question, but I think I already know the answer. Just confirm what I'm going to say, if you would, please, Sir, and if I'm correct, of course. You have been able to manage without grafting your *vinifera* cuttings onto American root stocks." Dave paused expectantly. "Am I right?"

"American root stocks?" don Pedro asked with a puzzled look on his face.

"Yeah, you know, so they won't get *phylloxera*."

"Elena, what is this *norteamericano* talking about?"

"Bill will have to explain it to you. It's a bit complex to take in all at once," she responded with a wink.

Dave was startled at the answer which appeared to involve no knowledge of *phyloxera* whatever. He recognized that he would have to obtain the answers he needed through some rather concrete questions.

"I'm sorry," Dave apologized. "Sometimes I go too fast through things. Uh, let me ask you this, please, don Pedro. Many years ago when you brought the vine clippings from California, how did you go about planting them?"

"I did not."

"I'm sorry, you said you didn't?"

"*Si . . . o . . . no.* No, I didn't plant the vines. I put the seeds in the ground."

Dave looked at the older man with a blank expression. His intended follow-up questions were quite obvious.

"Ah, *si, si*, yes, yes. They told me much up in California about what to do with the vines . . . cutting here, cutting there. But I am a simple innkeeper, not a . . . professor like them.

"Oh, I was going to try to do it all, though. I had all those vines unloaded off the ship. But, *Senor*, how was I going to get them all up here to Santa Rosa? I was much younger then, but I was still just one man. I bought a burro in La Navidad, but eighty kilometers with such a load . . . ah, *Dios Mio*, it would have killed both of us!

"So I picked twenty or thirty grapes of each type and brought them up here. The vines, they went in the sea."

Dave was obviously fascinated. "And the seeds, how did you remove them from the grapes and plant them?"

"Highly technical, as you *norteamericanos* say, highly technical. Pedro dug little holes, Pedro put the grapes between his fingers, and all the . . . what was inside . . . squirted into the little holes."

"And they grew?"

"*Claro que si*. Everything grows here," don Pedro exclaimed, motioning with his hands in an upward movement imitating the lush vegetation surrounding his little bar and restaurant.

"Thank you, *Senor*, thank you so much for telling me all of this."

The couple emerged into the bright sunlight.

"You are a very inquisitive *hombre.*"

"Yeah, I suppose I am."

The sleek black car headed north along a dirt road.

A small lane angled off to the left. Curiously, Dave thought, it got wider as they traveled along its course.

They drove past small homes in front of which children were playing.

Workers in the fields removed their hats and waved them at Elena as they passed.

She swung the car into the grand circular drive. Stone lions flanked the stairs up to the gray mansion.

"This is not just a simple farm," Dave concluded to himself.

Elena brought the Jaguar to a halt beside the fountain.

Dave had to scramble to keep up with the young lady as she strode across the pebble stones.

An elderly dark-skinned woman emerged from the double doors of the house's front. The two women embraced.

"*Mi Elena, mi carida Elena,*" the woman said with tears running down her cheeks.

"*Carmen, eres mi madre verdedera ahora.*"

Dave followed the two into the massive marble-floored entrance hall. Elena plopped her purse and sunglasses onto a table in the middle of the room. She snatched her regular glasses from her purse and put them on as she spoke rapidly and hurriedly to Carmen.

Elena introduced Dave, as Bill of course, to Carmen. She explained that the older lady had been her "Nanny," an explanation that was hardly necessary under the circumstances.

"*Y El Patron?* How is your father with your mother now gone?"

"Very well, indeed. As a matter of fact, he's living in Alaska with a lady who's younger than me!"

"*Dios mio!* He always was a man of great energy. But Alaska?"

"Sherry's family has investments up there, in oil. Besides, you know how Father always hated the heat."

"Haaa," Carmen responded with a wave of her fleshy hand. "I grew up with your father here on the *estancia*. A kind and good man he is. But a complainer, oh, oh. He complains of everything his whole life, since he was a boy. You may depend upon it, Elena, that in no time you will be getting letters from don Antonio crying about the cold and the snow."

"Well, that hasn't happened yet. Of course, they do seem to spend about as much time in Hawaii as they do in Alaska."

Carmen laughed heartedly. "Perhaps he will now be truly happy, at long last."

A young man appeared with their suitcases.

As they trudged up the grand staircase, Carmen remarked offhandedly and between rapid exchanges in a Spanish-Indian dialect with the younger woman, "We'll put *Senor Guillermo* in your brother's room, no?"

"*Si*," Elena answered with similar casualness.

Dave hoped that his disappointment didn't show on the outside!

The light gauze-like curtains fluttered gently in the breeze as the little group walked to the end of the long hall. Carmen swung open a massive wooden door, and the young man took the case belonging to the male into the room. Dave followed dutifully. It was, he thought, a bit like being placed in a jail cell. But it was at least a pleasant enough cell! The large bed appeared uncomfortable, but as it was a corner room, there was a refreshing cross-breeze.

"When you are ready, *Senor Guillermo*," Carmen called back into the room, "I've prepared a light lunch for you."

As the two women retreated down the hall, he could hear Carmen commenting, "That is all you have wanted since you got back from the States, a light lunch. Ah, look at you, *Nina*, how skinny you are."

Dave experienced the meal as something of a study in contrasts. The cold-cuts were neatly and thinly sliced, like at a fashionable cocktail-buffet back home. But they were to be placed on thick, obviously home-made bread. A carafe of don Pedro's wine was the centerpiece for the occasion.

The wine was a Chardonnay. His tasting of it reinforced the impression he had formed earlier at the restaurant. It was, somehow, both unusually tasteful and delicate. Perhaps there was something to this pre-*phylloxera* thing after all. But then one could never be sure, there being so many complex factors involved. Again, though, Dave's thinking rambled on, what you feed cattle does affect the taste of the beef. And type of soil changes the quality of wines. So why not what the nourishment passes through? He would most certainly take all this up with his wine club back in D.C.

As the couple walked away from the mansion, Elena inquired into how Dave had found his room.

"Lonely," was his pitiful reply.

Elena smiled sweetly, almost maternally.

"Oh, Bill," she began slowly and softly, "I do hope you understand. Carmen and the others have spent their entire lives here on the *estancia*. They are unfamiliar with the changes that have taken place outside."

Dave was, in the main, a respecter of tradition. And he did, in fact, understand. But he did feel that the circumstances justified a bit of pouting on his part. So he gave the beautiful young lady his most doleful look. It had, in all probability, been inspired by the Basset Hound with whom he had grown up in Ohio.

"*Ah, no te precoupes, cielo.* The servants, I mean the help, never come back upstairs after I dismiss them."

Dave's countenance brightened. "How will I know when the coast is clear?"

"I believe it best that I come to you. I think I walk a lot more softly then you. Additionally, someone misguidedly might come to protect me from you. I don't believe anyone would rush upstairs to protect you from me."

"Doesn't seem too likely," Dave acknowledged cheerfully.

"You know, Carmen asked me if I wished her to sleep upstairs. I responded no, that you were a perfect gentleman." She reached out and caressing his cheek, continued, "Which you are, but perhaps not in just the way Carmen understood it!"

"She certainly has a way of making a guy feel better about things," Dave thought to himself.

A huge verdant meadow stood before them as they emerged from the stand of nut trees through which they had been strolling. It was surrounded by a very solid-looking log fence.

"We could walk down to the gate," Elena commented, "but it's so much simpler to climb over, don't you think?"

As Dave turned to study the obstacle with which he was confronted, he could see the back of her tan trousers bobbing up as she moved swiftly from one rung of the structure to the next. He followed behind her.

Having achieved the open field, Elena set a course for a small hill on which stood five massive and ancient oaks.

As they strode rapidly through the lush grass, Dave caught sight of a gigantic bull a couple of hundred feet off to his right. Keeping his eyes trained on the potentially dangerous adversary, he urgently reached out and grabbed Elena's elbow.

"Oh, that's just Ferdinand. He's as tame as a kitten."

"Ferdinand?"

"*Sí.* We get that cartoon her, too. I named him myself."

Sure enough, Ferdinand watched the pair for a couple of seconds and then apparently decided that the grass was still the most interesting object in his home field.

They were both slightly but pleasantly winded by the time they got to the top of the hill. It was a sense of exhilaration.

The couple entered into something that put Dave in mind of a tent out of *Arabian Nights*. He had always had quite a fantasy life! The branches of the trees had spread such a thick and intertwining cover over the space between them that it was almost dark within. The absence of sunlight had left the "tent's" floor without the usual heavy undergrowth typical of the region. There was, instead, a luxurious carpet of moss. Exposed roots of the gnarled trees served as the room's furniture.

Elena motioned for him to sit, and she took a nearby "chair."

As Dave stared out into the bright sunlight beyond the branches, Elena said softly, "I used to come here often when I was a little girl."

Dave closed his eyes and leaned his head against the tree trunk. He breathed in the cool, dank air and reached out to hold Elena's hand.

"Tell me what you were like as a little girl."

"Oh, I guess you could say I was something of a tomboy. You see this scar on my elbow? Well, I received that when I fell just about where you're seated now. Miguel and I decided to construct the grandest tree house, and . . . ."

# CHAPTER 9

# "THEY LEFT WHEN IT WAS ALL GONE"

She moved. He could feel her sliding away from him. Dave reached out to stop her, but her hip brushed under the palm of his hand as he brought it down.

Opening his eyes, he could see Elena's silhouette against the dazzling curtain of light from the open and unshaded window. He instantly understood what had happened. During the night, during one of her visits to the "potty"—the refined young woman at times still enjoyed using the American slang she had picked up in finishing school—she had flung wide-open the room-darkening shades, thereby creating a natural alarm clock which would awaken her before those who slumbered below. She would, he knew, pad silently to her room where in an hour or so she would be "awakened" by her old Nanny and friend. While she wasn't "cool," at least as that phrase had been used by those with whom he had grown up, he was so proud of the lady who had just left his side.

He decided it best not to let on that he was conscious, let alone the depth of his thinking.

Elena leaned over and kissed him gently on the cheek. He felt that, under the circumstances, the wisest reaction would still be one of unconsciousness. This decision was severely tested when her soft but firm breasts slipped across his chest as she began to stand straight up.

"I am", he thought to himself, "a man of consummate self-restraint and control." Thinking thusly, but while laughing at himself, he clutched his pillow and went back to sleep.

Dave appreciated the fact that an effort had been made to give him "American coffee." It was served to him out of what appeared to be a percolator and into a regulation-sized cup. But, boy, was it thick! He didn't know whether to use the spoon to stir it or bring it to his mouth sip-by-sip like a chowder. Apparently, they had made it in their usual European manner and then added a few drops of water. Well, it was a nice gesture!

Elena was seated across from him. She wore a white blouse and a simple brown skirt. Wholesome was the word that came to his mind.

The gleaming black car maneuvered carefully out of the circular driveway, Elena at the wheel.

Moving through the intersection of the village, they turned right, heading west.

Three miles down the road they came to what can only be described as a ghost town. Had it not been for the fact that the buildings were of stucco, it could have been one of the deserted cities he had seen during the time he had lived in Nevada. Of course, there was no tumbleweed, he had to acknowledge.

Elena stopped the car in the very middle of the street in front of what had been the company store.

"This," she announced, "is our Tombstone."

"Looks more like Belmont to me," Dave said impulsively, recalling his poking around the sagebrush of Nevada.

"Belmont?"

"Yeah, finest ghost town I've ever seen."

"Where is it, Bill?"

"Nevada, between Reno and Las Vegas."

"*Ven, ven, entonces.* Come see our Belmont."

Dave stepped out of the Jaguar and onto a street half overgrown by the encroaching jungle.

They walked slowly through the deserted streets. The wind rattled the loose boards on the roofs of the houses. The couple walked into the store. The shelves were empty and laced with spider webs.

"What . . . what happened here?" Dave asked.

"Mines . . . An American mining company built this town," was Elena's reply.

"Mine? What did they mine?"

'Silver, but it ran out."

"And the people?"

"They left. There was no more work."

"But certainly," Dave said, "the company left something to help those who had worked for them."

"No, this is all that is left."

"But what became of the miners, the workers?"

"They went to farm, one supposes."

"Gee, not much left here."

"No, not much."


Dave leaned back against the bar in the old saloon and pulled Elena to him.


On the way back to the *estancia* and lunch, Dave inquired into the story of Cuidad del Plato.

"They came when I was a little girl. They offered work to all the men."

"Whose mine was it?"

"The company was called American Mining and Engineering. They built the city so the men could be close to the mine. There was intense activity for two or three years. The men walked up the hill one morning and the gate was padlocked. I suppose all the silver was gone. They left when it was all gone."


Lunch consisted of chicken breasts and rice. don Pedro's wine was present, of course.

"I took," Elena announced, "our friend out to Cuidad del Plato."

"It was good for our people while it lasted," Carmen commented.

"I was shocked to see the raw earth left on the mountainside outside of the tunnels. Back in the States the mining companies . . . uh, we are required to at least plant some kind of cover over areas like that."

Elena shook her head. "Sadly, there are no such laws in Cortesia. The mining companies did not even pay taxes."

"How can that be?" Dave asked.

All at the table merely shrugged their shoulders.

As usual, Monday came sooner than anyone would have expected. But, thankfully, this Monday was not a work day, but one of recreation if not of relaxation. Most importantly, Dave told himself as he drug the razor across the stubble on his face, he would be spending this entire Monday with Elena.

They parked outside the walls. There actually wouldn't have been a need at all to try to squeeze the car into the narrow, crowded streets. The wall around La Cuidad de Los Reyes, it turned out, was only an even mile in its entire length. So they easily could and would walk to the Palace.

Waiting for the ceremony to begin, Dave became aware of a number of men with closely cropped hair—soldiers, obviously. And their slightly darker complexions suggested to him that they were probably Cubans. Pulling his camera up to eye level, he pointed it in Elena's direction, but actually focused on the face of a gray-haired crew-cut man several paces behind her.

Elena smiled although she realized that her face was in the shadows. "Oh, well, "she thought to herself, "Bill is in the mining business, not photography."

Everyone cheered the "Royal Governor" as he left the Palace in the ancient carriage. Little girls threw flower pedals in his path.

The little motor which lowered the shades over the windows made a soft whirring sound. The room was now dark; the first of the slides was being projected on the large screen at the end of the conference table.

"Crew-cut there is obviously Dave's subject" the man in the three-piece suit noted. "Have you had any luck in running down who he is?"

The Colonel smiled. "Yes, Mr. Chairman, we think we can help you with this one." The officer pushed a button, and the brightly colored tropical view disappeared. In its place appeared a cold and grainy black and white picture of a group of uniformed men standing outside a massive stone building. Most were smoking. "This was taken during Castro's last visit to Moscow. We believe that the man with his arms folded on the right is the same fellow as in the picture your man in Cortesia sent."

"Who is he?"

"We're not sure of the man's name. As a matter of fact, for a long time we didn't even know that he was Cuban. He spent the bulk of '87 at various hush-hush military bases in the Soviet Union. He always wore undecorated khakis, and he spoke Russian. We knew he wasn't Russian because of his accent. We thought it was probably Spanish, but there was no way to be sure.

"Well, Fidel's visit got him into uniform and to Moscow, where we snapped him. Assuming that he's wearing his proper uniform, and there's no reason to believe he isn't, he's a general in their artillery branch. He was touring Soviet missile bases. That fits because Cuban missile personnel are assigned to artillery."

"It also fits with what Dave has been telling us. There's heavy involvement of the Cuban military in Cortesia, and they're artillerymen . . ."

"And women," added Ms. Sterns.

"And women, of course. Now, Sir, here's the next shot."

"The dark haired lady in all these is undoubtedly Elena de la Madrid. What have we got on her?"

"We know a lot about her," the Colonel replied. Riffling through his papers, he pulled out several sheets which had been stapled together. "She's officially only a minor aide in the Foreign Ministry, but she comes from a very prominent family, so she's been in the Cortesian press almost constantly during her thirty-so years."

"She's a fine looking gal," the Chairman commented appreciatively.

"She certainly is that," Colonel Smathers answered. "As a matter of fact, when she was in school, she was publicly urged to enter the Miss Cortesia Pageant. They figured she'd really charm them in Miami Beach. Sort of put 'Ol Cortesia on the map. But she's not oriented that way. Pity. Perhaps she . . ."

"What exactly does she do down there?" the willowy suntanned blond asked impatiently, interrupting the two men's drooling admiration.

"Uh, she works directly for the Foreign Minister entertaining, touring foreign visitors around, making sure their stays are comfortable, that sort of thing. He must rely on her a lot because she's gone with him in delegations to capitals all over the world."

Molly Sterns seized upon that word "entertaining." "Well," she said, brushing her sun-bleached hair back, "she must be a lot more entertaining than informative. We sure haven't gotten a whole hell of a lot of information out of her so far. What are she and Wilkinson doing together down there in Bananaland, anyway?"

"You know, Mr. Chairman, she may have a point there. As close to the center of things as this gal is, you would have thought we would have gotten more inside information. So far, almost everything we've gotten seems to come from looking through fences and the newspaper."

"Maybe he's saving it up, looking for some kind of pattern. Dave used to be a college professor, you know. He sometimes displays rather a need to try to make sense of things on his own. Molly, when you go down there next week, perhaps you can find out what's going on?"

"You bet I will."

# CHAPTER 10

# "HOW THE HELL HAVE YOU BEEN, CHUCK?"

" *S enor Robinson, Senor Robinson,*" the clerk called out as Dave strode through the hotel lobby after returning from a rather late night out with the lady.

"Yes, uh, *si,*" the American responded, obviously having been snatched back from rather intense pondering.

"A message for you, *Senor.*"

His heart sank as he crossed the floor, his shoes making clicking sounds, to the desk. His first thought is that it could be from "Her." They had just taken a long walk through the tropical night in which they had discussed their growing love and dependence on each other. She had drawn his head to her shoulder as they had stood on the dock, purringly telling him not to be afraid. But he still had his fears.

Has she herself become scared and wants to end it?

Might she, after all, have a commitment to someone else?

The horrible thoughts flicked through his mind.

The clerk handed him the message, and he opened it with trembling hands.

*Just arrived at El Presidente. Anxious to see you.*
*Janet*

Well, it was bad, but not as bad as it could have been!

He would, of course, have to put in a call tonight, he decided as he trudged up the marble stairs. But it wasn't an emergency, so he could take a nice, warm shower first.

As arranged, he walked into the dining room of the El Presidente, La Navidad's largest and least interesting hotel. It was called by locals "The Barracks."

There she was, at the center table eating breakfast with a group of co-eds and a young professor type in a tweed coat. Tweed in a country so near the Equator! "Where did they get these people?" he wondered. It's easy to see why they think *norteamericanos* are nuts. And from where did they get the young people? "Gee, you'd have to pay me Big Bucks to go on a trip with Molly. It would be like a mobile prison," he mumbled to himself.

The tall, thin blond rose and walked across the cavernous room to approach her old acquaintance. She planted a kiss on his left cheek. He hoped the wince wasn't noticeable.

"How the Hell have you been, Chuck?" was her opening remark.

He brushed his hand over the cheek, even though he knew full well that Valley Girls don't wear lipstick. There was saliva.

"Good, Janet, good. How do you manage to stay so thin?"

"Well, like I work out every day at the beach, you know."

"Boy, if they buy this, they deserve to be spied on," he thought. A "Valley Girl" from Kansas who works out at the beach. Get real!

One of the girls, brunette, busty, young enough to be his daughter, moved over a seat so he could sit next to Molly.

"Thanks a lot," he said silently to himself.

"Like you know, Bill, Andrew is going to take the group to the museum this later today, so you can show me the sights."

He hoped the smile he forced was at least half-way convincing.

As they walked through the Cathedral, Molly several times reached out and held Dave's hand. Their cover was, after all, that they were old, dear romantic friends. It was a tribute to his professionalism that he managed to squeeze her hand back and swing their arms together as they moved on in their "tour" to the National Palace.

The head waiter seated them at a corner table at the Frey Junipero. Dave had been less than truthful when he told her that this was the best place in the City for lunch. Somehow, he didn't want to take Molly to the little outdoor café that he and Elena had come to call "our restaurant."

"I guess you'll have to order for me," she said loudly. "No one in this filthy hell-hole seems to know how to speak English."

"I speak English," the waiter announced with obvious reserve. "What will Madam have?"

Dave winced. He literally wished that he could sink through the floor. He also wished that he could convince people that she was from another country, any country but the United States. But it was, he realized sadly, far too late for that!

"Janet," he said reproachfully as soon as the waiter had walked away, "you must watch what you say."

The woman was quite literally taken aback. She knew that she had in no way violated security. ". . . Oh, oh . . . like you mean that hell-hole bit?"

"Precisely."

She clasped her hands with her exceedingly long fingernails together and looked up toward the ceiling, striking a mockingly angelic pose. "However might I be forgiven?"

Dave shook his head. "Can't you see that all these people know about us Americans is how we behave while we're here?"

"Do I look like an Ugly American to you?" she shot back. "I don't think anyone would call me an Ugly American," she continued, stroking her arms in a human form of preening.

"Well, there's that old misconception again. In point of fact, the 'ugly' American was the only good one of the lot. All the other embassy personnel went around insulting the citizenry. But that shouldn't bother you . . . Janet. Maybe that's why you haven't taken the time to actually read the book."

"O-o-h . . . like excuse me, professor." Molly looked around quickly to make sure no one was listening. She leaned across the table at Dave and spat out the words, "I'll tell you something, Buster. Sometimes I think you've gone over."

Mercifully, the waiter brought the check rapidly. The poor man was probably as anxious for them to leave as he was to get Molly out of there. Dave had very much enjoyed his veal cutlet, but he knew that he would never again return to Frey Junipero. She had had the chopped steak smothered in gravy. Of course, she compared it negatively to McDonald's.

But she wasn't through yet. As he paid the bill, she commented, "This place is like really in the boonies. The john in my room doesn't work. We have to traipse down the hall like . . . like at camp!"

While Dave was careful to address the cashier in Spanish, she made it a point to respond to him in English.

Being temporarily without an indigenous audience to berate, she started in on him as they walked to his rental car.

"You know, Dave, I'm real concerned about your drinking. I noticed that you had a glass of wine with your lunch."

"But you had a beer. In fact, you had two beers."

"I had to. I'm not going to drink the filthy water around here. Anyway, I'll let 'um know at 'home' about this."

"I have no doubt whatsoever that you will," he responded dryly.

Dave walked toward the passenger side of the car to open the door for Molly, but she waved him off.

"I'll drive. You're too pokey."

He shrugged his shoulders and plopped into the seat as Molly walked around to the driver's side.

She slid under the wheel. Dave handed her the key, and she turned on the switch. The boxy little car shuddered and the engine started.

"This is a piece of junk," she commented with her typical disdain.

"Well, at least we can agree on one thing."

They were off with a jolt.

"You know, they have a seat belt law here in Cortesia."

She glared at him. "Shit!"

They returned to being "Bill and Janet" during the drive. There was the chance that the little import had been bugged, and the banging around Dave might have done to find the mic would have been about as good as announcing that he was a spy.

"Your mother told me that this country has a beautiful coastline. Let's go see it."

"Go right at the fountain roundabout just up ahead."

"How do these people live in those dirty hovels? Yuk!"

"I'm sure they enjoy them. After all, they've chosen to live that way."

Again the icy stare.

"You might think of keeping your eyes on the road."

"OK. Chuck."

He hated that nickname. He couldn't even remember when she had started to call him that. He had no doubt that it was some type of insult. It probably had something to do with Peanuts and Charlie Brown, but he really hadn't cared enough to ask.

As they drove up the coastal highway, Dave was struck by how utterly different this trip was from the others he had taken. The most obvious change was the jerking and chugging of the little box in which they were riding, which was in marked contrast to the solid smoothness of Elena's Jaguar. But what he missed most wasn't Elena's car.

Well, at least it was reassuring, it provided some consolation, that the deep blue water continued to crash majestically against the rocks. If he focused on this dynamic interaction of land and sea, perhaps he could forget that he was "alone" on this trip. Perhaps there was hope for the future.

"Pretty piss-poor surf, if you ask me."

Dave was vaguely aware of someone speaking, but he really didn't hear what she had said.

"Bill, Bill," she screamed at him, irritated by his obvious lack of attention. "Where the hell is your head?"

"On mining, always on mining," was his droll response. Molly countered with a disdainful sneer.

"I hear you've found a nice young lady to pass your time with here in Hades."

"Yeah, Elena de la Madrid."

"One of those voluptuous Latin types, I suppose."

"Yeah, you could say that," he answered with perhaps too big a smile on his face.

"They get fat when they get older. You know, 'early ripe, early rot'."

"Well, it must happen a lot after 30," Dave answered with a wave of his hand which was designed to make it seem a casual comment. He hoped to brush off the subject before he became angry and defensive.

Ah, a return to silence. By far the best part of this seemingly long journey, he concluded.

Molly turned the tiny compact off onto a rustic scenic overlook, a long spit of land which jutted out into the ocean.

She looked sternly at her captive passenger.

Dave nodded. He actually knew of no reason why they couldn't or shouldn't have their "little talk" here.

As they moved away from the vehicle, Dave walked in the slow, hunched manner of a man on the way to be executed. Well, if not executed, at least beaten. Of course, what he actually found himself thinking about the most was his fear that a friend of Elena's would see him with "her." He could wind up sacrificing a lifetime with Elena for an afternoon with Molly. Not much of an exchange! He caught himself. Did he say "lifetime"? Not very realistic under the circumstances. Well, he'd have to sort all that out later. Right now, he had plenty of other things to think about!

They walked down a vaguely cut path to the right of the outcropping of land on which she had parked and down to a collection of rocks at the base of an imposing, barren cliff. Not even any boats were around. Here they could have their talk in privacy.

Dave plopped himself down on the least jagged of the rocks. He folded his hands in his lap and looked up passively at Molly. There was no question as to who was conducting this particular meeting.

"Well, Dave, do you want to review what you've learned first?"

"Oh, let's go ahead and hear the bad news. I was getting a bit giddy," he replied with a weak smile.

The long tanned legs turned abruptly in the sand. "You're a real smart ass."

Dave flashed Molly a toothy grin.

"Well, I'll tell you what they're concerned about in Washington." She emphasized the word "concerned." "You've been spending all this time with this Elena person, and you're not getting shit out of her."

He straightened his back preparatory to attributing some of the tid-bits he had sent back to Elena, but Molly cut him off.

"What in Christ's name are you doing with her?"

"As needed," he replied in his most business-like voice.

"As needed," she responded with disgust. "You know, Dave, you're a Royal Chump."

The word "chump" took him by surprise. He was expecting something more like "letch."

"You never could see beyond a big pair of boobs." The pacing resumed. "You see, Dave, Ole Molly here stayed late one night and did some homework on your Miss Muffin." She could have just told him what she had found out about Elena, but again, she took delight in playing with him for a while. "Yes, Sir, I not only went over all the news items we had on Honey Buns, but I checked out everyone she had ever been seen with. And I even checked her out through the press outside Cortesia."

Dave stared at her, unable to comprehend what she was talking about.

"Ever wonder why Twittly Tits never got married? I'm sure it wasn't because she wouldn't put out, as you must know so well." The cat had its mouse, and she was enjoying playing with him. Dave squirmed on his rock.

"Yeah, she went out with lots of young men, guys in her own class, you know, aristocrats. 'Miss Elena de la Madrid was at Count So-and-So's party with Sir Such-and-Such.' Few months later, different guy who had been, as they say, 'born with a silver spoon in his mouth.' Get the picture, Dave?"

"No, I don't get the picture. As you so often point out, I'm slow."

"Well, I'll make it clear to you. Satchel Ass is a real pinko. The only friends she's kept over the years have been Commies."

"Her father was Army Chief of Staff."

"This is true, but I think you'll find that the Old Fart's victories all took place between two sheets . . . Know where he is now?"

"Alaska."

"Yeah, and with?"

"I know, a gal younger than Satchel Ass."

"Actually, he's screwing her in Kauai right now. The whole family's just a lot of high class trash."

Dave cocked his head again. Antonio more and more sounded like his kind of guy!

"Well," she continued, "what went wrong with her 'young men' was that they had ideological differences . . ."

"Ideological differences?" It was like an alien expression to Dave. He had never thought about it as applying to Elena's unmarried status.

"Yeah, these guys were upper crust, living off their inheritances and all. But Twittly Tits disapproved. She wants the wealth redistributed, you know, spread around . . ."

Dave gave her a vacant stare, which was genuine.

"Look, I'll spell it out for you. Half of her friends are card-carrying Communists."

David Wilkinson, secret agent of the Government of the United States of America, should have been shocked, outraged was a better word. But he wasn't. Sitting on that rock, it all became clear to him. Elena had been born into wealth and privilege. But she could feel what the other people felt. He had never known anyone who could listen, understand and empathize like dear Elena. All the times he had sat on her couch talking to her flashed through his mind. He had gotten lost in her deep, brown eyes. He had talked about his childhood, his fears and his dreams. The way she listened, the way she grew sad as he spoke of disappointments, the way she brightened at his successes, like in Little League, made him feel that she had actually been with him, that she could experience what he had experienced.

Of course, she could see "her people" working for pennies a day for a U.S. corporation that cared not a whit for them or their children. And, of course, she could feel their suffering in her heart. And she would want to do something. But what? Somehow change the system, that's what. So that group of "students" in her apartment that afternoon had actually been a type of cell meeting, liberal, antiestablishment certainly, Communist perhaps. He may actually have seen a Communist cell meeting! The thought strangely excited him, thrilled him.

"I do hope you had a nice trip," she interrupted.

He stirred himself back into the conversation. "You know, just because you hang out with lawyers doesn't make you one."

"You're so naïve. The Government's riddled with them. The Prime Minister is a solid U.S. supporter, but he's old and sick. His underlings are playing footsy with the Fidelistas."

"Yeah, that's true. *Senor Hernandez* is not at all on top of things."

"Well, what you ought to be doing is figuring out how the Commies were able to get into a conservative government like this one."

"Yeah, that's been puzzling me."

"Well, it's getting late, so let's go over what we've learned. The people in Washington had some questions about that big base up in the mountains. Specifically, what . . ."

It was good to be off the hook, but Dave was sure it was only temporary.

CHAPTER **11**

# "WERE YOU LOVERS?"

I t was an unusually cool day for Cortesia. A storm was brewing up miles out to sea. So far, the only effect of this had been a lovely breeze. If they were lucky, the disturbance would move off to the north, passing them by. If, on the other hand, it veered inland toward them, there could, judging from past experience, be major problems.

Elena wore a medium-weight tan suit and a champagne-colored blouse. She had bought the outfit during her student days in Europe. It was such a pity that she had so few opportunities to wear the nice clothes she had gotten "On the Continent," as they say, here in the tropics. She made it a point to take advantage of every opportunity to do so, however. She did not, though, appear to be taking a great deal of pleasure in the occasion. Elena had been quiet, even somber, during their walk from the Ministry. Her beautiful face, so reminiscent of Elizabeth Taylor in her younger years, seemed stressed. She was definitely preoccupied.

Dave was decidedly uncomfortable. He knew that "something" was wrong, and he couldn't help being afraid that he knew exactly what that "something" was. He fell silent too, into his own thoughts, as they walked mechanically to "their" café.

"Well", he said to himself, "you're really blowing it this time. Damn you!" Of course, he had meant to tell her about "Janet." But the time just never seemed right. Of course and come to think of it, he really couldn't think of when the right time might have been. Molly had made a point for the two of them to be seen walking arm and arm around the City for the past few days. He should have known that someone would have mentioned these apparent going-ons to Elena.

The hour was late, but he decided to rush in and rescue what of the situation he could. He might, he thought sadly to himself, actually have nothing to lose.

They sat down awkwardly at the little table to which they just naturally gravitated. Dave swept a large lock of hair away from his eyebrows as Elena watched in silence. He took a deep breath and cleared his throat.

"You know," he began in an already failed attempt at casualness, "an old friend of mine, of the family really, is in town."

Elena looked down at her folded hands with their flawlessly manicured fingernails. "Yes . . . uh, yes, someone did happen to remark that you had . . . uh . . . company."

Dave was seized with terror. Her response was such that he couldn't tell what it meant. What might she say next? He felt welling up within himself an amazingly strong impulse to tell her the truth, everything. But, no, he couldn't do that. Or could he? "No, no, no," he said to himself as he struggled for breath.

"I hear that she is quite pretty, tall, thin and blond. She sounds like the type who is, how do they say, in fashion in your country."

That was encouraging, he thought to himself. At least she wanted to know about the situation. There was hope, he hoped.

"I don't know," he stammered. "Look, it's not what you must think."

"Maybe it doesn't matter what I think. Perhaps it is none of my business."

"No, no . . . I mean yes, yes, it is your business. At least I want it to be. I love you so much."

"I love you, too," Elena said thoughtfully. She took off her glasses and looked at Dave, turning her head slightly to one side. "But maybe that's the kind of woman you want, one with a lithe figure who looks like she just came off the beach. Here you just have me. Maybe that is why we have been having problems."

Boy, she sure gave him plenty to think about!

"First of all, you're beautiful."

"Wouldn't you say more 'wholesome,' somewhat like a school teacher?" she mumbled, again lowering her eyes.

"No! You're gorgeous."

Dave put his index finger under her chin and gently lifted her face up until their eyes met. He was rewarded with a faint smile which he found very, very reassuring.

After permitting himself a small sigh of relief, he continued. "And, I don't want someone like that. Maybe I did once, but I know better now. Elena, you've helped me understand things I've never understood before."

The smile on her lips broadened momentarily, but she turned her head further into his hand that was stroking her soft cheek. Clearly, she wanted more of an explanation.

Thoughts raced through his mind. It was so paradoxical. He was, indeed, here in Cortesia under utterly false pretenses. But in terms of Molly he actually had nothing to hide. There was, in fact, less than nothing between them, at least not now.

"Janet . . . Janet Sanders, that's her name . . . , is the daughter of a lady who goes to the same church as my parents do. We both grew up in the same town in upstate New York. She's here leading a student tour, and her mother asked my mother for me to show her around. That sort of thing. She's a very demonstrative person," he added lamely in an effort to pass off their hand-holding as being merely a component of such rituals as the perfunctory kiss on the cheek between women and men who fancy themselves part of the "Hollywood Set."

How, he wondered, could he prove what he was saying? The idea briefly flashed through his head that he could introduce her to "Janet." That would, at least theoretically, make the whole thing seem above-board. But it certainly wouldn't work in the present instance. Beyond, undoubtedly, provoking an "international incident," Molly was a sure bet to make some comment, probably crude, which would let out the fact that he and she had, in fact, had sex. Of course, he could explain that that was a long time ago. But what he couldn't explain to Elena was how lonely and, yes, frightened he had been during his first overseas mission.

"Were you lovers?" she asked in a soft voice, almost a whisper.

The question took him by surprise. He hadn't really expected such directness from the refined young lady. "Briefly, a long time ago," he replied, almost without thinking.

An island of honesty in a sea of deception! He had shocked himself yet again.

Why, he wondered, had he responded with such candor, particularly when it was so unnecessary?

She closed her eyes as though experiencing a fleeting pain. Then the soft smile returned. "It is over then?" she asked.

"Yes, over," he replied in a chocked voice.

Her understanding smile changed into a slightly mischievous grin. "When does this . . . Janet person leave our country?"

"This Janet person," he intoned with an air of finality, "leaves our country tomorrow."

"We will wish her the most felicitous of journeys, of course." She patted his hand in an almost motherly fashion.

"*Bien viaje, bien viaje,*" he repeated as he stared into her deep brown eyes.

The waitress, with Dave not even looking up to see her face, put their plates in front of the couple.

Biting into the fresh seafood, he certainly felt very much on top of things. But this sense of well-being was only temporary. He realized that he had forgotten an important point that the Elena had made. She had said that they had "problems."

"You know," he said after taking a sip of the very delectable Chardonnay, "you said we had 'problems.' Of course, I wanted to . . . ." Something seemed to catch in his throat, ". . . follow up on that. Am I doing something wrong?"

"No, *Cielo*, it is not that you are doing something 'wrong,' as such. It is just that something keeps happening that I don't at all understand."

There was a long pause.

"What do you mean?" he finally managed to ask.

"Well, it is a little hard to explain. We go places and have lovely times. And we talk. Oh, how I love our talks. We seem to, as they say in your country, relate so well. But there are times when you become, *Como se dice? Evasivo . . . .*"

"Evasive?"

"Yes," she smiled weakly. "There are times when I ask about things like your childhood or your job, and there is a long pause, like you're trying to think of what to say, or perhaps what not to say. Is it that you don't want me to know certain things about you? That would hurt me very much . . . I love you. There's nothing wrong, is there? I mean, you're not in some kind of trouble?"

"Oh, no, nothing like that." He looked directly into Elena's eyes and squeezed her hand. "I promise you that I've done nothing wrong."

"There have been times when I've worried about that. I believe you, Bill, and I am most relieved."

"If there's one thing I am it's law-abiding," Dave said, ending at least that phase of the conversation.

"Then, My Dear, what is our problem?"

"Uh, I . . . I don't know. I guess maybe I'm just not used to being in an intimate relationship. You know, you're an exceptional woman. There aren't many as sensitive and perceptive as you."

Elena didn't know if she was being complemented or put off.

As it turned out, it was a bit of both.

Some wispy clouds appeared in the sky as they walked again on the cobblestones.

"I have," she said somewhat self-consciously, "a rather sad errand to accomplish this afternoon."

"Sad?"

"Yes, at the cemetery."

"I'll accompany you," Dave said in a subdued voice. He assumed that Elena planned to visit the grave of her mother. He knew that she had been dead for about three years.

She approached a street vendor and bought a bouquet of blue flowers. Dave was hardly a botanist, so he hadn't the foggiest what they were.

Turning left on the way back to the Ministry, they ascended some steps he had never even noticed before. The narrow, sinuous staircase delivered them to a great wooden door with iron clamps. It stood in the middle of a gloomy stone fence.

Elena transferred the flowers to her left hand and reached for the middle of the ring. But the door opened of its own accord. A man in a white suit emerged from the portal. He was in his late forties. He wore a somber expression on his face. Dave had seen him in the halls of the War Ministry, as well as, come to think of it, at the meeting in Elena's apartment. The distinguished man and Elena exchanged wordless nods.

They entered through the gate the gentleman had left ajar for them. The graves within were old, some so old, in fact, that the ground above them had sunken into the earth. The wind beat the branches of the huge oak trees into a rhythmic, mysterious dance. Elena reached out and put her hand around Dave's arm as they walked toward the back of the cemetery.

"This," she said in a hushed voice, "is the oldest cemetery in Cortesia. Crew members from the first ship from Spain are buried over there," she explained, pointing to a row of small, identical headstones.

Elena had a very different look on her face. There was a touch of sadness, no, no "inspired" would be a better word for the quality of her expression. They had come to what was obviously one of the newer graves in the back of the cemetery. Simple though it was, it had the only marble headstone that Dave could see.

## EDUARDO SANCHEZ GUTIERREZ
## 1920-1983
### *Nuestro Carido Professor*

Elena added her flowers to those that had already been neatly arranged on the bare soil of the grave. Elena knelt down and made the Sign of the Cross, the first act of religious devotion Dave had ever seen her perform. He withdrew a few paces, hands clasped together in front of him.

She looked at him expectantly, quizzically, as she rose to her feet. What, she was obviously thinking, must this *norteamericano* think of these proceedings?

"Who was *Senor Guiterrez*, a relative of yours?" he asked as they walked back down the narrow staircase.

"No, he was a teacher, a professor at the University, as a matter of fact. Today was the anniversary of his death."

"What did he teach?"

"Political economics," she replied sort of absent-mindedly.

"Must have been pretty popular."

"That, as you are so fond of saying, is an 'understatement'," she replied with a gradually brightening countenance. His gift for understatement had, apparently, helped lift the pall.

After escorting Elena back to the Ministry, Dave made his thrice-weekly walk-by of the docks. With the exception of the expected departure of one of the tankers, it was the same collection of ships. So he wouldn't have to write "home" about this this time. It suddenly struck him that whoever in the government was reading his mail, and Molly had told him that the lab had found definite evidence that that was happening, must wonder why a little old lady in upstate New York would want to hear about "harbor happenings." "And people think spying's become all satellites and computers," he said to himself, shaking his head.

As he strode back up the hill he decided that he wouldn't walk to the Interior Ministry with its, to him, incomprehensible geological records. He had during the day developed a "curiosity," and the University seemed the place to satisfy it.

*La Universidad Real de Cortesia* was centered on a plateau jutting out from the mountains immediately above the old section of the City. The last part of the trek up was arduous, to say the least. But the magnificent view of the Old City and the harbor somewhat compensated one for the exertion.

The University was a study in contrasts. But because it so resembled most U.S. universities in this regard, this didn't impress itself much upon Dave. Gray Greek Revival buildings were neatly arranged into a "quad" on the small, level area of the plateau. Brick, "Frank Lloyd Wright" buildings were scattered rather haphazardly up the slopes. Obviously the science buildings or "Ag Hill," he thought to himself as he looked up the foothills behind the more classical-appearing structures.

The guy in the corduroy suit with the battered briefcase obviously worked here.

"Pardon me, Sir. Could you direct me to the Economics Department?" His use of English had been unthinking and automatic.

"Oh, A Yank," the man exclaimed. "Certainly, certainly. Second building on the left."

"Thank you so much." He wondered if he wore that suit during the usual, tropical climate of Cortesia. He rather imagined that he did.

The thick walls of the second building on the left imposed a bone-chilling type of coolness. It perhaps would have been refreshing if it were hotter outside, he reflected to himself.

He entered the first office he came to down the hall. The young woman at the desk was somehow familiar. She wore a dark business suit. Her black hair was tied back into a bun, and she also wore heavy dark-rimmed glasses like Elena's.

"*En que puedo sirvirle, Senor?*"

"Oh, I simply wanted to speak to one of your faculty members."

"One of the faculty?"

"Yes, just anyone who might have a few minutes."

"Well," she said as she rose from her desk, "we'll surely find someone."

They walked down the long hall until they came to the first open door. At a desk pushed up against the far wall sat a rotund man in light blue pants and a white shirt which was open at the collar.

"Dr. Mendez," the secretary announced, "this gentleman wishes to speak with one of our professors. Might you be able to spare him a few minutes?"

"But of course," the portly chap intoned.

"I'm Bill Robinson from the United States."

"Ah, this will give me an opportunity to practice my English, for which I am grateful to you . . . Well, to the point, how can a poor professor of economics be of help to you?"

"Well, a friend of mine was talking about a man who used to teach economics here. He's now deceased. His name was Eduardo Guiterrez. What she said about him aroused my curiosity, and I wanted to learn more about him. Did you happen to know him?"

Dave realized full-well that what he was doing was risky. After all, up to this point he had studiously avoided any direct questions about political matters. But he figured he could justify this on the basis of his close personal relationship with Elena and the rather natural desire to learn more about and understand someone who had been so obviously influential in her life.

The professor's eyes brightened. "Know him? Ah, yes, we all knew Eduardo well. Charming man, but, how you say, controversial?"

"Controversial?" Dave asked, feigning surprise. Mendez' opening comment suggested to Dave that he might just have found a key to some of the things that had been puzzling him for a long time.

"Well, I'd say that 'controversial' is putting it quite mildly. You see, back during the Batavia regime, he wrote a very controversial book which, basically, argued for the redistribution of wealth."

"Redistribution of wealth?"

"Indeed. And, as you can easily imagine, he was at times rumored to be a Communist. But the Old Boy was cagy. He never, never used the term Communism or even Socialism. The name Marx never appeared in his works. And he wrote a number of scathing articles denouncing the totalitarianism and brutality of various Communist regimes of the time. So he largely succeeded in being cleared of those charges.

"But his position was very interesting. He noted, of course, the tremendous disparity between the way our upper and lower classes live. One reason for this, according to Dr. Gutierrez, was, forgive me for saying so, *Senor*, American exploitation."

"I understand completely," Dave responded with a deferential nod of his head.

"Well, with all the gold and fruit going to the north through our harbors, it certainly cut down on the size of the 'pie,' as we economists like to say."

Dave smiled.

"But the way he formulated the other problem, the one here in Cortesia itself, was truly unique and interesting. He didn't at all base the unequal distribution of wealth on the means of production or 'Capital.' No, rather, he laid great stress on education. He felt that the factor which kept the children of the poor trapped in that condition was their lack of funds for education. He felt, I paraphrase here numerous writings and lectures, that if the poor could be educated that they would naturally rise in society. He believed that this 'rising in society,' as he termed it, would be associated with their receiving a greater share of the material wealth. Now exactly how this redistribution of the wealth was to take place was not immediately clear, at least to me. Here Eduardo was a bit vague. Perhaps on purpose?

"It seems to me, though, that what he was saying was that the lot of the disadvantaged would improve via two main mechanisms. Firstly, education would make them more economically competitive. They could obtain better jobs, and they'd be able to run a business on their own. Secondly, he seemed to hint that changes in a more equitable direction would take place as a result of the greater participation of the 'educated poor' in the political process. Certainly, so many of his students have gone into government service, even though the financial rewards would have been far greater in private industry or outside Cortesia.

"In any case, Gutierrez devoted the 'action' part of his life to opening up educational opportunities to disadvantaged youth. He cultivated a sort of 'absent-minded professor' image. He wore, how you say, . . . un-ironed . . . ooo . . . baggy trousers, and he would stop people on the street and ask directions back to the University! Most did not take him all that seriously. But those of us who knew him well knew what a brilliant man he was.

"So the people in the government said, 'Ah, this old man is actually harmless, and education is a good thing.' So they went along with much of what he had come and asked for. As a consequence, Cortesia has been the only country in Latin America, outside of post-revolutionary Cuba, to offer completely free education up to the doctorate to young people who cannot afford tuition or books. It was our one point of liberality." The professor made an expanded wave with both arms.

"It was remarkable to see these young people four years later with all the social skills, even the accent of the aristocracy. A real Pygmalion story, you might say. They're indistinguishable from his students who are truly from the upper class, and he did attract a surprising number of those. You must understand, Eduardo and his students took up a lot of time with their 'children,' taking them to concerts, teaching them how to speak, buying them conservative clothes, etc."

"Isn't the aristocracy threatened by all those liberals in the government?"

"Ah," Mendez ejaculated with a wave of his fleshy hand, "they've grown so fat and old that they wouldn't notice a camel in their swimming pools. Besides, who is going to do the work here in Cortesia? Most of their sons and daughters are off on the Riviera squandering their money. Why, around here, you can practically become a Minister by default. Not yet the Prime Minister or Finance Minister; they've managed to hold onto those."

"You've been very helpful, Sir. I'm much indebted to you."

"*De nada, Senor.*"

The wind had picked up and there was an ominous, heavy feeling in the air as Dave exited the ivy-covered building.

# CHAPTER 12

# "AND IT RAINED FOR FORTY DAYS AND FORTY NIGHTS"

The rain beat on the window sill as they made love that night.

Elena, as was her custom, had turned on the radio softly. The station was playing Cole Porter's "Begin the Beguine." One heard that genre of music so often here, Dave reflected to himself dreamily. In so many ways, life in Cortesia was like traveling decades back into the past.

She yawned slightly as they lay together under the bedclothes. "We're getting the fringe of the hurricane," she commented softly.

Dave snuggled closer to her back and rubbed her long, dark hair. "Is it going to hit land?"

"They say it will strike about two hundred and fifty miles north of here. That will be beyond Cortesia's borders. But such storms have hit here before. I so pity the poor people who will have to live through it."

"Uh, huh," Dave commented drowsily, allowing his head to sink deeper into the incredibly fluffy pillow.

Elena turned in the bed to face him. She pushed herself up slightly and swallowed. "You know," she began softly, "I must go away for a day or so. To a . . . uh . . . meeting."

"Oh, what kind of meeting? Gee, I'm free. Maybe I could go with you?"

"I'm afraid, not, Dear. I, of course, would love to have you there, but I don't think the others would understand."

"Where are you going?"

"Oh, merely back up to the *estancia*."

"And what kind of meeting could the Government be having up at your family's ranch?"

"Oh, it's not the Government as such. It's just some of us who are concerned about the way things are going."

"The way things are going?"

"Yes," she said, wiggling somewhat in the bed. "We want to make Cortesia a better place to live."

There was an uncharacteristic air of defiance in her voice, and Dave decided not to pursue the topic any further. He did, though, work in a hopefully casual reference to the fact that he had "run" into someone at the University who had known Professor Gutierrez and that he thought that he understood a bit of what she meant. He hoped by this quick comment to head off the effect that any word getting back to her about his asking questions about their "movement" might have.

"I'll go up in the morning and be back by Thursday at the latest."

He drew Elena to him and they began to make love again. He felt a bit insecure, but a sense of faith that all would be well in the end swept over him.

Back in his own room and fast asleep, Dave was suddenly jolted back to consciousness. There was an urgent pounding on the door. Despite the stereotype of members of his profession, he was a very sound sleeper. Groggily, he shook his head and put on his bathrobe.

A young woman stood outside his door. Her hair was drenched, and she was shaking water off her eyeglasses.

"Elena!"

The phone rang at the National Palace.

"*Hola*," answered the Sergeant of the Guard.

The caller stated, "The American Ambassador wishes to speak to the Prime Minister, please."

The Prime Minister had by this time been helped from his bed to a desk a few feet away. A cup of coffee was placed before him, but it went untouched.

"*Si.*"

"Your Excellency, this is John Morehead."

"*Ah, Juan, como esta?*"

"Quite well, thank you, Sir . . . Uh . . . uh . . . His Excellency must certainly be aware of the inclement conditions which prevail."

"Of course, *Senor*."

"Well, the Government of the United States has no wish or desire that a great man such as yourself should have to undergo the . . . the . . . rigors of such an event of nature. Uh, knowing full-well His Excellency's wish to share the fate of his People, yet and still, there are times when duty dictates, shall we say, an 'alternate course of action' . . ."

"Yes", *cough, cough*, "get on with it, *Senor*."

"Well, Your Excellency must realize that there are times when urgent consultations are a necessity."

"Well, of course, such times do occur."

"Exactly so. And . . . it would seem that such a time has come at the instant moment. There is a team of FBI agents assembled in Miami as we speak, and they would very much appreciate your consultation and advice on the War on Drugs, so to speak."

"*Si, si.*"

"Well, you can see the overwhelming importance of your departure for Miami at the earliest possible moment."

"*Si.*"

"I mean purely for reasons of international security."

"*Claro que si.*"

"And we know, Prime Minister, that your Air Force is of the highest quality. But, of course, as the Patriot you are, you will want to deploy it to the maximum benefit of your people . . ."

"This is true, *Senor Ambassador.*"

"Well, Prime Minister, I have arranged for a U.S. Air Force plane, a 707, actually it's one of the President's aircraft, to land, with Your Excellency's permission, of course, at the International Airport in a few hours. Your Excellency, family and staff may take it to the . . . uh . . . urgent negotiations in Florida."

"*Si, entiendo.* It is most important that I attend this meeting. A matter of the greatest urgency."

"Exactly so, Your Excellency."

"Bill, the storm is going to hit us direct and hard. We must leave La Navidad now."

"Elena, come in, you're shaking."

He took off his bathrobe and put it around the young woman's shoulders.

"Go to where?"

"To the *estancia.*"

"The *estancia?* I thought that was where you were having your mysterious meeting. I thought I couldn't be there?"

"I don't care about that now. You must come with me."

"My Dear," he said, stroking her drenched hair, "aren't we being a bit hysterical? I mean, after all, this is a sturdy hotel, reinforced concrete. It's not going to blow away." Suddenly, Dave realized his foolishness in succumbing to the knee-jerk reaction to try to allay or treat irrational fears. He'd be pleased as punch to go off with Elena in any kind of weather.

Her loud words shook him out of his self-kicking. "No, *mi cielito,* but you must understand what is going to happen. When the storm hits there will be no services, no 'Law and Order.' The rules of the jungle will prevail. There will be looting and stealing. It's happened before, and it will occur again this time."

At the airport a 707 with the flag of the United States of America on the tail touched down on one side of the field.

On the other side of the field a cargo plane taxied to a halt. The flag on its tail was, in some ways, a curiously revered flag of the United States. The flag was Cuban. The bay door opened, and five military ambulances rolled down the ramp. People began to emerge from the passenger compartment. The doctors and nurses went into one of the buildings for their scheduled meeting with local health officials. The others walked up the ramp to begin the process of unloading relief supplies.

A black limousine pulled up to the U.S. aircraft. The airman at the bottom of the ramp saluted smartly as the old man made his way slowly and painfully up the stairs. Another luxury vehicle pulled up, and the American Ambassador emerged from it and followed the older man up the ramp.

"Good morning, Prime Minister," the Ambassador greeted him. "We're grateful that you've taken the time to consult with us on these urgent matters."

"You know, *Senor*, that the prime Minister of Cortesia is always honored to be of service to his distinguished allies."

Dave and Elena walked through the hotel's parking lot to a waiting Jeep Cherokee. Dave recognized the young man at the wheel as one of the people who had attended the meeting, or whatever it was, at Elena's that Saturday afternoon. The rain turned into a veritable deluge. There were several rudely dressed people in the back seats whom Dave learned later were food service personnel form the ministry in which Raul, their driver, held a middle-level position.

The trees swayed dramatically in the wind as the sturdy vehicle turned onto the mountain highway. The windshield wipers couldn't keep up with the accumulated water, and the going was agonizingly slow.

Farmers were out in their fields making vain efforts to save their crops from the oncoming engine of destruction. They must surely have realized that the sheets and blankets they spread over their young plants would never stay in place. But, it seems, there are times when people simply can't bear to just do nothing.

They stopped for fuel at a rustic filling station in a tiny mud-street village at the foot of the steepest pass of their journey.

"Ah, it's Salvador," Elena exclaimed as the driver jumped out of the Jeep to begin pumping gas.

An old Ford truck stood on the side of the little parking area. A tall, lanky dark-skinned man strode over to the vehicle in which Dave and Elena sat. Sal touched the brim of his soaked straw hat in an informal salute to the titular heiress of the *estancia* on which he was the foreman.

"*Que tal, Elena?*"

"How good it is of you, Salvador, to come out like this."

"Everyone helps everyone. *Correcto?* Is that not what you say?"

"Yes, yes it is," she replied with a prideful look on her face.

Turning from the philosophical to the practical, the middle-aged farmer asked, "How are the roads down to the City?"

"Not good and not getting any better. The going was so slow for us. But Big Bertha there will handle the mud so much better than this vehicle. So I don't think you'll have any trouble. But hurry!"

"You may believe that I will. I fully plan to be back in my own bed this night . . . Now, tell me, please, is there any particular sector of the City to which you want us to go?"

"Well, come to think of it, I believe Cristobel. It's right on the coast, and it's been badly hit in the past. Just offer refuge to anyone who can squeeze into Bertha, particularly the children. Assure them that while they're not going to luxury they will be safe from the storm over the mountains. And we will provide them with food and shelter. Tell those who wish to come but cannot find space in the truck that our neighbors too are dispatching vehicles to help them leave. We'll go ahead to the house to make the necessary arrangements."

"*Si, Senorita.*" Sal, who could remember the day of Elena's birth, said with a self-consciously respectful nod of his head. "I go."

Dave reached over and squeezed Elena's hand.

As they pulled into the *estancia,* the clouds above were moving in a strange semi-circular pattern. Elena pointed up at them.

"You see, we're directly in the storm's path. But the mountains will protect us. Of course, we'll get rain and lots of wind. But we'll be safe here."

There was a festive air as Dave and Elena entered the Manor House. Seven or eight couples, they didn't stay still long enough for him to actually count them, were milling around the grand entrance hall and the adjoining sitting rooms. He had seen many of them in offices in the Capital from time-to-time. It was difficult for Dave to be sure exactly who he had seen before and who he hadn't. They were all dressed so differently this noontime. They, both male and female, wore wash pants with oversized open-necked sport shirts. But their grooming certainly hadn't suffered in the transformation. The men were all clean-shaven, and the ladies' makeup had been impeccably applied. They all wore earrings, and the rarified scent of perfume floated above the evolving party.

"Ah, Elena, welcome home," cried one of the young men as he rushed out to the middle of the floor, beer mug in hand. He embraced her and gave her a light peck on the cheek. Making a sweeping gesture with his hands, he continued, "As you can see, we've already made ourselves quite at home."

"That is as it should be," she replied. "After all, we are doing all we can for our People today."

Turning toward the center of the room and raising her voice, she announced, "I think some of you may know my special friend Bill Robinson."

Those who heard nodded at Dave, and several of the men who were close by walked over to him and introduced themselves and their spouses/dates.

"You'll have plenty of time to get to know everyone," Elena commented. "We'll be locked up here together for several days."

They made their way to the sideboard of cold cuts which Carmen had laid out for the assemblage. One of the men handed Dave an exceedingly cold beer. Elena pulled a bottle of U.S. cola from a large bowl of ice and water. "If you had to be in a hurricane, this was the way to do it!" Dave thought to himself

Carrying his and Elena's bags up the stairs, Dave commented dryly, "Are you going to show me to my cell now?"

She stopped at the head of the stairs and turned toward him, smiling. "I have some bad news for you. With so many people here Carmen has left the house to go stay with the other workers. Space is at a premium, so you'll have to 'bunk in with me, Pardner.' Things are so tough, we may have to make our own bed," she said, raising her eyebrows.

As he lugged her heavy case, sweating and puffing, he couldn't help speculating as to one, if a person could actually come to like tropical storms, and two, if the development of that kind of affection was possible, if this was a very moral attitude to have!

She walked to the window of the large room that had been hers for as long as she could remember. Throwing open the lacy curtain, she peered out. "And it rained for forty days and forty nights," she muttered half to herself.

Dave walked behind her and put his hands on the lady's hips. He kissed the back of her neck and peered over her shoulders through the window. The clouds were black, and the rain was falling with noticeably increasing intensity. The branches of the trees moved in strange, unreal ways.

"Yes," he said softly, "it's something cataclysmic."

Elena turned abruptly. "I'm scared. I want you to hold me . . . in bed."

She grabbed his hand and pulled him, though in truth Dave needed no encouragement, to the massive dark-wood bed that occupied one wall of the room. Sitting on the tall bed, she quickly unlaced her boots and kicked them across the room. Elena popped her heavy eyeglasses on the marble-topped table beside the bed.

Dave stepped back a pace to watch what would happen next. She unbuttoned the khaki shirt she wore. She tossed the brown garment on top of her spectacles. He had never noticed before how thick the band of her brassier was. But, he supposed, for purely physical reasons that's how it had to be. Her jeans came off next. There was, he thought, a delightful incongruity in the silk panties she wore. But then, he considered, a woman probably wouldn't have a separate set of undergarments for informal wear.

Elena threw the top covers off the bed and jumped nimbly between the sheets.

Dave had simply stood in front of her, enthralled by the scene being played out before him.

She pulled the sheet up around her neck in reaction to the last blast of thunder. Her eyes widened in fear as she stared somewhat vacantly at her lover, giving him at the same time a puzzled and beseeching look.

He had never seen her afraid before. She trembled as the lightning crashed and the rain beat on the roof harder and harder. Her long nails dug into his back as they made love in the darkening room.

Fortunately, one of the men, although professionally a "civil servant," was an amateur chef. Pablo directed the activities in the kitchen that evening. The outcome was a truly delectable beef stroganoff. They ate it to the accompaniment of thunder and the howling of the wind.

Truckloads of people rolled in from La Navidad during the day and night. The *estancia's* staff was well prepared for them.

The next day was a day without dawn. Dave awoke to the scent of Elena's body and perfume. All was darkness, and the rain beat incessantly on the roof of the old mansion.

She moaned and turned in the bed. Dave never tired of feeling her breasts brushing across his chest.

"What time is it?" she asked.

"7:30."

*"Dios mio! Tango que levantarme. Tenemos mucho trabajo."*

"Yeah," he responded, failing to see the urgency.

She sprang from the bed and disappeared into the bathroom.

Five minutes later she emerged, teeth brushed and only a pale pink gloss on her lips.

"The meeting starts at eight SHARP."

She scrambled back into the same outfit she had worn yesterday, topping it off with her heavy dark-rimmed eyeglasses.

"You can sleep, my Dear," she said, kissing him on the forehead.

"Yes, I think I will."

Dave rolled over and went back to his dream, which was nothing more than that the lady who had just left had not left.

Her scent was still on the pillow. The dark sky gave no clue as to the time. But it felt as though he had slept another hour or so. The rich aroma of coffee invited him to get up, which he did.

Arriving downstairs, he found the main floor of the stately mansion all but deserted. A young boy, all by himself, was clearing away the dishes from breakfast.

Puzzled, he asked the young fellow where all the people had gone.

"Downstairs in the ballroom," he was told.

Clearly this meeting, or whatever it was, had begun. And it had been made quite clear to him that he wasn't welcome, so he would have to try in some fashion to "stumble in," or at least listen in. What was he to do with himself? He would be, as they say, at loose ends for most of the next couple of days. But one of the sitting rooms had what appeared to be a reasonably well-stocked library. He didn't know whether he could actually spend eight or ten hours a day reading, but, for the moment, it appeared to be better than nothing.

The Assistant Secretary of State for Latin American Affairs rose as the Prime Minister of Cortesia was helped into his nondescript office.

"Mr. Prime Minister, we are honored that you have agreed to meet with us in the midst of the crisis in your country. We also appreciate your agreeing to move the meeting here to Washington from Miami. The Government of the United States is following with the greatest concern the devastation wrought by the tropical storm that struck your country earlier today. We are fully aware that it must grieve Your Excellency to be absent from his People during their time of suffering. You may be certain, Sir, that we would never have requested your presence were it not that matters of utmost urgency and importance had been brought suddenly to our attention. Our two Peoples, Mr. Prime Minister, have shared a long history of friendship and . . ."

The old man made an impatient wave with his hand, obviously signaling the young blow-hard to get on with it.

The Assistant Secretary cleared his throat and continued, "We are well aware, Mr. Prime Minister, that your Government maintains relations with the Government of Cuba which, of course, the Government of the United States does not recognize."

"Quite so," he replied, well aware that it was general knowledge that virtually all developing nations played the larger powers off against one another. Not very idealistic, perhaps, but after all, would you rather get one paycheck or two?

"What concerns us is the extensive presence of the Cuban military in your country."

"Extensive presence? I am afraid I am not following you, *Senor*. There are, from time to time, a handful of military advisors. But my generals tell me they have much to learn from everyone."

"Our sources indicate that the Cubans are in Cortesia at about the strength of a regiment."

"Sources? Regiment?"

Jennings held out his flabby hands, almost in a gesture of surrender.

"Oh, oh, no," he sputtered, "we're not spying on you, heavens, heavens no . . . But, as you must know, we routinely interview American citizens who return from overseas, mostly businessmen. Cortesia, of course, was not the focus of our 'debriefings.' But quite a number of returnees spontaneously brought to our attention things they had observed in your country. These reports, when put together, take shape into an ominous pattern. We, quite frankly, find this pattern disturbing. And, assuming I'm reading your reaction properly, Your Excellency, you may well be similarly distressed. Allow me to show you what we've put together."

Jennings pressed a button on his intercom, and an Army colonel entered the office. He carried a large folder under his arm.

"Colonel Smathers, show the Prime Minister the maps."

The officer withdrew a map of Cortesia and balanced it on the Assistant Secretary's desk. Withdrawing a pointer from his jacket, he began tapping on various locations.

"We know, Sir," he began, "that the Cubans maintain a permanent military mission at Costa de la Obscura. We estimate its strength at . . . And here in the mountains . . . We've been able to identify the following Cuban warships in Cortesia's waters over the past . . ."

His Excellency's mouth literally gaped open as he stared at the map with all its red markings.

# CHAPTER 13

# "OUR TIME HAS COME!"

D ave walked into the elegant Victorian-styled sitting room with the walls lined with bookshelves. Glancing over the collection, he came across a large, leather-bound copy of Don Quixote. It had been a long time since he had read that. He wondered how well he would get through it in Spanish.

Looking around for a comfortable place to sit and read, he noticed that there was a fireplace across the room. He didn't know if they actually needed it in this tropical country. Perhaps it was just for show. But then, again, they were at a fairly high altitude. During the course of his speculations, he had approached the fireplace and was examining the interior, trying to see whether he could detect signs of burning. As he did, he could hear voices arguing in Spanish. As he knelt down to finger the charred remains of a log, he realized that the fireplace must share a common chimney with a corresponding fireplace in the ballroom below. What luck!

He pulled a wooden chair closer to the brick structure and settled in to "read" the classic work. It involved no small strain, but he seemed to be catching more and more of the dialog as time went by.

"'*Patiencia, patiencia*.' I've heard that word 'patience' so often that I've come to hate it." The speaker was a dark haired man in his late thirties. "All of us have worked our way up, rung by rung, in the Government. And we have some powerful 'friends,' including now even the Ministers of Foreign Affairs and War. But what's more important than that is what we don't have. And what don't we have? We have no control over how resources in our country are allocated. And we have no Constitutional guarantees of our property rights in Court. We are, lamentably, totally at the mercy of a group of 'Robber Barons.'"

"Aradio, Aradio, we all know that what you say about justice is true. But I fear that at times you overlook the good we have been able to accomplish." It was a woman's voice, and Dave recognized it immediately as that of Elena. "We have been able to obtain help from our friends abroad. There is the new hospital in the city and the orphanage just ten miles down the mountain from here."

"But, Elena, what a shame it is that we have to go begging from others when there are such riches in our own State Treasury. Should not we be caring for our own children, our sick and our old? Why should our money go into the coffers of the fat rich or sent to the Great Empire to the north?"

"No, no, of course that's not right," she replied. "I'm merely attempting to point out that our . . . that is to say dear Eduardo's methods are reaping results even as we speak. Of course, so much more needs to be done. But we must not stoop to the level of rabble in the streets. Eduardo would be so disappointed in us . . ."

"Two things," he said, turning to the others in the cavernous room, "we must note. First we don't want to be 'rabble,' and secondly, we mustn't disappoint Eduardo. Respecting Dr. Guiterrez, he was and is, indeed, beloved. But he has been dead for almost a decade. Do you realize that there are some in this very room who never even knew him? You must understand, my friends, that we live now in a different time from that of our Mentor. One wonders what he would have thought were he here today. Perhaps he would conclude that the first phase of our struggle had been completed. Perhaps, indeed, he would, in the light of events, believe, as I do, that the time for a different course has come."

"A different course?" a young man in jeans questioned. "What do you mean?"

"I think you already know what I mean. We must seize the power while it is there for the grabbing. Hernandez, our so-called 'Prime Minister,' is old and ill. All the men around him are either senile, sick, alcoholic or, as in the case of the Finance Minister, all three. I tell you, now is the time to act. Our time has come!

"Do not, I beg you, be put off by Ms. de la Madrid's comparison with 'rabble.' What does Elena know of rabble? She was born of the Aristocracy in this mansion. She speaks of the poor, but she knows nothing of poverty . . ."

"I think you've gone a bit too far," another young man protested from the rear. "Our Elena has led the fight for reform . . ."

"Yes, but always, always within the 'System.' And a corrupt system it has been, too. Our riches, and Cortesia is rich in resources and in its people, have poured out of our borders. We must seize the opportunity to see that Justice is done. We must act now!"

Elena was on her feet. "And what," she pleaded, "and what would my friend have us do in place of what we are doing now? Would he have us embark upon a civil war in which many, children even, would be killed?"

"No, Elena, no one wants war. But the time has come for us to seize control of the Government. Practically all of the workers, I mean those who truly work, in government service are with us. We can take over the Government at any time we choose."

"A *coup d'etat*?"

"You may call it that if you wish. The Army would back us up. Their loyalty is to our friend the War Minister, not the senile old fool who is the so-called PM."

"Then, I ask you, how would anyone be able to tell our 'government' from that of any other self-declared, self-serving mob who happened to seize control of a 'banana republic'?"

"Believe me, Ms. de la Madrid, we represent the People of Cortesia."

"And how exactly do you know that? Where, I beg you, is your Mandate from the People you purport to represent?"

"Ha! There's the rub, indeed! How can there be a 'Mandate,' as you so quaintly put it, in the absence of free elections? As you all know full well, the 'elections' we have are no more than a sham. Only a 'Freeholder' can vote. And who is a Freeholder? Someone who owns property, that's who! Eduardo gave us Castilian accents and fine clothes, but it was not within his power to give us land. But you, Elena, have land," he said with a sweeping gesture of his arms toward the *estancia's* widely flung and rich fields. "Do you vote? The rest of us cannot, you know."

"This," she said with downcast eyes, "is my father's land. He did deed over to me a parcel of it on my nineteenth birthday. So I can vote. But I never have. Why vote? There are no choices."

"Exactly so!" Aradio shouted. Only the landed, the Aristocracy, vote, so who do they elect to the Chamber of Deputies? Themselves, that's who! And they have such little interest in Matters of State that they meet only rarely, only when it's too rainy for their Thoroughbred races, it would seem. And so they're nothing more than a 'rubber stamp' for Old Man Hernandez and his cronies. So they, who technically hold the purse strings, vote money from the resources and sweat of the Cortesian People in any way he wants. That's why we have to go begging for help for our own People!"

"This is outrageous! It's insufferable!" a diminutive, thin woman with a long brown and gray ponytail yelled from the corner of the room.

"Yes, we must do something and now," Aradio said in encouragement of the evolving drift of the meeting. "We must develop some form of organized opposition to the exploiting old fossils who are presently in charge."

A worried look crossed Elena's face. "You know, Aradio," she said, "that political parties are illegal in Cortesia."

Several of those assembled joined Aradio in a hearty laugh. "Ah, our little rich girl doesn't want to 'rock the boat,' as they say, in her favorite totalitarian country."

"Yes, Elena," the small brunette chimed in. "Sometimes you're almost a reactionary. It's like you want to run a little private social services agency in the midst of a society and government that are blatantly exploiting the People. It reminds me at times of that Fascist Reagan's 'Volunteerism.'"

A young man in jeans, apparently the junior member of the group, stood up to protest. "I think you're being way too tough on Elena. If you only knew all that she has done for me personally over the years. She has a good heart. I know she wants what is best for our People. If we disagree, it is only on methods, not goals."

"But what a difference in methods," Aradio retorted. "And I'll tell you about the most dramatic of the differences. Elena and I talked, more correctly argued, about it. We have right here in Latin America a brilliant example of how a People cast off the shackles of an exploitive dictatorship and turned that nation's riches to the good of the common people. Yes, yes, I make reference to the Cuban Revolution."

"Yes, the Cuban Revolution," Elena said, shaking her head contemptuously. Softening, she continued, "Look, I know and appreciate full well that the lot of the poorest people in Cuba has improved since Castro came to power. But just look at how they did it! Look at what they've lost in the process!

"Don't you recall what happened when the Fidelistas came to power? Those who were not worshipful of Fidel were lined up in front of ditches and shot. Is that what we want here in Cortesia? I don't . . ."

"Elena, how insulting! Certainly you can't believe any of us capable of such things." His words were punctuated by a shocked mummer from some of the others present.

"Oh, I don't think it beyond reality. And I don't in the least doubt your sincerity. Despite our differences, I know all of you to be people of Good Will. But revolutionary movements have a way of getting out of hand. The 'end justifies the means' mentality may become so strong that people find themselves doing things they would never have dreamed of doing. You see, I'm something of a student of history, and . . ."

"I'd say she was dragging us off the subject," the mousey brunette spat out.

"Yes, Elena, I think you are," Aradio pronounced as though a Judge sitting on the bench.

"Oh, am I?" Elena said, obviously both irritated and feeling the strain of the group pressure around her. "Well, let's look at the 'fruits' of such revolutionary zeal. Do you know how many Cubans there are, representatives of the Castro regime I should say, in our country right now?"

"They have been exceedingly helpful to us," a young man responded. "Even as we speak, the Cubans are leading the way in giving aid to our People during the crisis of the ongoing storm. And what have the Americans done? Ha, they sent a Presidential jet for that old coward Hernandez so he wouldn't get his feet wet, that's what!"

"Granted, yes, the Cubans have done a lot of good for our People. But in my job in the Foreign Ministry I get to see a lot of what's going on throughout the entire country and in many agencies of the Government. And I can tell you that for every nurse, every doctor, every social worker Fidel has sent us we are now 'host' to five soldiers, soldiers of the Army of Cuba. And what, we may well ask ourselves, have the soldiers of the 'People of Cuba' been doing over the past decades? They've been suppressing the People of Cuba, that's what! You know, you can't just leave Cuba. They won't let you! And do they really vote in Cuba? No! With all the changes going on in the former Communist world, Cuba is practically the only holdout. Why, they've made no progress whatever. And they are the very people that some of us have chosen to allow to roam free on our land. I say this is dangerous, and . . ."

"Dangerous? How do you mean?" Aradio demanded in a haughty tone.

Elena paused. This was not an area into which she had wished to be drawn. Perhaps, on reflection, her debate opponent had seized an opportunity to trick her into it.

"Well, we must be aware that recent U.S. administrations have been, shall we say, adventuristic. Both Reagan and Bush have sent troops into countries almost without warning, when there was no threat whatever to the security of their country. I can't help fearing that that could occur here also. And that, I'm certain, would be a monumental setback to Cortesia. We could see a return to outright military . . ."

"Ha, you see what's she's saying," Aradio shouted in forensic triumph. "We mustn't do things. We mustn't choose our own friends. And why not? Because the Mighty United States of America will be displeased. And how, she admits, would the Americans show their displeasure with us for being 'bad children'? They would invade us! So we must simply not get out of our 'place.'"

There arose a mummer of seeming approval from the group.

Encouraged by these reactions, Aradio gleefully interjected a rhetorical question. "Might, I wonder, if Ms.

de la Madrid's reverence for the wishes of the United States relate in some way to her intimacy with a *yanqui*?"

There were snickers, some decidedly nervous.

A man rose from the middle of the group. Everyone became quiet in apparent deference to his status as the senior person present. It was the distinguished-looking *caballero* that Dave and Elena had encountered several days earlier in the cemetery, as well as even earlier in Elena's apartment at the conclusion of their "meeting."

"I have," he began slowly, almost somberly, "been giving some thought to these issues for some time, years as a matter of fact. There is no doubt in my thinking that we have come to a critical point in the road to progress for our People. I, perhaps, knew Dr. Guitterez, our Mentor, better than anyone else. At least, it was my honor to have spent the most time with him. And I can tell you that Eduardo knew full well that such a time as this would come. He told me often that he did not know when it would happen, nor the particular circumstances, nor whether he would live to see it or not. But come it would, he knew, and come it has.

"We have, as our Elena has pointed out, made great progress over the years. And I want very much to stress the word 'we.' All of us, in our own ways, have been dedicated to the purpose of improving the conditions of our People. When and where we differ, it is only in our heads, not in our hearts. I know all of you well, and I know this to be true.

"It seems to me that a number of important issues have been raised during our discussions today.

"To me, the dull, and as they sometimes say, pedantic person that I am, the central issue is that of organization.

Of course, political parties are not allowed under the terms of the 'Constitution' of our country. The idea is that we are so harmonious a People that differences should not arise among us. Of course, that's not true. There are and should be different 'interests' among our citizens.

"It is a fact that we here in Cortesia have no political process as such. What we have is, one could say, an 'oligarchy,' a ruling class based primarily on wealth, but secondarily on pretensions to Spanish Nobility. They, exclusively, determine how wealth is distributed. The Prime Minister and the Chancellor of the Exchequer are always one of them. And, as we know, the Prime Minister is chosen by the Chamber of Deputies, which, as our friend Aradio has so correctly pointed out, is elected solely by the landed.

"Of course and following Eduardo's strong example, we have been able to play roles in the Government. We've 'wormed our way in,' as the Americans might say, into some powerful positions. In fact, we have friends and supporters at the highest levels in both the War Ministry and the Foreign Ministry. I think it is, therefore, ironic that we present to the world a more enlightened image than is the reality here at home.

"All my Honorable Friends, and here I speak particularly of Elena and Aradio, have made valuable points today. Indeed, progress has been made. But, one must, regrettably, admit that there is much more to be accomplished.

"I find myself agreeing in part with Aradio and in part with Elena. I believe that our current *modus operandi* has achieved its maximum effect. We have been able to do much good from within the system, but we have not been able to change in any basic, fundamental way the inequitable distribution of the wealth of our fabulously rich country. It seems to me, therefore, that the time of individual effort has passed and that we are now in need of some form of organized movement toward progress for our People. I do not, though, know exactly what form that organization should take. I do know, though, that any form of organization we might adopt would put us in great peril, much as was true of the Founding Fathers of the United States.

"I agree, however, with Elena that we should not follow the example of Cuba. It is the easiest mistake in the world to assume that the opposite of what is bad is good. What we want, I suggest, is neither Adam Smith nor Karl Marx. What we want is freedom, opportunity and, yes, bread for our People. Not firing squads!

"It seems to me that we should all take some time to reflect and consider where we should go from this juncture. Perhaps we can meet again in a month or so. I know I may seem a 'weak sister,' to use again American slang, but it is a momentous thing on which we are contemplating embarking."

Elena handed the speaker, Roberto Cordoba, Undersecretary of War, a note as he sat down amid a hushed and thoughtful silence. Rising again, he announced, "I have here a list of our duties in caring for the people from the City for the remainder of the day. Aradio and Isabella are to go to assist in the preparation . . ."

Back in Elena's room, Dave opened his briefcase and took out a few pieces of stationary.

*Mr. George Simpkins, Director*
*Explorations and Acquisitions*
*Eastern Mining*
*3000 Rockefeller Plaza*
*New York, NY 10112-3373*


*Dear George:*


*There certainly are a number of very attractive properties here in Cortesia. I must report, though, that the owners and authorities here are very uncertain, divided in fact, on the question of whether they wish us or our competition to develop these properties. This is a much, much more complex and delicate situation than it must appear from your vantage point. I can only urge that you exercise the utmost in tact and caution in any negotiations you might have with the Cortesians.*

*I have updates on some of the specific properties we've corresponded about earlier. In Section G-15 of your map, from what I've been able to learn from the records, there's not the concentration of silver that we had previously thought. Copper, on the other hand, is . . .*

# CHAPTER 14

# "EVERYTHING IS COMING APART!"

The large, awkward vehicle made its way slowly down the mountainside along the slippery, mud-clogged roads. The couple had spent two days "in retreat" at the *estancia*. Information from the radio indicated that it was now safe to return to the City.

A puzzled look came over Dave's face as Elena made a sudden and unexpected turn to the right about halfway down the road to the nearest village.

"I want to stop by the orphanage to make sure that all is well," she explained. "The telephones are out of service, as you know. I must get them a wireless. Really, we should have foreseen this." She smiled sweetly through her expression of concern.

"Orphanage?" he asked, pretending that he had never heard of its existence.

"Yes, it's run by an Order of Sisters from Brazil. You see, Bill . . ."

He hoped the slight, involuntary squirm wasn't detectable.

". . . whenever I travel with the Minister I approach various organizations in the countries about our needs here in Cortesia. I have a little 'traveling road show.' I believe that's the American expression."

He chuckled. Elena's rare use of slang was in such contrast to her precision of speech in both English and Spanish that it always amused him. He found it somehow refreshing. He put his hand on her knee.

Elena gave an audible sigh of relief when they turned the bend and could see that the large wooden structure was very much intact.

The Sisters greeted them warmly and gave them a brief reassuring tour of the bright, clean facility. Several of the older children knew Elena and unhesitatingly came up to embrace her. They were offered lunch, but they declined, preferring to travel on to don Pedro's cantina for a meal accompanied by his *vinifera* wine.


The return to normalcy in the City was swift. The tropical storm had not lived up to its fearsome expectations. La Navidad had been spared all but minor damages, and injuries had been few. Most importantly, there had been not a single fatality.

Elena was at her desk in the Foreign Ministry at the usual time the next morning. She was composing letters for the Minister's signature to thank those countries who had sent aid to Cortesia during the storm.

As the morning wore on, she became aware that something was different, possibly wrong. She couldn't quite put her finger on it. It was as though people who were usually around were absent, and people who normally weren't there were today. At first she passed it all off as merely part of the recovery process from the disruption of the just passed crisis.

But there actually seemed to be so much more to it than merely that. In fact, she noticed a sharp contrast between the moods of the clerical and support staffs and those of the Deputy and Under Ministers. The secretaries and the mail boys wore smiles on their faces. They obviously felt very much delivered from the Valley of the Shadow of Death. Those at the Sub-Ministerial level, on the other hand, wore tense, worried expressions on their faces. They shuffled from office to office, seemingly oblivious to those around them.

During her trips to the coffee room, Elena heard snatches of comments made by these nervous men in their tailored suits.

"He didn't say why. The meeting was just cancelled. That's all I know."

"His secretary took the report but said the Deputy Minister couldn't meet with me today. He wasn't even in the office."

"Emilio, what are you doing here? I thought you were at the conference over in . . ."

She came to the realization that, for whatever unknown reason, the air was heavy and oppressive. And the rapidly rising barometer and clearing skies wouldn't make the eerie atmosphere go away.

Elena and her immediate colleagues would only gradually and over time come to learn of the dramatic confrontation which had taken place only hours earlier.

At the National Palace, the largest of the Greek Revival buildings atop the small hill in the center of the City, the Ministers of War and Foreign Affairs sat uneasily in the anti-room to the Prime Minister's ceremonial office. They were both perplexed at having been called to this meeting. There was no agenda, and it was so early for the old PM.

The sound of the approaching boot steps of a military aid echoed down the hall.

"The Prime Minister will see you now," the lieutenant announced formally.

They were ushered wordlessly into the ornate office.

The old man was dwarfed by the huge chair in which he sat and the massive desk in front of him. General Piedra, the PM's personal military aide, was seated in one of the chairs beside the desk. Surprisingly, he did not rise as the two Cabinet Members entered the room. Four or five other uniformed men were standing in the corners of the Prime Minister's office.

The two halted in the middle of the chamber, sensing before reasoning it through that something was seriously amiss.

"Good morning, Prime Minister," the Foreign Minister said with a forced smile, obviously trying to encourage a more congenial atmosphere.

The frail person behind the desk glared at them. At first his expression was stone-like, but it shifted to an uneven sneer.

"You are traitors!" he shouted at them.

"Traitors? I don't understand," gasped the War Minister.

"Yes, my country is infested with the soldiers of Communism. And you two scoundrels are the ones chiefly to blame."

"Sir, what Communist soldiers?"

"What Communist soldiers?" the PM said mockingly. "What Communist soldiers? Ah, what feigned innocence. And how unworthy." He let out a bizarre sound which was about equal parts laugh and cough.

"His Excellency knew that there were Cuban advisors within our borders. I informed you myself. As his Excellency knows, we consult with many nations . . ."

The Prime Minister banged his hand on the desk. "So we have a whole <u>regiment</u> of advisors? You must think me impossibly senile. Even I know that advisors don't come in regiments!"

The two men had no answer. Silence prevailed for several moments.

"Uh, if the Prime Minister would like our resignations, I'm certain my colleague and I would a . . ."

"Resignation!" Again the loud laugh/cough. "No, traitors don't resign. They are punished. You may consider yourselves under arrest!"

The soldiers in the corners of the room moved in upon the former Ministers.


"The Prime Minister will be speaking in a half-hour."

Elena glanced up from her work, pushing her glasses back up on her small nose. But the speaker had left. Apparently he had been somewhat carried away by the excitement of unfolding events.

No one was working by this time. The staff simply sat and, literally, shuffled papers. They were adrift on a sea of uncertainty.


"How about lunch, Honey?"

That sound was, perhaps, the most pleasing ever to strike her ears.

"Bill, yes, Dear, I would love lunch."

She rose and kissed him gently on the cheek.

He could sense the tension in her body.

"What's wrong, Elena?"

"I don't know, actually. It's just that something's not right. I'm not at all certain what it might be. It's just that everything's so strange today, like something awful is going to take place."

Instead of the usual soothing music at the outdoor café, there was a strained, hoarse voice on the loudspeaker.

> *. . . This cancer at the very heart of the Government of Cortesia is, as I speak, being rooted out. The former Ministers of War and Foreign Affairs have been placed under arrest. They have delivered us into the hands of our enemies. They are traitors of the most vile and contemptible sort . . . .*

Elena arose involuntarily at the sound of her boss' title.

"The Minister. Under arrest . . . ." she mumbled as though in some sort of trance.

Dave stroked her hand to comfort her. He pulled her back into her seat. It struck him that he was, in all probability, a player in this unfolding drama.

> *. . . And I know there are others of their ilk among us. But I can assure you, Loyal Citizens of Cortesia, that they too will be cast out.*

Her skin paled and her hands trembled. It was all Dave could do to keep breathing.

> *. . . This crisis has forced me to take drastic action. My loyal friend and aide, General Piedra, has declared Marshall Law.*

The two sat in stony silence as the General read the conditions of the Marshall Law, the Curfew and the Suspension of the Rights of bail and to an attorney.

Elena gasped and grabbed her chest.

Dave stroked her shoulder protectively. He looked at her with frightened, worried eyes.

She took off her glasses and tilted her head to one side.

"You understand, don't you?" she said in a strange monotone. Her expression softened, and she whispered. "Then get away from me. You may be in danger, too."

Dave paused, a mass of past memories, hopes and fears swirled through his brain.

"No, I won't leave you," he finally got out in a voice which was both choked and defiant.

They walked slowly, arm-in-arm, back to the Ministry. Even without saying it, they both knew that their only short-term hope lay in acting as though none of this had anything to do with them. They were simply a salaried government worker and a representative of an American mining firm. Friends, perhaps lovers. Nothing more.

Dave kissed Elena goodbye beside the usual column. It may not have been noticeable to others, but the kiss and the embrace were a little slower and sadder than usual.

Dave walked alone down the street. He turned to watch her trim figure disappear into the darkness of the interior of the cold stone edifice.

Army vehicles seemed everywhere, and soldiers with machine guns patrolled the streets.

They sat largely in silence that evening in Elena's apartment. They sipped cognac, looked at each other and sighed. They were both scared, and they valued so much being together in their fear. But Elena knew she shouldn't be talking with anyone about what was going on, much less a foreigner. Moreover, she had come slowly and painfully to realize that her lover was not what he pretended to be, at least not professionally. First of all, he really knew practically nothing about mining. Once, just making conversation, she asked him what kinds of mining properties he had been sent to find. "Anything that's marketable," he had responded evasively. He did, though, go on to rattle off with studied casualness a number of minerals, "gold, silver, zinc, tungsten . . ." The problem was that two years previously she had gone with the Minister overseas to assist him in treaty negotiations. Great stress was placed in those negotiations on a clause relating to the importation of tungsten by Cortesia. There is no tungsten in Cortesia! For years she had heard this geological fact bemoaned by those who were trying to develop various competitive light industries.

Further, it had become pretty clear to her that "Bill's" actual education and training had been in the social sciences, say economics, political science or sociology or psychology. Certainly, he could discuss topics in these areas much more knowledgeably than anything technical. And it was all too obvious that he was unusually interested in matters political, and yes, it had to be admitted, military.

Elena had also noticed something quite subtle but rather consistent about the way her companion communicated with her, and with others as well. Quite often when she would say something to him, instead of commenting on it, as most people do, he would repeat back part of what she had said. This would take such forms as, "Ah, so your brother felt . . ." or "It sounds like you went through a rough time with that one . . . ." Often he would merely nod his head or say "Hmmm." The effect of this was to make you feel that he was intensely interested in what you had to say and to keep you talking. It felt nice, actually.

She had observed that he used very much the same technique with others, particularly when they were discussing politico-military affairs. His interactions with Major, now Colonel de la Castile were good examples of this. Elena had never actually been able to bring herself to use the word "spy." But in her heart of hearts she knew there was little doubt that's what "Bill" was. And there was, of course, no doubt about for whom he was working.

Dave reached out and stroked her long, luxuriant hair. He wore a pained, apologetic, almost panicky expression on his face.

Paradoxical and nonsensical though it was, she wanted him to stay with her. Sometimes what you sense inside a person is more important than external circumstances, even facts. She so hoped she wasn't, as they say, being used. But she felt safer with him beside her. She put her head against his chest and made a kind of babyish, snuggling movement.

They were startled by a knock on the door.

Elena padded in her stocking feet across the room to pull open the huge wooden door.

She stepped back, wide-eyed, as Roberto Cordoba walked quickly into the room. He was dressed in work clothes and an oversized straw hat. He more resembled a peasant than the suave government functionary Dave knew him to be. Roberto could read just from her expression that Elena was surprised that he had dared to come here. "Too risky to use the phones," he explained simply. "Everything is coming apart," he blurted out, throwing his hands up to his temples.

"Yes, I know," she answered softly, almost serenely.

"Of course, of course. It's all too obvious, isn't it?" He stroked the back of his neck, pushing his head backward while sighing. "I had so hoped that it would never come to this. So did Eduardo."

Recovering somewhat from his agitation, born of the special responsibility he felt as the senior member of "The Group," his eyes scanned the usually inviting, comfortable parlor. His head came to an abrupt halt when he spotted the American seated on the couch.

Dave gave him a weak smile. He knew full well that his presence had not enhanced the level of comfort of the Cortesian.

"You may speak freely in front of him," Elena said nervously, taking a gigantic leap of faith.

"Well, then," the man continued, regaining some of his poise, "the situation is grave, and it grows worse by the hour. Two more Ministers have been placed under arrest. And there are rumors that several Deputy Ministers have met with a similar fate. When I left the War Ministry there were soldiers wearing the epaulets of the Palace Guard going through personnel records. I am not certain for what they were searching. Perhaps some hint of liberality, perhaps an 'unfortunate association.'" He shrugged his shoulders. "In any case, I don't believe I'm being an alarmist when I say I think all of us are in danger."

"No, Roberto, you are not an alarmist."

"I was able to get a message to de la Castile through his brother, my colleague at the War Ministry. The Colonel has agreed to meet with us tonight."

Elena gasped audibly at the implications of what she was being told. Things had gotten so bad that they must turn to a sympathetic Army officer!

"I want you to come with me. I respect your opinion, and I know that you have tried, the abuse you have taken, to avoid what has . . . lamentably come to pass . . . If we must take . . . uh . . . direct action, it must be with the full certainty that it was absolutely necessary . . ."

Roberto, appearing noticeably grayer than usual, looked at the beautiful woman searchingly.

"I . . . that is we," she said glancing briefly in Dave's direction, ". . . will go with you."

# CHAPTER 15

## "NO ONE GUARDS THE GUARDS.
## NO ONE SPIES ON THE SPIES"

T he three walked down the front steps of Elena's apartment building and got into the front of Roberto's late model Volvo, which he had carefully hidden in the alley.

A number of military vehicles patrolled the streets of the Capital.

They took the main highway to the south of the City. Dave glanced questioningly at Roberto as he turned onto the road that went to and only to the Military Reservation.

The driver permitted himself a slight chuckle in the face of the grave situation. "That's correct," he announced, "we're going right into the bear's den."

"Is that wise?" Elena asked.

"Why not?" he answered with a shrug of the shoulders. "de la Castile is, technically, one of the guards. No one guards the guards. No one spies on the spies. Besides, they do not at this point know what role everyone is playing. If they think about it at all, they will think we have come to inform on our colleagues."

He brought the vehicle to a smooth stop beside the guard post.

"Your business, *Senor?*" the young corporal asked, obviously straining to make his voice deeper than it naturally was.

Instead of responding verbally, Roberto handed the young man his identification card as an official of the Ministry of War.

The guard, visibly impressed, stammered, "How may I be of service to you, Sir?"

"Please direct me to Colonel de la Castile's quarters."

"The Colonel is temporarily billeted in the BOQ, which is at the end of the second road, to the right, Sir."

The corporal saluted as Roberto moved the Volvo smoothly away from the guard post and around the square with its flag and the traditional menacing canon.

The door opened almost immediately in response to their knock. They were obviously expected.

The thin, distinguished-appearing field officer pulled the door open slowly. His khaki uniform, open at the neck, was unadorned except for his nameplate, the three crests denoting his rank and the symbol for the Communications/Intelligence Branch on the other collar.

"Please do come in. Make yourselves at home, at least to the extent that these Spartan quarters permit. May I offer you something? Wine? A cocktail?"

The Colonel's manner was so courtly that for a few seconds Dave forgot how truly serious was the business on which they were there.

Roberto and Dave accepted the offer of wine. Elena declined. Dave could tell that her "nervous stomach" was acting up. Any alcohol, obviously, would provoke a very negative reaction.

Having delivered the drinks, the Colonel, who had not poured anything for himself, sat down in a straight-backed wooden chair across from the long couch on which his three visitors were seated.

He looked at them intently for a moment and began speaking slowly. "Of course, I would have to be extremely naïve not to have some idea as to why this meeting is being held. But since Dr. Cordoba did, in fact, request this meeting, perhaps he should set its tone."

Roberto cleared his throat and gulped. "The Colonel is well aware of the national crisis presently afflicting our country. Indeed you, undoubtedly, Sir, have much superior information as to its extent."

De la Castile looked thoughtfully over his hands with the palms together and nodded.

Roberto continued, "At this point, as best we know, four Ministers have been taken into custody . . . ."

"Five," the Colonel interjected.

"Five," Roberto continued. "One supposes the PM does, in fact, have the Constitutional authority to discharge his Ministers. But is it within his powers to deprive them of their freedom?"

De la Castile shook his head and shrugged his broad shoulders.

"Regardless, the arrests appear to be extending ever downward into the rank and file of government workers. I saw soldiers at the Ministry of War going through personnel records this afternoon. So I believe I'm not sounding a false cry of alarm when I say that many civil servants are in danger of being deprived of liberty."

"It's just as you say," the officer acknowledged sadly. "The 'arrests,' the 'purge' if we are to use the technically correct term, has extended to below the level of political appointees."

"And what crimes have these individuals committed?" Roberto asked.

"They are unspecified. In cases in which some type of document is given the detainee, only a single word like 'disloyalty' is given in explanation," was the answer.

Roberto paused for a moment of thought. "In your opinion, Sir, are these detentions, this 'purge' legal?"

"I am a soldier, not a lawyer."

"I, it happens, am a lawyer. I know that they are not legal, even according to our rudimentary Constitution. Would you accept my opinion on that matter?"

"I respect your opinion, Dr. Cordoba. And, for what it's worth, I believe your analysis to be correct."

"Then what in heaven's name can we do?"

The Colonel sat back and stared into space for what seemed a very, very long time.

"Ah, what to do. There's the question," he sighed. "I hope you will understand the great . . . uh . . . ," he waved his graying head back and forth several times, searching for just the right word, ". . . ambivalence I feel in your putting this issue before me.

"You will appreciate the fact that a soldier, that is to say a truly professional soldier, wishes above all else to avoid matters legal and political. Many a military career has been ended by a soldier taking it upon himself to make political statements. And the almost inevitable result of all this is that the soldier's usefulness to his country is ended, not to mention that he foregoes his pension."

The visitors, Dave included, looked downcast. It seemed that they were being told in a roundabout, lecturing way that they had come to the wrong person in their search for help.

Sensing their discouragement, Colonel de la Castile permitted himself a small, benevolent smile. "But," he continued, "these are extraordinary and dark times. And, at such times, general rules and principals do not always apply."

The mood in the room brightened perceptibly.

"Almost a quarter of a century ago I took an Oath. The current crisis inspired me this day to do something most of my fellow officers have never done and actually reread our Oath. What I promised to do was to 'obey and support the leaders of the People of Cortesia in the performance of their Constitutional Duties.' Well, as Dr. Cordoba has informed us, the actions of the Prime Minister and his closest associates are not Constitutional. Therefore, I am not required to obey their orders. Indeed, if one takes one's Oath seriously, which I acknowledge most Latin American officers do not, then I am honor-bound to oppose them." He paused, allowing the significance of what he had just said to sink in with his audience, and just perhaps with himself as well.

The three smiled. But, as though they all shared the same face, the smiles gradually faded into an anxious, open-eyed expression. The three alternated in looking at each other, silently communicating their joint recognition of the true gravity of the evolving situation.

"As I said, I feel great ambivalence about all that is taking place. I have expressed to you my misgivings and regrets. This is not an easy time for a soldier. I must admit that I did not fully appreciate the complexities of Government Service when I embarked upon this career." He smiled warmly and extended his arms out to them in an outstretched, palms-up gesture. "And yet, I am honored, truly honored that you have chosen to come to Arturo Rodriguez de la Castile at this critical point in history." He held his head high in a mockingly regal attitude. "Honored, yes honored. That both pleases and frightens me." As he spoke he lowered his head. His voice deepened and softened at the same time. "You see, in order to explain, I must put false modesty aside. You have come to the right man." His voice had descended to a veritable whisper. "I have the power to right the great evil which stalks our poor land." His eyes narrowed, he clinched his fists and his voice increased in volume. "And I will use it!

"But," he said with a pointing gesture, "unsupervised, uncontrolled military might has inherent within it the seeds of disaster, the seeds of catastrophe. And that is what I shall unleash. Mrs. De la Castile's little boy, as my U.S. colleagues sometimes express it, is going to direct a formidable military force totally on his own. In a situation such as this, power is everything. I have, as I shall explain to you, that power. But who will stop Arturo de la Castile from taking personal advantage of this power once he embarks upon this righteous war? I shall tell you. de la Castile will stop de la Castile."

The Colonel picked up his briefcase and withdrew a single, plain sheet of paper. Using the ink pen he took from beneath the flap over the pocket of his khaki shirt, he wrote:

*La Navided*

*28 August 1992*

*I Arturo Rodriguez de la Castile y Munoz make before witnesses known to me the following declarations:*

*I hold the rank of Colonel in the Army of the Republic of Cortesia.*

*It is my judgment, based in part on the advice of counsel, that the actions of the individual who currently occupies the Office of Prime Minister of Cortesia are consistent with neither the Constitution nor the Rights of Man. It is, thus, necessary that I take upon myself the Command of the Armed Forces of Cortesia.*

*In taking this action, I remain a citizen who happens to be a soldier. No gain must accrue to me or my heirs as a result of the actions I am compelled to take.*

*Therefore, I shall remain a member of the uniformed service of my country. I shall obey the civil authorities appointed above me.*

*The only condition under which I would ever in the future participate in the Government itself would be following the resignation of my commission and as a purely private citizen facing popular election.*

*Any violation of the above set out conditions would constitute High Treason, punishable in the most severe form possible.*

  *(s) Arturo Rodriguez de la Castile y Munoz*

  *(s) Elena Margarita Carmen de la Madrid y Portuando*

  *(s) Roberto Guillermo Cordoba y de Granada*

  *(s) William R. Robinson*

After the three witnesses had signed, the Colonel handed the document to Elena for safe-keeping.

Having placed personal ambition aside, the Colonel stood up and assumed a very definite air of command.

"I am afraid," he informed them, "that we do not have the luxury of time. Mr. Hernandez' thugs are denying Liberty to innocent civilians as we speak. We must act, and we must act now!"

"Tell us what to do," Roberto implored.

"I cannot tell you what to do. I believe, though, that you should remain here in the Capital. I have arranged to fly back up to Costa de la Obscura, our military headquarters, as you are well aware. I have spent most of the day conferring with my brother officers. To a man they have agreed to support whatever actions I might take."

Dave was dumbfounded by what he was hearing. de la Castile was now speaking of assuming command of the nation's armed forces with about the same matter-of-factness of someone telling his friends of his intentions to purchase a new automobile.

"Forgive me, Colonel," he finally blurted out. "I know it's none of my business, but I can't help wondering how you're able to do all this so quickly. I mean . . . uh, won't the generals fight you? Haven't they been listening in on your conversations?" de la Castile and Roberto exchanged knowing glances.

Roberto took it upon himself to answer the foreigner's question. "You must understand that at this point in our history the rank of General in the Army of Cortesia is a purely political appointment. It is an honor, rather like being knighted. It does, though, appeal more to the friends of the Government who make, shall we say, pretentions to *maschismo*. Some of them were junior officers when they were younger but did not work their way up through the ranks, nor do they have any advanced training in military science. For all practical purposes, functional command is now in the hands of career officers like Arturo, mostly majors—there are few colonels."

"So, you see," de la Castile continued the narrative, "the so-called 'generals' wouldn't know how to listen into our coded conversations. I doubt that any of them have even heard of a 'scrambler.' In any case, we must move swiftly, before too many of our supporters find themselves behind bars.

"Roberto, I would recommend that you remain here in my quarters. You will be safe here. As soon as things are secured, I will send a radioman to accompany you everywhere you go. I realize that your group has no formal structure of leaders, but you are now the closest thing to Civilian Authority we have. You can keep in touch with your colleagues here in the Capital and keep me advised as to their sentiments."

He looked searchingly at Elena, obviously contemplating the pros and cons of a contemplated course of action.

Finally, the silence was broken. "Elena," he said softly, "I would like you to come with me, please. I think it advisable for a civilian to be present . . . . I don't believe the danger to be great, but I can, of course, offer no guarantee."

Elena was obviously stunned by the Colonel's request. She looked back blankly for a few moments, and then she turned her glance beseechingly toward Dave. Her first thought was that she didn't want to leave "Bill." She briefly contemplated asking that he be allowed to accompany them. But she realized almost immediately the utter impossibility of this being granted. The implications of having a foreigner with them, particularly an American, were obviously prohibitive. She couldn't, to her regret, even suggest it.

"I'll go with you, of course," she answered in a chocked voice.

The men shook hands, and Elena wordlessly embraced both Roberto and Dave, giving the latter a small kiss on the cheek in the process.

Dave watched with a combination of longing and dread as the Colonel and Elena stepped into the drab colored staff car and the taillights disappeared into the night on their way to the airstrip.

Some minutes later, a sergeant knocked on the door and announced that the Colonel had instructed him to drive "Mr. Robinson" back to town.

So Dave would await the results away from the Principals. He felt a sense of emptiness. He wondered, of course, how these Great Events would turn out. More importantly, though, he wondered when he would see his dear Elena again.

CHAPTER **16**

# "SIR, I RELIEVE YOU"

T he small executive jet whispered its way through the moonless, starlit night. Elena and the Colonel sat across a table from each other in the passenger compartment. de la Castile had spent most of the flight on the wireless coordinating as much as possible in advance the events which would, barring complications, take place upon their arrival at Cortesia's military nerve center. He and Elena, though, had had some time to converse.

"There is one 'general officer' who is sometimes in residence at Costa de la Obscura. His name is Borges. He's an older, portly man, sort of a Falstaffian character. This is actually more of a retirement home for him than anything else. I forget what he did to earn his rank. I guess he either gave some money or had some negatives! In any case, he's technically in command. We don't, though, anticipate much difficulty with 'El Gordo.'"

As the plane banked for its descent, her gaze was pulled to the glare of floodlights ahead. They formed a rectangular pattern, surrounding some sort of field. It was, she mused, like a gigantic stadium in which some drama, possibly a dangerous drama, was soon to be played out. de la Castile's handsome face darkened a bit.

"Major Blanco," he said, directing his eyes up to the ceiling, "has passed the word to the Cuban officers that there will be a military takeover and that it will be of a 'liberal' nature. We can only hope they will recognize . . ." He held his up his hands in a gesture of casting fate to the winds. ". . . assume, believe that the new Government will be their friends and . . . and not intervene."

The intensity of the sound of the wind rushing across the plane's wings increased.

"I must apologize, and I trust that you will convey this to your colleagues, for my rambling and I am sure tedious discourse back at the Capital. Perhaps you can see that all this is not easy for a soldier."

She thought for a moment, her head to one side and now playing nervously with her eyeglasses. "I understand completely, Colonel."

A gentle thud, the muted screech of rubber against concrete. They had arrived.

The copilot came back and turned a large wheel which allowed the cabin door to be moved to one side. The dimly lighted interior of the craft was suddenly flooded by light from the outside.

The Colonel climbed down the ramp first. Glancing over his shoulder he could see forms before him on the tarmac. But the glare of the floodlights prevented him from seeing who they were. As he looked back up the ramp a gentle, refreshing breeze ruffled his hair, reminding him to put on his cap, which had been neatly tucked into his webbed belt. He held one of Elena's elbows as her feet searched for the descending steps in that eerie amalgam of darkness and blinding light.

Turning, he could finally make out the beak-like features of Major Epidio Blanco. The Colonel stood erect and saluted, appearing to very much be making a point of his role as a soldier.

He assisted the lady into the rear seat of the waiting jeep.

It was but a short drive to the arena Elena had seen from the air.

General Borges had been awakened when the floodlights entered his bedroom. He had rolled over and groaned, none the better for all the rum and wine he had downed the evening before. "El Gordo" pulled the thin sheet over his head.

"What in hell is going on out there?" his wife, who both outweighed and "outranked" him, asked.

"How would I know? The goddamned sons of bitches are always prowling around at night, like a bunch of damned cats."

That was that for a bit of time, but the continuing commands barked out on the parade field and the approaching plane had moved "Mrs. El Gordo" to punch "The General" in the chest.

"Very well, very well, I'll get to the bottom of it."

"What in Christ's name is all the racket about?" he demanded on the phone.

There was a pause on the other end of the line. "Sir, General, I don't know . . ."

"Don't know!" he exploded. "You bastards better damn sure know."

"Sir, I'll get the Watch Commander, Sir."

"Major Caballo here, Sir."

"What in God's name is going on out there, you fool. You've awakened Mrs. Borges and . . . me."

There was a long pause.

"Uh, Sir, Colonel de la Castile is arriving, and the men have been mustered to greet him."

"de la Castile arriving! Men mustered to greet him! My God! What is this, the Second Coming?"

"General, I don't know. I was simply told that . . . ."

BAM! The phone was slammed down.

El Gordo pulled on a pair of pants from the closet and a shirt. He didn't notice that the two had never been part of the same "uniform of the day."

Rushing out of the frame house, he strode breathlessly and ponderously to the Fort's Center. The Fifth and Eighth Corps were aligned in parade formation around the field. A jeep pulled up to the top of the formation.

As the general lumbered across the parade field, the Acting Corps Commanders were, quite obviously given their double takes, at a loss as to how to deal with his unexpected presence.

A Cuban captain and sergeant stood behind a barbed-wire fence on one side of the field. The captain reached out his hand, and the enlisted man placed a walkie-talkie into it.

de la Castile bounded from the jeep and saluted Colonel Perez, who stood in front of a small group of staff officers at the head of the parade ground.

"El Gordo" rushed up, spitting and sputtering in his anger.

"What is the meaning of this?" he demanded, shifting his gaze incredulously from Perez to de la Castile and back. de la Castile came to a rigid attention and saluted. "Sir, I relieve you," he announced in a voice loud enough to be heard across the entire field.

The portly man pulled a sagging suspender back over his shoulder. Wide-eyed, he blurted out, "Relieve me. Relieve me? By what authority?"

The Colonel paused, staring at his "superior."

"I am assuming Command in the name of Justice and The People of Cortesia," he declared with obvious *orgulloso*, pride.

"Justice! The People! Have you gone mad, de la Castile? You're a pompous, arrogant son of a bitch, that's what you are! I'll see that you're shot for this!"

"That," he remarked calmly, "is a distinct possibility."

"Have this man arrested," Borges shouted shrilly to Col. Perez.

Perez looked sadly at the older man, apparently embarrassed by the ungainly appearance of one purporting to wear the same uniform as himself.

Perez' none too respectful stare and inaction infuriated Borges. Turning awkwardly around to face the ranks of men assembled, he shouted, "Fall out and arrest these traitors."

"Stand fast," Perez counter-ordered. This command was echoed and amplified by the Sergeant Major who stood beside him. The words "Stand fast" were repeated down the columns.

No one moved.

The silence was palpable, actually physically oppressive.

But the heaviness lifted as each man present, in his own way, came to realize that at long last officers sympathetic to the Cause of Freedom and Human Rights had assumed command of the bulk of the fighting forces of the Republic of Cortesia.

What "General" Borges came to the realization of was the totality of his impotence. He held his fleshy hands up to the sky.

"Judas!" he spat out.

"Mr. Borges," de la Castile responded calmly, "you may consider yourself confined to quarters until further notice. You will find that your command phones have been disconnected, but the standard phone in your residence is fully operative. You may phone anyone you wish, including the Press. You are, though, to make no effort to intervene in, interfere with or confuse military communications. I must, regretfully, inform you that any violation of these conditions will force us to incarcerate you."

El Gordo spat on the ground and stormed from the parade field like a chubby little boy displeased by the rules of a marble game. de la Castile asked Colonel Perez to put the men at ease. He stepped forward and in a gesture strange for a military man, he removed his cap.

The great distance and lack of a loudspeaker precluded, he thought, a long speech. But he felt compelled to at least try to explain to the men what was taking place. A World War II interchange between a Soviet and a U.S. general popped into his mind. "General," the Soviet Marshall announced proudly, "when I tell my men to do something, I don't even have to tell them why." "Hmmm," the Western officer responded matter-of-factly, "when I tell my men why, I don't have to tell them to do it." He recognized this as the operative principle in this dangerous situation. Events were so extraordinary and the upcoming actions for soldiers so unusual that he realized that to hold things together he would have to do as much educating and persuading as ordering.

"Gentlemen, we are assembled here at a critical and dangerous moment in the history of our Beloved Nation.

"We are soldiers. We are good soldiers! We have sworn to uphold the Constitution of the Republic of Cortesia. The man who currently styles himself the Prime Minister and those with whom he surrounds himself have embarked upon a course of illegal, un-Constitutional actions. As you undoubtedly have heard, they are arresting and jailing civilians without charges or any pretense of Due Process. As good soldiers, we must and shall oppose them!

"I ask each of you to act as Patriots! We do not take these actions for gain or self-glorification. Indeed, the safer course for all of us would be that of acquiescence and inaction.

"Your Officers stand solidly for the Constitution and beside me. They will keep you informed of all developments and pass on the appropriate orders. You may be sure that we will do all in our power to avoid the shedding of blood.

"May God bless you all!"

There was a pause as he looked at each Corps in turn.

"Sergeant, please dismiss the men. They will need their rest."

As the men dispersed, de la Castile, Perez and an aide walked without discussion, automatically as it were, toward a squat concrete building in a grove of trees on the opposite side of the field from the runway. de la Castile glanced back and motioned with his hand for Elena to accompany them.

A guard in fatigues brought his rifle to Present Arms as the four, the lady now in the lead, descended the steps and walked into the bunker.

The centerpiece of the dimly lighted, cavernous room they entered was a huge relief map of Cortesia and the surrounding countries and seas. Soldiers stood around the large table on which it lay with forked sticks, ready to move about the symbols of divisions, missile launchers, important personages, etc. as the situation changed.

Arturo both enjoyed this room and considered it overdone. The strategic complexities of a small country like Cortesia did not require such an elaborate set-up. What had happened was that a former Nobleman/Commanding General had been honored, for purely political reasons, with a tour of the War Room in the Pentagon. So impressed was he that he just had to have his own version of it back home. In front of them lay the results of the General's delight in the playthings of advanced age. Regardless, though, of the dubious need for such, this room afforded one of the best in fixed communication facilities in the world.

As de la Castile followed Elena into the chamber, everyone stopped working, stood up and applauded.

The Colonel struck his swagger stick sharply on one of the metal handrails.

"I don't," he said with a frown on his face, "recall anyone announcing a celebration. There is serious work to be done." Not very charismatic, he thought to himself. But charisma was something he wished actively to avoid. He had seen better men than himself sacrifice their Causes and their Honor on that alter.

The Colonel sat down in the center chair of what very much resembled the bridge of the Enterprise on the Star Trek set.

His first call was to Dr. Cordoba. "What," he asked, "is the sentiment in the Capital?" His second call was to the Commander of the La Navidad Military Reservation and the third was to the Commander of the Naval Base.

CHAPTER **17**

# "WHAT FOR GODSAKES IS GOING ON DOWN THERE?"

"Yeah," the Assistant Secretary of State groaned into the phone beside the bed.

"It's Hobson, Sir, at the Situation Desk. So sorry to wake you, Sir, but we're getting reports of some unusual activity in Cortesia."

"Unusual activity? What the hell does that mean? Speak English, man! What for godsakes is going on down there?"

"Well . . . uh, Sir, we don't know exactly at this point. It seems that a colonel by the name of de la Castile, about their best I might add, has taken command of the main military base at Costa de la Obscura. Obviously, he wasn't invited to do this. General Borges, the Base Commander, called the Embassy. He demanded that we call in the Marines and have de la Castile shot!"

The yawn at the other end of the line was audible to the duty officer. "Has anyone spoken to the Prime Minister?"

"No, Sir. When they called the Palace, some guy who called himself 'Captain Something or Other' answered. The Attache' asked to speak to the PM's Military Aide. He went to consult with somebody, we don't know who. When the captain returned, he said that no one was available then but that a statement would be issued in the morning."

"Damn it! A coup. A dirty, lousy left-wing coup."

"That's how it appears, Sir."

"And just when we had things worked out with Old Man Hernandez."

"Yes, Sir . . . uh . . . is there any action you want us to take tonight?"

"Oh, . . . oh," the bureaucrat answered dopily, obviously shaking himself into as much clarity as possible. "Is there any indication of danger to U.S. citizens or our interests down there?"

"No, Sir, no one has called in, and the Attache' said that they had checked with security at the mines. Nothing unusual. No signs of fighting whatever."

"Well, I think we can let this wait until morning. I mean, this kind of thing goes on down there all the time. Get me in to see the Secretary as soon as you can after mid-morning."

"Yes, Sir. Goodnight."


Dawn fingered its way down the mountain valleys and into the still, quiet streets of the Capital of the Republic of Cortesia. As the vendors set up their wares and as the women swept the streets, there was no way they could be aware of the momentous changes that had taken place while they slept. In actuality, it looked much more like the recent turmoil had ended and that normalcy had returned. No more olive drab trucks rumbled through the streets. No more soldiers, machine guns slung across their backs, roamed the City. Their officers had called off their aimless maneuvers and ordered them back to the barracks and to bed.

Hours earlier at the Palace, a small group of soldiers loyal to de la Castile had occupied the lobby. They had strolled, almost casually, into the old building during the early hours of the morning. Dr. Cordoba and his radioman accompanied them.

Captain Diaz informed the corporal at the desk that they were here on urgent Government business. It was, he said, imperative that Dr. Cordoba meet immediately with the Prime Minister.

Diaz stepped back a few paces as the corporal relayed the message upstairs. A moment later the corporal repeated what he had heard: "Surely, Captain, this matter can wait until in the morning."

The captain approached the desk and glared down at the enlisted man. "No," he said firmly, "it cannot wait until morning."

The corporal's eyes widened as he looked past the captain and at the fatigue-clad, armed men with him.

"You may inform the Prime Minister that we're on the way up for our meeting. And please advise the other members of the Guard that you have all been relieved."

The Members of the "Palace Guard" had been selected more for their aristocratic backgrounds than their military training or zeal. They abandoned the building immediately.

As the small group emerged onto the upper floor, they were greeted by the sight of the bath-robed Prime Minister hobbling down the hall, his portly valet in his wake. The old man was in a state of considerable agitation. He had obviously discovered that his lines of communication to the outside world had been cut.

"What is the meaning of this?" he sputtered and demanded.

The soldiers stopped in their tracks, uncertain as to how to deal with that obviously complex question.

Roberto stepped forward.

"I am Roberto Guillermo Cordoba."

"Yes, yes, I've seen you. You're a petty bureaucrat at the War Ministry."

Roberto nodded, acknowledging that at least the old man had been able to place him in space and time.

"The un-Constitutional and unreasonable acts of your government, Sir, have forced the democratic forces of Cortesia to take action. Colonel de la Castile has assumed command of the Armed Forces, and we are in the process of forming a provisional government until truly democratic elections can be held."

"Guards, Guards!" the old man shouted in a hoarse voice crackling with rage.

No one came.

"They are gone," Cordoba said softly.

It was surprising that the former Prime Minister of Cortesia could slump even more.

"You may, if you wish, Mr. Hernandez, remain in your rooms here, or we will arrange for your immediate transportation by air to the country of your choice."

The rising sun found the former Prime Minister of Cortesia the "guest" of the Generalissimo of a neighboring "Republic."

The manager of the country's only television station sat alone in the station's small, unpretentious lobby. The sources his staff relied upon for news had, of course, advised him of the events that had transpired during the night. So he was not the least surprised to receive a call requesting air time for the "Provisional Government."

At 8:00 AM, as scheduled, three men walked into the station. Roberto, who had changed into a dark suit, walked up to the manager and extended his hand.

"I am Roberto Cordoba."

"*Buenos dias, Senor Doctor Cordoba. Amilio Coppa, a sus ordenes.*"

Roberto introduced the men with him to the manager. And this is *Corporal Garcia*. And, of course, you know Captain Diaz."

"Captain." Returning his gaze to Roberto, he said, "We have done the best we can in preparation for you. If you will accompany me, please, Gentlemen."

They entered a small studio. Outside of the equipment, it contained only a plain wooden table and a straight-backed chair, behind which stood the silver and scarlet flag of Cortesia.

"Will you require something . . . uh . . . something more elaborate, *Senor?*"

"No, *Senor*, this is exactly . . . what we need." Roberto was obviously moved by the simplicity and appropriateness of the setting which had been arranged for his speech. He somehow regarded it as a sign of support.

"We've announced that a representative of the, uh, uh . . . new government would address the People at 8:30. Of course, if you need more time, we . . . ."

"I'm quite ready, thank you," he answered, betraying for the first time a trace of anxiety in his voice.

Roberto seated himself behind the desk and carefully placed the three sheets of paper he carried on the bare, cold surface before him.

The station manager gave Roberto his only instruction. "I'm certain, Dr. Cordoba, that you know to begin when the red light on the camera comes on." The waiting speaker nodded. And then they left him alone in the room.

A man in coveralls walked briefly into the studio to make adjustments to the two cameras.

There was a long silence.

The little light appeared.

> *"Good morning, my fellow citizens of Cortesia.*
>
> *"I am Roberto Guillermo Cordoba. I am a Doctor of Law, and until the recent upheavals I was a Member of the Council to the Minister of War.*
>
> *"As you undoubtedly know, the government of Ernesto Hernandez began several days ago to arrest civilians without even the pretense of formal charges. This action is not only illegal according to the Constitution of our Nation, but it is inherently abhorrent to anyone who is at all concerned about the Rights of Man.*
>
> *"Because of these deplorable actions of the former government, my colleagues and I have assumed control of the mechanisms of government of Cortesia. I say my 'colleagues.' We are bound together by no common interest other than the*

*wish to see a truly democratic form of government prevail in our beloved Cortesia.*

*"We are painfully aware of the fact that we, at this point, have no explicit Mandate from the People for our actions. We pledge to you that elections in which all adults may vote will be held at the very earliest date possible. Until that time, I have formed a caretaker government which will insure that vital services are provided and Citizens' Rights, as guaranteed by our basically sound but underdeveloped and sadly neglected Constitution, are respected. But this interim government will refrain from taking actions that would have any long-term effect on the future of our Nation.*

*"Now, as to the process of holding elections, a number of steps must be taken. Firstly, there's the matter of . . . ."*

"The Secretary will see you now."

The Assistant Secretary raised his bulky frame from the couch and lumbered into the grand and imposing office of the United States Secretary of State.

"It's good of you to see me on such short notice, Sir."

The urbane, silver-haired diplomat nodded without rising from his chair.

"I'm certain, Sir, that you've heard about the coup in Cortesia during the night."

"Yes, of course, there was a rather full account in the morning pouch. But what I don't understand is why people are making such a big fuss over all this. I mean, this kind of thing goes on all the time down there, doesn't it?"

"Yes, it does, but there are some special things about Cortesia. First of all, Sir, we've discovered a large Cuban military presence in the country. I informed the PM about it just last week. He went back to sack the traitors. I guess that, seeing that their little game was up, they turned on him.

"The second reason, and I didn't know about this myself until a gal named Molly from Intelligence came over to brief me this morning, Cortesia is the only source for a certain metal in our Sphere of Influence. Damn thing starts with a 'B,' but I can't pronounce it. What I do know is that it's vital to our Strategic Defense . . . uh . . ."

"Star Wars."

"Yeah, Star Wars. But, you see, no one down there knows what we do with the stuff. It's a tightly kept secret on our side. When we buy it, whether from American-owned or locally-owned mines, we purchase it in the name of a toy company."

The Secretary laughed, breaking for a moment the building tension. "A toy company! The Democrats would love to hear that Star Wars is being built by a toy company."

"Yes, Sir," the Assistant Secretary mumbled, uncertain as to whether or not he should join in the laughter.

"Well, what do we know about those who have taken over down there?"

"They seem to be a rag-tag, loosely organized group of far-left liberals. Intelligence has photos of many of them crawling all over Cuba. Molly, that is Ms. Sterns, singles out a woman named Elena de la Madrid as a particularly bad apple."

"Have they made any announcement of their plans?"

"Yes, their self-proclaimed leader, a lawyer named Cordoba, just finished making a radio-TV speech. One of our monitoring stations picked it up. He said they did it for the people and they're going to hold open and free elections as soon as possible."

"Free and open elections. Hah! That's the rebel equivalent of 'the check's in the mail'."

"Quite so, Sir."

"Hmmmm. Well, I'll call the President right away. Keep me up to date."

"Yes, Sir."

The Monday State Department briefing began with the following comments:

> "The Government of the United States deplores and condemns the illegal takeover of the reins of government of the Republic of Cortesia.
>
> "We have enjoyed friendly and mutually beneficial relations with the Government of Prime Minister Hernandez. This un-Constitutional coup conducted by subversives controlled by Havana is both a tragedy for the People of Cortesia and a grave threat to the peace and stability of the region. We will not extend recognition to this new, self-proclaimed government.
>
> "There are U.S. citizens in Cortesia, and we have legitimate business interests in that troubled nation. Any effort of the rebels to interfere with the ongoing, legal enterprises of U.S. citizens will be met with the most serious consequences."

During the question and answer period, the inevitable exchange occurred:

Q: "What, if any action has the Administration decided to take with respect to the situation in Cortesia at this time?"

A: "We're consulting with our allies and studying our options. Perhaps I'll have more for you later."

CHAPTER **18**

## "WE'RE RIGHT IN THE MIDDLE"

D ave paced up and down on the tarmac, anxiously awaiting Elena's return.

The small, white jet appeared to come out of the setting sun as it cleared the mountain peaks and began its descent.

His eyes were fixed on the back of her khaki pants as she made her way down the ladder to the ground.

They embraced about half-way between the plane and the tiny terminal.

"Boy, I've missed you," Dave said joyfully.

"I've missed you too," she responded softly.

They walked with his arm around her waist through the lobby. A number of the waiting passengers glanced at them, apparently having seen her picture in news reports about the members of the Provisional Government.

They sat together for a moment in her car.

"You look tired," he said sympathetically.

"I am."

"Do you want to go out for a drink and supper?"

"No, no thank you. I want to go home . . . . You know, I've never really had a family. I'll prepare us a nice supper."

Dave was somehow touched by what Elena had said, even though he hadn't fully worked out the meaning of her words.

They drove in silence through the streets of La Navidad. Several times he glanced over to the passenger's seat and saw that she had removed her glasses and was rubbing her eyes. He knew that she was under a terrific strain.

"Sit down, Honey. I'll pour you a drink," he said as they entered her apartment.

She plopped on the sofa and kicked off her shoes. There was an audible sigh of relief.

Dave brought them both gin and tonics in tall glasses with lots of ice. He sat down beside her, placing his hand on her knee. He looked into her eyes, inviting her to speak.

She merely smiled weakly.

"Tough times?" he asked gently.

"Yes, as you say, tough times."

"Do you want to talk about it?"

"Yes, I'm very tired, but I do want to talk about it a little. We can talk more tomorrow. Roberto radioed up mid-afternoon. He said the American Ambassador had phoned him. He warned us to give it up. Said the U.S. was considering what steps to take and that military action had not been ruled out.

"The Cuban General tried to get in to see de la Castile all day. Arturo finally agreed to see him as I was leaving."

He cupped his hands together and spoke very slowly to Elena. "I heard on the short-wave radio just before leaving to pick you up that Radio Havana has announced that Castro will regard any attack on Cortesia as an attack on Cuba."

"My God," she moaned, throwing her forehead into her hands. "We're right in the middle."

They held each other as darkness fell on the City.

The phone's ring stirred the couple not from sleep, but from what could best be described as a state of nervous exhaustion. Both now realized that Cortesia had, indeed, been an island of peace in a sea of conflict. They knew that they would miss that, and they now wished that they had savored it more.

Elena walked barefooted over to the small marble-topped table on which the ringing phone sat.

"*Hola.*"

"Yes, I know. Bill told me."

"Certainly, I'll see you in the morning," were her last words before hanging up the phone.

"We're having a meeting at nine in the morning," she announced to Dave. Elena made a gallant effort to smile and said, "Well, Dear, I believe I promised you supper. If you'll freshen the drinks, I'll make the preparations. Does pork sound good to you? I've got a Gewurztraminer that should compliment it beautifully."

"Sounds great to me," he said in something of a monotone.

The conversation during supper related, obviously by mutual and implicit consent, to anything not related to the ongoing turmoil in Cortesia. Mostly, they swapped stories about their childhoods. Dave told Elena about his first out-of town journey without parental supervision. He talked about how he and a buddy had boarded a bus and rode into Columbus to walk around, do a little shopping and have lunch at a fancy restaurant. He described how grown up and sophisticated that had made the two thirteen year-olds feel. Elena listened with her usual open-eyed attentiveness. She asked several questions about the experience. There was, though, one question that she didn't ask. That was how a kid growing up in upstate New York could make it to city named Columbus on a bus for lunch!

Dave cleared the table as Elena poured water into the sink. As usual, she washed and he dried and put the dishes into the cabinet.

"Well," he announced after the task was completed, "it's quite late. I guess I'd better go."

Elena turned to him and put her hands on his shoulders. Dave could feel the dampness of her apron through his trousers. "No," she said softly but firmly. "I don't want you to go. I want you to stay with me, Bill."

As they looked at each other, her eyes narrowed and she tilted her head to one side. "Bill," she continued in a breathless and trembling voice, "I can't help wanting to know. Is that really your name?"

His heart seemed to stop. His brain whirled in a sea of conflict. Suddenly, though, a great sense of serenity descended upon him, quite unexpectedly.

His voice sounded almost like that of a robot as he heard himself say, "No, my name is David. Everyone calls me Dave."

Her huge brown eyes were hypnotizing. She smiled sweetly.

"I love you, Dave."

"I love you, Elena."

"I trust you, Dave."

"I won't do anything to hurt you."

"I know. And someday you'll tell me everything."

"Yes, someday I'll tell you everything."

She stepped back slightly and moved her hands down to his hips.

"You know, you have everything you need here, even extra clothes from the times you changed here so we could go out in the evenings."

"Yes, I have everything I need here."


There was a rap on the door of Roberto Cordoba's office at the War Ministry, the same one he had occupied as an Under Minister for over four years now.

Roberto glanced up from the papers he was studying and invited Aradio into the cramped room.

Skipping the usual amenities, Aradio began, "We have a problem we need to talk about."

The gray-haired man behind the desk smiled. "A problem? By my count we have a multitude of problems!"

Aradio frowned. "No, no I mean within ourselves."

Roberto leaned back further in his chair and shrugged his shoulders. "Oh, we've had our differences over the years. But Old Man Hernandez was good enough to settle for us the issue of how to proceed. Besides . . . ."

"Well, let's settle something right now," the younger man said sharply, cutting Roberto off. "We're meeting at nine, about an hour and a half from now. It's the first chance we've had to sit down and discuss things, our first formal meeting."

"Um-mmm."

"Am I correct that anyone can bring up anything and that we will operate on the basis of group consensus?"

"That is certainly my assumption. I seem to have misplaced my manual on Provisional Civilian Governments."

Aradio frowned again.

"Look," Roberto said benignly, "this is going to be an even longer road to travel if we don't take with us our senses of humor."

"Well, I don't find what I need to discuss with you at all humorous. It's about Elena and the American."

Cordoba stroked his lip with the tip of his index finger and thought for a few moments. "Oh?" was all he could come up with right away. But then he said hastily, "Of course, she may associate with whomever she wishes."

Aradio pounded his fist on the simple desk. "At the risk of our Country, our lives, our freedom?" he gasped.

"I fail to see how one . . . uh, one relationship between a Cortesian and an American is going to have such cataclysmic results."

"Look, we know absolutely nothing about this man. He's an enigma. On social occasions he almost never talks about himself. He just asks questions, questions and more questions. And what does he do with his days? Is he out looking for mines? No! He's snooping around, like down at the harbor. And doesn't it seem to you strange that everywhere he admits to have traveled to actually look for 'geological prospects' has been right next to a military installation?" Aradio stood up for his dramatic finish. "I tell you, Roberto, that *gringo* is a spy!"

Roberto motioned with his hand for the agitated young man to resume his seat.

"That thought had crossed my mind," he said as a temporary look of concern swept over his face. "But, again, we can't tell Ms. de la Madrid with whom to be involved. And we don't know that William Robinson is a spy. He checked out perfectly when Arturo made inquiries about him shortly after his arrival."

Aradio shrugged his shoulders, obviously unimpressed.

"Besides," Roberto continued, "we actually have nothing to hide from the United States. We're moving toward democratization, and we've made no move against private property, whether internally or externally owned."

"Well, the press releases out of Washington certainly don't convince me that the Americans understand all that."

"I concede the point. But it's our job to convince them."

"I just can't see how you can accede to such arrogance. It's their job to keep out of our business! You know, we have powerful friends. The Cubans will help us."

'Wait, wait," Roberto said, holding up his hand and shifting nervously in his chair. "You're talking about foreign policy here. And we don't know at this point what position the elected Government will take with respect to alliances."

"Oh, that's true," Aradio said a bit sheepishly. "But still, I think it quite comforting to know that we're not alone in the world . . . But then back to the point I am raising, Elena and the American. We may well in the future have something to hide from the Americans. I urge you to recall that the United States Government has been quite pointed in informing us that they have not ruled out military action."

"This is true. And from my observations of the couple, I do not believe that Elena is going to give him up. But for a variety of political and practical reasons we don't want to deprive ourselves of Elena's services . . . her counsel, her prestige, her help. Perhaps a compromise would be in order here. I'm certain that we can arrange things so that Elena will have no information about military matters, like troop dispositions, antiaircraft emplacements, etc. That's not her area anyway. How do you feel about that?"

"It sounds like a very workable compromise, at least for the time being," Aradio replied with the faint hint of a smile of a person who had just won a minor victory.

As they exited the office to attend to pre-meeting chores, Aradio commented, "You know, Roberto, you're so naïve. It's fortunate for your parents that you weren't born a girl."

Dr. Cordoba stopped in his tracks and turned toward the other man. He poked Aradio's chest gently with his forefinger. "You see," he said, "I told you that a sense of humor would help us get through this."

CHAPTER **19**

# "WE ARE NOT EMPOWERED TO COMMIT OUR NATION"

A s usual, the guards raised the silver and scarlet flag of the Republic of Cortesia over the Palace as the sun made its appearance over the mountain tops. But, in reality, the old building was deserted. Government workers throughout the Capital continued their work of maintaining vital services, water, welfare relief, etc., but the Halls of Established Power were empty. What Central Government Cortesia had was meeting in a small conference room used by mid-level executives in the nearby Ministry of War.

Cordoba could not help noting as he entered the room that the participants had seated themselves in a highly symbolic manner. Aradio and Maria sat on the left side of the table, and Elena and Hector de la Fuente occupied the two seats opposite.

"*Buenos dias*," he greeted them, feigning a tone of brightness.

"We meet today not as a government but as an agency for the creation of a representative government for our Nation. It is my position that anything we do should most definitely fall into the category of 'caretaker.' The sole exception to this, in my judgment, is that we must, must arrange for elections with universal suffrage at the earliest possible time.

"Elena, I wonder if you would be good enough to take charge of the process of arranging for these elections?"

"I would be honored, Roberto."

The meeting was temporarily interrupted by the entrance into the room of Colonel de la Castile, who had just flown down from Costa de la Obscura.

Cordoba continued, "Now with respect to the elections, we have a number of fundamental questions with which to grapple. Heretofore, we've had here in Cortesia what purported to be a Parliamentary form of government. Of course, the Legislature was only a rubber stamp . . . ."

"Ummmm-mmm," de la Castile interrupted. "If I could have the Committee's indulgence, I should like to go ahead and make my report. As a military officer, I do not believe it appropriate for me to be involved in political discussions."

"Forgive me, Colonel," Roberto said with a deferential nod of his head.

"Ladies and Gentlemen of the Committee, I am pleased to report that peace prevails throughout all areas of the Republic of Cortesia. There has been absolutely no resistance to the Provisional Government. It seems that all of the supporters of the old regime who were in the Armed Services merely went home and hung up their uniforms! It appears that the practice of promoting on the basis of family connections does not yield a High Command that a leader can depend upon in time of need. I have been able to rescind the stand-by alert that was put in place seventy-two hours ago. We are now in a very routine mode of functioning.

"I do, though, need to report to you on a meeting I had yesterday with the Cuban Commander, General Alvarez. He kept congratulating us on our 'Glorious People's Revolution' and calling me 'General.' I told him it was not a 'Glorious Revolution,' that it was merely the restoration of Constitutional Law and that I was only a colonel."

"Do you want to be a general, Arturo?" Roberto asked as the others chuckled.

"Not that way," he said with a smile. "Well, the General made a proposal. That was that we integrate our commands during the crisis. I told him that, first of all, there did not appear to be a 'crisis' and that, secondarily, I was not empowered to take such a step which had such obvious foreign policy implications . . . ."

"I received a complementary proposal from the Cuban Foreign Office through their Ambassador," Roberto interjected. "I'll give you a full report later."

"I told the General that I would bring the matter before this body."

"Thank you, Colonel," Robert intoned in formal appreciation. "Of course, in light of your earlier report, I hardly see the need for such drastic . . . ."

Maria interjected, "I believe strongly that we ought to accept the General's offer. The United States is beginning a campaign of old-style imperialistic saber-rattling. We may need to protect ourselves, and it is obvious to me that it is vital to our security and the Rights of the People of Cortesia that we avail ourselves of any assistance that is pro-offered."

"I believe that would be a most dangerous step," Elena said, looking searchingly at Roberto in the knowledge that his would be the deciding vote in the matter. "To involve ourselves in such joint military ventures with the Cubans would, I think, send a powerful signal to the Americans that their worst fears are correct. I think it would have the effect of increasing the probability of their taking . . . uh . . . adverse action against us."

"Oh, oh, no, no, we mustn't do anything to offend the U.S.A.," ejaculated Maria with obvious bitterness. The slight woman with the graying ponytail seated beside Aradio raised her hands into the air, clearly preparing to launch into a speech of some intensity.

"Please, Maria, allow me to finish," Elena said, her voice betraying a touch of weariness. "Another danger I see in this relates to the fact that while it might be easy to combine our efforts, I'm not so certain that disentangling ourselves would be quite so simple."

Hector, the meticulously dressed young man seated beside her, leaned forward in order to enter a comment. "I believe that what Elena is telling us is most definitely true. As an Assistant to the Minister for the Army, I have had extensive contact with Cuban military personnel. They have been involved for over three decades in a military build-up such as Latin America has never seen before. And, of course, they had tremendous assistance from the Soviets prior to the collapse in the Kremlin. They possess weapon systems officers in other countries have never even heard of—missile launchers, radar detection devices, just to name a few. And they have all this time been preparing for a United States invasion of their island. They have developed a highly militaristic tradition, and their chain of command has the rigidity of the SS.

"What I'm trying to develop from all this is that any army that integrates its command with that of the Cubans is going to be automatically overwhelmed by their more powerful units. Their resources are so much greater than ours that a Cortesian officer would almost feel silly, I guess presumptuous would be a better word, to try to have any significant input into the functioning of such a combined force."

Everyone turned their eyes to Colonel de la Castile.

He sat there in silence.

"Bull," Maria shouted, her outburst ending in a squeaky wheeze.

Dr. Cordoba held up his hand in the manner of a policeman halting traffic. He couldn't help noticing a disapproving look from Aradio. "I really believe, Ladies and Gentleman," he said, "that this is a topic which should be deferred. First of all, I cannot help noting the Colonel's discomfort at being party to these discussions. Secondly, Hector's point is well taken. In considering this issue, we are in danger of, as the Americans say, 'putting the cart before the horse.' Military policy should flow from foreign policy, not the other way around. Given that we are a provisional government without a foreign policy, in such matters we are not empowered to commit our nation. There are, though, a number of immediate security matters to which we need to attend."

Roberto, who had appeared increasingly uncomfortable as the meeting progressed, paused and cleared his throat nervously. "Uh, Elena, you know, you have so much to do in beginning preparations for the elections that you may want to absent yourself in order to commence work." He looked at her searchingly, almost pleadingly.

Elena shot back a short distance in her chair. She let out an involuntary soft gasp. It was immediately obvious to her that she was being "dismissed."

Roberto smiled at her weakly.

"I . . . I, that is . . . uh, yes. I do have much to do. Please excuse me," Elena stammered as she pushed her chair back and walked toward the door.

Her moving away from the table spared her from seeing the grins of satisfaction on the faces of Aradio and Maria.

Roberto jumped from his chair to open the door for the wounded Elena.

"You know," he said soothingly as she moved in sleep-walking fashion in front of him, "we'll take no action on foreign policy in your absence."

"Yes, of course, Roberto, I have no need to know about such matters," she replied, a non-sequitur as a response to his words, but not to the context.


Dave had finished his morning reading and was having another cup of coffee while writing a letter "home" when he heard the sound of a key turning in the door.

"Hi, Dear," he said without looking up from his work. "Gosh, you're home early. How was the meeting?"

"Short, at least for me."

Detecting a note of distress in her voice, he looked up at her. "Is something wrong?"

She allowed her arms to fall helplessly to her sides. "Well, when they got to the point where they were going to discuss 'security matters,' they, in effect, invited me to leave."

Dave felt a stabbing sensation in his chest. He got up, walked over to her and put his hands on her shoulders.

"Maybe it's the company you keep."

"Yeah, maybe it's the company I keep," Elena replied with a faint smile.

"I'm sorry."

"No, don't be. I want to have someone. I want to belong to someone."

"You have someone."

Dave patted her bottom twice as the embrace ended. "Say," he said more brightly, "I've made you some coffee."

"Yes, yes, I'd like that very much."

He poured the creamer and artificial sweetener into the cup as Elena described what had transpired at the meeting.

"Well, one good thing, I guess, is that they've asked me to take charge of arranging for the elections."

"Great," Dave replied as he settled himself beside her at the kitchen table. "That is, ultimately, the most important thing in the whole business."

"Yeah."

"Yeah! I guess I've taught you to say 'yeah.' You used to always say 'yes' when you spoke English."

"Yeah, I guess I did."

The Seal of the President of the United States appeared on all four monitors.

*"The door opens, the reporters rise, Ladies and Gentlemen, the President of the United States."*

*"I have," he began, "a few announcements, and then I'll be happy to answer any questions . . . , uh, . . . you might have.*

*"We in the Administration are quite concerned about the recent action of the Federal Reserve Board in raising the Prime Interest Rate. At a time when our nation's economy is struggling to recover from the recent foreign-caused recession, it seems the height of imprudence to at this time . . . .*

*"We deplore and condemn the military coup which occurred several days ago in the Republic of Cortesia. The People and Government of Cortesia have been magnificent friends and allies of the United States. We are emphatic in our stance that we do not recognize the current regime, and our only contact with this rabble of young, impudent hoods has been by way of urging them in the strongest possible language to step aside and allow for the return of the Constitutionally legitimate Government of Prime Minister Ernesto Hernandez."*

*And during the question and answer period, the following exchange occurred:*

*"Sir, what, if any, steps is the Administration considering in order to remove the 'illegitimate regime' in Cortesia?"*

*"Well, Hayden, the United States is most definitely going to play a vital role in removing that . . . uh, illegal regime. I don't really think it*

*wise for me to specify the exact measures that we're going to take. Obviously, there are going to be economic sanctions. We're consulting with our allies on the exact form of these right now."*

*"Mr. President, have you made any formal decision with respect to the possible use of force in Cortesia?"*

*"No, no we have not. Certainly we all hope that it doesn't come to that. But, as I've said, we regard the coup as a most serious and dangerous matter, and we're simply going to have to do what it takes to . . . uh . . . straighten this thing out."*

CHAPTER **20**

## "NOTHING WORKS ANYMORE"

Dave and Elena walked through the parking lot beside her apartment building. Many of the automobiles had been in the same spot for weeks. Others had been missing, apparently unable to even make it back home. Fortunately, Cortesia was blessed with rich soil and dedicated farmers, so the populace continued to be well fed. But the little republic had no plants to manufacture spare parts for cars or such needed maintenance items as air filters and transmission fluid. The embargo was taking its toll on the life of the people.

As they walked down the hill toward the Ministry, the sun was already warming their faces.

"Well, today's a big day," Dave said in as upbeat a manner as he could in his attempt to break the tendency toward silence so early in the morning.

"That's right. I get to announce the date of the election this morning. I'm real glad that we were able to make arrangements for it to take place before the U.S. election, if only by a few days."

A weary yet contented look on the young woman's face turned rapidly to one of surprise and alarm.

"Look," she said excitedly, pointing beyond the harbor and out to the open sea.

Quite out to sea, presumably beyond the twelve-mile territorial limit, a group of huge warships sailed southeast along Cortesia's rocky coastline. They were vastly larger than any vessels possessed by the little republic or any other nation of Latin America, for that matter. They were a threatening and menacing presence.

The two looked at each other anxiously. It didn't take words for the couple to conclude and agree that this specter only increased the gravity of the situation.

Two people were seated at the simple wooden table as their images were flashed to TV screens across the Nation. One was a thin, well-dressed man with graying hair. The other was a dark-haired young woman whose voluptuous beauty was tempered by a conservative business suit and horn rimmed eyeglasses.

> *"I am Roberto Cordoba, as many of you, my fellow citizens of Cortesia, know. I am currently the Chairman of the Coordinating Committee of the Provisional Civilian Government. I need to also make sure that you know and understand that I am also a declared candidate for the Presidency of Cortesia. As such, I have offered my resignation to the Committee. Regrettably, the Committee has,*

*to date, been unable to agree upon a successor for me, so I shall be forced to continue in this interim capacity until the election.*

*"In continuing with this uneasy arrangement, I need and wish to make two things clear to you. First of all, I am not an incumbent in the Presidency. Secondly, this interim government is serving in a purely caretaker fashion. We are maintaining as best we can vital services, but we are refraining studiously from making any policy decisions which could affect the political future of Cortesia. In this way, my supporters and I hope to avoid even the appearance of taking advantage of our temporary positions in the transitional government.*

*"Clearly, the most important task of this interim government is to arrange for fair and early elections. Our colleague Elena de la Madrid has bravely taken on this most important, indeed critical, assignment. Ms. de la Madrid is with us this morning to outline the procedures for this historic event, the first truly democratic election in the history of the Republic of Cortesia. Ms de la Madrid . . . ."*

Elena's voice trembled for the first sentence of her speech, but she rapidly regained her composure.

*"My fellow citizens, I am pleased and honored to announce to you that our elections will be held on Sunday November 1ˢᵗ. All citizens eighteen*

*years and over will be eligible and are encouraged
to vote.*

*"Of course, we considered it desirable to
institute a registration procedure for the election.
Unfortunately, this method for accounting for
the votes proved impossible at this point. Time
alone would have made setting up such a system
quite difficult, but our current inability to replace
computer components and obtain the needed
'software' has made it virtually impossible. In its
stead, we are going to utilize a system like that
used at carnivals and amusement parks in other
countries. We are going to stamp the hand of
everyone who has cast his or her ballot. The ink
we will use, I am assured, is one that cannot be
removed, even with the most vigorous scrubbing,
within twenty-four hours of its application. We
apologize for having to resort to this perhaps
juvenile tactic. I can promise all of you who are
listening today that the ink we will be using is not
harmful. Next week, we are conducting meetings
with tribal leaders from the Interior to explain
both the procedures and the innocuous nature of
the stamp."*

As Elena and Roberto exited the station, they walked
past the front desk. The woman seated there picked up the
telephone. A distressed look appeared in her eyes, and she hit
the cradle a few times. Glancing up at Cordoba, she spat out
the words, "Nothing works anymore."

"Well, they can't stop the fish from coming in," Dave commented as he bit into his lunch.

"No, they can't," was Elena's simple and perhaps distracted reply.

Up the hill, the Committee met with Elena's chair empty.

"We are meeting," Roberto began with an obvious note of seriousness in his voice, "to consider various . . . military possibilities. The Colonel is with us today and, I understand, has a presentation." de la Castile stood, pointer in hand, before a large map of Cortesia at the head of the room.

"I am," he began, "informed by the Chairman of this body that there exists the possibility of an invasion of our borders."

"You mean a U.S. invasion," Aradio interrupted rudely. de la castile nodded.

"We could not withstand it. It is hopeless." Aradio sat back in his chair. "It is all hopeless," he whined.

"Our Cuban comrades will save us," Maria chimed into the general hysteria. "They are all that stand between us and total destruction."

The Colonel bounced the pointer a few times in his muscular hands. He spoke slowly, softly.

"I would beg, please, to differ with both of you. Assuming that the Cubans weren't here at all . . . ."

"God save us," Aradio ejaculated.

Arturo held up a hand of restraint.

"Let's try," he said with purposeful calmness, "to look at the situation with some objectivity. The United States of America has been involved in three major military conflicts in recent years. The two most recent and uppermost in our thinking are the invasion of Panama and the War in the Persian Gulf. The third, though, is the Vietnam War.

"Clearly, the biggest U.S. victory was the Gulf War. You may recall that prior to it Saddam Hussein predicted a grave U.S. defeat. His prediction was based on the theory that the United States suffers from something he labeled 'Vietnam Syndrome.'"

"Well it pains me to admit it, but the Americans proved him wrong on that one," Maria interjected.

"Did they? Granted, a quick analysis of what occurred would, indeed, bring one straight to that conclusion. But let's look at it a bit more deeply. Now, I don't want to bore you with a lecture on military strategy, but if the Committee wishes to know what we're dealing with . . . ."

"It's vital that we know. Please continue, Colonel."

"As you wish, Dr. Cordoba. Now to understand the conclusion . . . or opinion I will ultimately be offering this afternoon, it is necessary to analyze in some detail both the U.S. victories and defeats in recent years.

"The greatest U.S. defeat ever was, of course, Vietnam. Now, U.S. soldiers will tell you that Vietnam was a political, not a military defeat. In other words, they will tell you that they could have won the war if only the politicians had backed them up . . . and let them do what they thought should have been done. And they more recently cite their great victory in the Gulf as proof of the validity of their position. There is, I think, some truth to their formulation, but it's clearly overdrawn. Remember, please, that at the height of Vietnam the Americans had a half million men engaged in a country, say, about twice the size of our own. I will grant them the point that if this entire force had been unleashed to subdue all opposition in any way that the U.S. Army could, indeed, have effectively occupied and controlled the entire country. What I don't believe is that the process would have been accomplished as quickly or as handily as was effected in Kuwait.

"In order to understand my reasons for making this last statement you need to have a little insight into American tactics and training. In, I believe, anticipation of the inevitability of war with the Soviet Union, the United States has continued to maintain the basic model of warfare which we may label the 'Post-World War II Western Concept.' There are two major components, we might even say steps, in this type of warfare. The first is to bring to bear on any given 'target' various sources of firepower from as many directions as possible. Then the target is ultimately destroyed through a varying process which basically relies on 'fire and maneuver.' This is the simultaneous advancement toward a target of several distinct but coordinated units which cover each other with firepower, thus protecting each other as they alternately move against the objective.

"This strategy, obviously, requires a number of things of the 'enemy' to be successful. There has to be a certain degree of target identifyability and stability. Western belligerents, with their need for command centers and various support services, are typically most kind in providing these kinds of targets. The second requirement for this kind of warfare is a certain amount of space in which these often large units may maneuver, such as does exist in Mid-Eastern deserts. It's a 'brilliant glimpse into the obvious,' an amusing phrase I picked up while training in the U.S. by-the-way, that the jungles of Vietnam were horrible for an army so oriented."

Hector raised his hand like a student in a classroom. "But Panama is a jungle, and the Americans won there. Doesn't that disprove your thesis?"

"I don't think so. For one thing, the terrain of Panama is nowhere so forbidding as that of Vietnam, or Cortesia for that matter. But the most important reason for my arguing that the U.S. 'victory' in Panama is not terribly relevant is that Noriega, being a . . . uh . . . a crook, surrounded himself with other crooks. So what they were facing was not so much an army as a gang of mobsters. And even I would acknowledge that the U.S. is more than a match for that!

"Given the American style of warfare, I think you can see that our Republic is ideally suited for an effective resistance to an assault that might be launched by The United States of America."

Several gasps could be heard in the small conference room.

Punctuating his remarks with a pointer tapping on a wall map, de la Castile continued his presentation as though unaware of his audience's emotional reactions.

"Our coastline is composed of rocky cliffs. There are but two harbors, at Coast de la Obscura and here in the Capital. Both posses narrow entrances and are heavily defended. An amphibious assault would be suicidal.

"In terms of a land assault from one of our neighbors, they would run, right at the borders, into jungle so impenetrable that their customary tactics would be completely ineffective . . . ."

"What about parachute drops?"

"There are very few places in our country where there is even a minimum of open space for such to even be thinkable. We know where they are, and we would be there.

"In my opinion, there are but two ways in which a successful invasion of Cortesia could take place. The first would involve massive bombing, much as the U.S. conducted against Germany in World war II . . . ."

"*Dios mio*," one of the men moaned.

"Indeed. There would, of course, be massive civilian casualties. We would be powerless to put up any but token resistance to this form of combat. It is, quite obviously, up to the Members of the Committee and its successors to make the determination, in light of pressure from world opinion, as to whether or not the U.S. would resort to this tactic . . . .

"The second potentially effective strategy involves the gradual infiltration of units by land, sea and air and the subsequent conduct of what may be labeled, generically, as 'guerrilla warfare.' This is the type of combat for which the United States is peculiarly unsuited . . . ."

"Now wait," Aradio interrupted, "I've heard that the U.S. has special training now for just that kind of fighting."

"Oh, they have some career officers and enlisted personnel who have received such training. But the great bulk of their personnel are of the so-called 'citizen-soldier' type. This, translated into the . . . uh . . . modern vernacular, means that they are young people who are in the U.S. military for brief periods of time for the purpose of obtaining vocational training or later support for their education. Many, many are from poor families. Many are members of ethnic minorities which have suffered discrimination. By-in-large, the real campaign in which they are engaged is one of improving themselves and upgrading their condition in life. I would predict that, if asked, most U.S. soldiers wouldn't even be able to tell you where Cortesia is, much less be enthusiastic about suffering in the 'conquest of Cortesia.'"

There were a few snickers, apparently reflecting a sense of reassurance in the room.

The Chairman took advantage of the pause to ask a question. "Excuse me, Colonel, but if I understand you correctly in your earlier remarks, I believe you made note of the fixed installations of the American style of warfare. Would not our facility at Costa de la Obscura qualify for that category?"

"Yes, Sir, you are quite correct that it would. It would be completely indefensible from U.S. airpower and would have to be abandoned should hostilities commence. Fortunately, for our purposes, Costa de la Obscura is less of a central command center as believed by the generals and politicians and is, or at least can be, in actuality, merely more of a training base. You see, our soldiers are 'cross trained.' We have learned the Western style of warfare, of course. We've also trained with the Cubans and," the Colonel paused to give emphasis to his words, "the Chinese. We've always known that the latter form of combat would be more relevant in the periodic border skirmishes we have with our neighbors. In these battles, which, as you know, we have always won, we have always operated from mobile command centers in the mountains. Believe me, up there, you can't tell a colonel from a private.

"I think, to return to the main point I was trying to make, that the political significance of what I'm saying, for your considered judgment, is that whatever invasion route the U.S. might take, an outright assault or gradual infiltration, there will be American causalities, massive in the first case, continual and mounting in the second. Here is where we get into the so-called 'Vietnam Syndrome.'

"This Committee must, in my judgment, make a determination, an . . . estimate . . . of how many flag-draped coffins it will require to be returned to the United States before they will give it up. I don't know what that number is, but there is a number beyond which they will not go. Thank you for listening to me."

"My God, man, you're advocating war with the United States of America!"

"No, *Senor Sanchez*, I am not. War is merely an extension of foreign policy. I am simply giving the Committee my judgment as to what it might expect should that . . . uh . . . regrettable step be taken . . . Again, thank you for listening to me."

# CHAPTER 21

# "YOU MIGHT AS WELL SEND THIS ONE TOO"

Dave and Elena sat on the floor of her apartment. Dave was wrapping a "souvenir" to send "home." In view of the general turmoil that had gripped Cortesia and thus their lives, this would seem to be a very unusual thing to be doing at this particular time. But Elena knew full well what he was doing as he selected certain portions of the newspaper and wrapped them carefully around the little statue.

"Here," she said, handing him the page she had just read, "you might as well send this one too."

Dave adjusted his glasses, which were perched precariously on his nose. He began to read, noting with both pride and pleasure that it was not necessary for him to translate the article into English for him to comprehend it.

### Poll Shows Socialist Gaining
*La Navidad, Cortesia*            Jose Belenger

*A poll was conducted this weekend just past of 200 likely voters in next month's Presidential Election.*

*Aradio Sanchez, who has emerged as the Opposition Leader to Dr. Roberto Cordoba, appears to have closed the gap somewhat with the current Chairman of the Provisional Civilian Government. Twenty percent announced their plans to vote for Sanchez. A third plan to vote for current Chairman Cordoba. The remainder described themselves as "undecided." Should this trend continue and Sanchez prevail, all indications are that a Socialist victory would signal a major shift in both domestic and foreign policy for Cortesia.*

*Sanchez has called for the nationalization of all foreign-owned investments. He advocates closer ties with Cuba. In recent weeks he has increasingly come to refer to Dr. Cordoba as a tool of U.S. Capitalism and Imperialism.*

*The election is slated for November 1st, with all citizens eighteen and over eligible to cast ballots.*

"Yeah," he sighed, "you're right. I need to send this."

"Not what 'they' want to hear, is it?"

"Not hardly."

Elena slid herself across the floor to be closer to Dave. "You were speaking about your childhood last night. By-the-way," she said looking him straight in the eye, "I really like it when you do that. It makes me feel comfortable, closer to you."

He stared at her warmly.

"I was thinking about something you were talking about, and I wanted to know more about it. You were telling me about your visit to your grandparents' farm, and it struck me how different the cultures you were exposed to were. I'm wondering what effect that had on . . . ."

Less than a mile out to sea a small fishing trawler plied its way through the choppy waters. On the hull with its cracking paint had been stenciled the words "The Wanderer" and "Long Beach." The engine coughed and sputtered as the vessel moved through the mist, paralleling the coastline.

Two men stood on the boat's deck. Both wore yellow slickers and the cloth stocking cap of the working fisherman.

"I was just downstairs, uh . . . below. It looks like we're not going to get home any time soon," the older man said with disgust. "We're going to have to make a few more passes. Every time we've come through, the bulk of the signals have come from different positions. The radio operator says it sounds like they have the world's biggest collection of radios."

"Maybe they're moving them around," the younger man suggested.

"But why? Why would you keep moving your command posts when you're not even under attack, much less in danger of being overrun?"

"Sure beats me, Major," he said with a shrug.

"The only exception is Costa de la Obscura. Steady flow of traffic out of there. And it's increasing. They obviously haven't abandoned it!"

"No, Sir."

About two hundred miles to the northwest, the Command Center of Costa de la Obscura seemed like a big, empty barn. The two young radiomen who were the room's only occupants were dwarfed by the massive panels of electronic equipment and displays. One spoke into a microphone, while the other used a telegraph key. Reading from stacks of paper on the desk in front of them, they would transmit a message and pause. After about ninety seconds, they would start again. Sometimes they would adjust the dials on the console to switch frequencies. The telegrapher allowed himself a few snickers occasionally when he transmitted "orders" from officers he knew were not within a hundred miles of the base.

Footsteps rang out in the hollow room as a lieutenant walked up behind the two.

Plopping a new stack of papers on the desk between them, he said nonchalantly, "Get these out right away, Boys. The security of our country depends upon it!"

One of the young men twisted in his chair. Looking up at the officer, he commented, "Well, if that's so, Sir, we're in big trouble."

The Lieutenant managed a little smile. He then turned on his heel and walked back to the office in which a small group of writers was making war on paper.

A buzzer sounded from just below the gunwale of the ancient-appearing craft. Sergeant Williams picked up the headset. He shivered slightly in the bone-chilling mist.

"Major, we've got a medium-sized vessel rapidly approaching. Metal. Obviously military. Intention clearly interception."

"Thank you," Major Stone responded, suddenly assuming an air of formality and stiffness. "This was bound to happen. That's why we spent all that time with the fishermen. Get your sea voice on, Sergeant."

"Aye, aye, Sir."

Moments later, "Sir, they're attempting to contact us by radio."

"Don't respond."

There was an eerie silence that stretched long in time.

Several deafening blasts of a fog horn, and the two men could make out a steel hull paralleling their course some fifty yards to starboard.

There was a series of sharp sentences spoken in Spanish over a booming loudspeaker.

Grabbing an electronic microphone, the Major responded, "How's that?"

After a pause, the larger vessel responded in English, "Cortesian Coastal patrol. Heave to."

"Kill the engine."

"Yes, Sir."

The military ship maneuvered carefully to lie beside the battered fishing boat. A Cortesian Lieutenant Commander stood at the rail, bullhorn in hand.

"What ship are you?" the naval officer inquired in slow, carefully pronounced English.

"The Wanderer out of Long Beach," came the reply.

"You are in the waters of the Republic of Cortesia. Prepare to be boarded for inspection."

"Ye can't do that, Captain. The Santiago Treaty gives us the right to fish these waters without no interference," the Major answered.

"Fish yes, spy no."

The Marine at the Lieutenant Commander's side did not understand a word of the English, but he knew from the tone of voice of the speakers that a disagreement had arisen. He pulled the machine gun he carried from his shoulder and held it tightly in his hands.

"There are no fish in these waters at this season. Prepare to be boarded."

Two armed Marines jumped onto the wooden deck, taking with them ropes to lash the two vessels together.

The officer saluted upon descending to the smaller craft. "Augusto Guillermo Suarez, Lieutenant Commander of the Royal Navy of Cortesia, *a sus ordenes.*"

"Welcome, Captain . . . uh, Commander. We've nothing to hide. Have a look-see for yourself if it pleases ye."

The officer glanced over the topside. Nothing remarkable there. Descending the ladder, one of the "fishermen" and one of the Marines following, he entered the cabin. It appeared to be quite typical for fishing vessels of that type. There was fishing tackle on the floor, and cabinets lined the walls. The tackle, though, was completely dry. It clearly had not been used recently. Besides, the Commander <u>knew</u> that this was a spy ship. They had observed it repeatedly moving along the coast in these fishless waters. There was no other explanation for this otherwise nonsensical pattern.

He kicked the fishing equipment aside. Nothing there but the bare deck floor. He instructed the young man who seemed to be sleeping on the cot in the cabin to move himself and his bedding aside so that he could inspect the cabinets. The cabinets' doors opening revealed boxes of food, large boxes of food. The Lieutenant Commander, almost in desperation, began pulling the boxes down from the shelves. It took a little while for him to hit pay dirt, complex electronic equipment hidden behind the boxes of food.

"Pretty, how you say, fancy for so simple a fishing vessel."

"There's nothing . . . illegal about carrying a radio, Captain."

"Perhaps not. But I do not know what all this . . . this is. I do know, though, that what you are doing is in the territorial waters of the Sovereign Republic of Cortesia. It is, therefore, necessary that you and your . . ." he glanced around the cluttered cabin as one who is smelling something foul, ". . . ship be taken into custody."

"I . . . This is outrageous! I protest."

"Your Government will be notified immediately. They will provide whatever assistance you may require."

Dave interrupted his shaving to tune in a bit better the short wave radio. He was listening to Armed Forces Radio, hoping to get some news about the ongoing Presidential Campaign back home.

> *"The State Department has lodged a protest with the Government of Cortesia over last night's seizure of an American fishing boat. Calling it a gross violation of International Law and the Santiago Accords, the U.S. is demanding the release of the vessel and its crew. Cortesia has been given twenty-four hours to affect their release or, as the State Department put it, 'face the consequences.'*

*"U.S. citizens are reminded that the United States does not recognize the illegal regime now in place in Cortesia, and travel to that country is banned."*

Dave kissed Elena softly on the back of her neck as he passed the vanity table at which she was applying lightly her makeup.

"Do you think it was spying?" she asked.

"Yeah, I think so."

Elena put her glasses back on and looked at him intently.

"Oh, I don't know. I just think so," he replied to her silent question. Continuing he said, "I mean, last night would have been a lousy one for fishing."

In Panama the last of the five thousand soldiers had just arrived at the airfield for "training." Their presence was in no way a closely kept secret. As a matter of fact, the U.S. and world press had been pointedly informed that the troops were in Panama for a dual purpose. On the one hand, they would be receiving additional training to "brush up their expertise in jungle warfare." However, the Pentagon went to some lengths to make it clear that they were not raw troops. As the spokesman stated, "While the immediate mission of these units is that of training, they are ready and available for deployment should conditions in that already unstable part of the world require such action."

That evening after work, Dave and Elena walked slowly up the cobblestone streets and back to The Apartment. The current crisis and the strain it had brought to them, as well as to everyone else in Cortesia, had, it seems, given them permission to abandon any hiding of the fact that they were a couple, in every sense of the word. He had moved the great bulk of all his clothes, etc. there. He only maintained his hotel room because the "Company" sent his mail and "paychecks" there and left messages for him at the front desk.

A loud explosion interrupted his pouring of their evening cocktails. Instinctively, he looked across the room at Elena to make certain that she was unharmed. She was holding on to the edge of the sofa as she allowed the shoe she had just removed to drop to the floor. They both rushed out onto the balcony to see what had happened.

A pillar of smoke arose from a building on the harbor.

"That's the Coastal Patrol Headquarters," she announced excitedly. "They're bombing in retaliation."

A second jet appeared from the sky and streaked toward the column of fire. They stood spellbound, like two deer hypnotized by the lights of an approaching automobile. A second inferno was unleashed, this one farther up the hill.

"There are homes up there," Elena shouted.

"He missed," Dave commented, actually to himself, as his voice could not be heard above the sound of the explosion. He placed his hands on the railing and bowed his head.

"*Dios mio*," she groaned, grabbing her stomach as though in pain.

Dave put his hands on her shoulders and guided her back inside. The smell of burning and chemicals was becoming strong.

They collapsed on the sofa, holding each other.

"Elena, Dear Elena, we could go away. I could arrange it. I could . . ."

She looked at him with that so familiar tilt of her head, even managing a faint smile. "You know I can't do that."

"I know," he sighed.

CHAPTER **22**

## "I GUESS BOTH"

The top sheet was a knotted tangle on one side of the bed. The bottom sheet was wet with their perspiration. It had been a sleepless, fitful night for Dave and Elena.

He brought in steaming cups of coffee for himself and Elena. He rubbed her shoulders gently, and she turned, unclothed, toward him.

"Good morning," he said, attempting to be cheerful.

She brushed a lock of dark hair across her moist forehead and strained her eyes in an obviously not totally successful effort to bring his face into focus.

"Oh, *Buenos dias*," she replied after a pause.

"*Te quiero.*"

"I love you, too," she answered softly. But her expression grew serious as she remembered the true nature of the situation in which they now found themselves.

"Look," he said, groping for words. "I need to do something. I'll need the Jeep . . . I can't promise that I'll do any good, but I won't do any harm."

"I know, of course, . . . Dave. Just hold me before you go."


Dave drove the ponderous vehicle several blocks out of his way to view the site of the bombing. An entire row of stucco shanties had been completely leveled. Only a few charred walls, none over three feet high, remained. A little black dog sniffed through the ruins, looking for her family.

The Jeep roared up the hill along the same road into the interior, the same highway he and Elena had taken so many times to the *estancia*. Despite the seriousness of his mission, Dave decided that no harm would be done by a stop at Pedro's for lunch. Then it was back on the road. But instead of taking the left fork to the *estancia*, he took the right, which cut through the densest part of the jungle of Cortesia.

The border town of Lagrimas de Maria, while technically a Provincial capital, was in reality only a country village. Farmers walked their cattle along its often muddy streets, and the *siesta* was still observed.

He entered the local cantina. The tiny bar was crowded with off-duty soldiers. They were unarmed but still in uniform. Clearly, they were on some kind of alert, most probably because of the closeness of the International Border. The local beer was pretty raw stuff, but at least he was no longer thirsty after he had finished the mug.

He asked the barkeep for directions to the "Provincial Office Building."

The muscular man with tattoos on his arms laughed. "We have nothing so grand as that, *amigo*. The place you seek is where the government has an office. It is also the City Hall. It is also a Quonset hut!"

Dave walked down the now dusty street to the make-shift governmental headquarters. He was fully aware of the fact that an American in this part of the country would attract a great deal of attention. So the best he could do, he concluded, was to appear as open and above-board as possible.

It took a few minutes for his eyes to adjust as he walked into the Quonset hut from the bright sunshine.

To his right, apparently the "Provincial" side of the rickety structure, sat an overweight middle-aged woman in a simple short-sleeved dress.

"I am Bill Robinson of Eastern Mining," he announced courteously.

"An American," she responded flatly, literally turning her nose up at him.

"Uh . . . that's right," he conceded. "I'm looking for mining properties, and I'd like, please, to review the Provincial records on mineral rights in the area."

She eyed him suspiciously. "I . . . I don't know. These are not, how you say, normal times. I shall have to check. You will have to wait."

Picking up the old black phone on her desk, she asked for "The Major."

"There is a *gringo* here," she said, making no effort to prevent Dave from hearing her words. "He's demanding to see our records on mining claims." She paused, then answered, "I don't know."

Her lips curled maliciously as she listened to the officer on the other end of the line.

"*Si, Senor.*"

She shrugged her shoulders and looked up at Dave. "Major said you could look at them. He said something about life going on."

She rose with some effort and made her way to a file cabinet behind her desk, from which she pulled an overstuffed folder. This she took to a large table at the back of the structure. She plopped it on the wooden surface. This, apparently, was the signal to the American that he had been granted permission to be seated and go over the records.

Dave sat down. After wiping his glasses, he began reviewing the contents of the folder. He flipped through them rapidly. He knew exactly what he was looking for. Unfortunately, the maps showed that none of the potential mining properties was located along the border in this area. "This is going to be a long night, Ole Boy," he said to himself with a resigned sigh.

He pulled his suitcase out of the Jeep and walked through the cantina to the little room he had rented for the night. The iron-framed bed squeaked loudly as he placed the bulging canvas-covered bag on it. He unzipped it with one motion and then withdrew a map and a bottle of Scotch. He poured a few fingers of the whisky into a reasonably clean-appearing glass on the bedside table. He sat down gingerly on the ancient bed and, utilizing the suitcase as a desk, he began studying the map.

He moved his finger along the road running northeast of the city. About a mile and a half away this road came quite close to the border, say less than a mile or so. And the map showed the existence of a town, at least large enough to make it onto a map, just a bit over a mile into the territory of Cortesia's neighbor.

He decided it best to at least try to get some sleep. As he finished the Scotch, he pulled the flimsy curtains over the window in an effort to darken the room as best he could. Stripping down to his underwear, he hopped between the sheets.

If what followed in that creaky bed rested his body, it certainly didn't do much good for his mind. Thoughts raced through his head. He could see himself, as though in a dream, almost twenty years ago, a young, eager, dedicated agent, determined to make a success of his career. Some of his early missions flashed in front of him. At one point, he actively questioned himself as to whether it was a dream, or if he was really back in that cold gray, city in Bulgaria. . . . Then, after what seemed to be a pause, some scattered, disconnected scenes from his childhood. Suddenly, he was back in Cortesia. He and Elena were at the outdoor café. They were sipping wine . . . They were talking, happy . . . It was before all of "this," he concluded vaguely. . . . Dave relaxed and moaned contentedly . . . The image began to grow misty, vague. He strained to bring it back into focus, but it only got worse. He felt himself being pulled away from the café and Elena. He clutched at something, trying to stay. Perhaps it was the table, or perhaps it was a chair. He couldn't tell. It was all too foggy, too confused . . . . When the fog began to clear, he was, incredibly he would have realized had he been fully awake, standing out to sea, looking back at the harbor of La Navidad . . . A huge gray ship moved in front of him, completely cutting off his view of the City on the Cliffs. Its decks were crowded, packed with guns. A gigantic American flag flew over the guns, creating a deafening flapping sound . . . He kept thinking that the ship would pass. But it just kept coming and coming. "That ship is in my way!" he shouted, he cried . . .

Dave sat up suddenly in the bed. He was trembling, sweating. He looked around. He wondered if anyone would come to investigate the scream. He knew he hadn't been in the harbor of La Navidad. But whether he had really screamed or not, that he didn't know . . . No one came, good.

He thought of having another Scotch to calm himself. But he concluded that, in the words of the Manual, that would be "inadvisable." He contented himself with a wet rag drawn over his forehead.

Back in bed, he lay there, watching the fan move slowly, slowly above him.

A cool, moist breeze came down from the jungle-covered mountains. It made the lacy curtains flutter, and it awakened Dave.

He sat up and held his head in his hands. "I'm clearly confused," he muttered to himself.

His watch on the little table read 8:30, just about the right time, he decided. He showered and stepped into fresh underwear. He flung open his case and looked at the shirts he had brought with him. Elena had ironed them for him, he reflected. He decided that the blue denim was a good compromise between the white most men in the region wore and the very dark dress shirt. The darker shirt would indeed, he reasoned, be better suited for his mission, but this was so much so that it might provoke suspicion.

Dressed now, he strolled into the cantina. People were just beginning to arrive, following the custom of late Spanish suppers. He ordered a *cervesa*. He'd just have two, he declared to himself, this one and another beer with supper.

The barkeep served him supper right there on the bar, allowing the tables to be used by the families that had gathered there for their evening meal. He had a beef taco. How different it was, he thought again, from what passed as a taco back in the States. What he was cutting into with knife and fork consisted of small, lean strips of beef smothered in onions and gravy. These delectable items were tenderly encased in a soft, doughy tortilla. "One could get used to this kind of food," he concluded to himself.

A man and a young woman entered the little eating establishment and occupied two stools next to Dave. Somewhat to his surprise, the man stood up, walked behind his companion and approached Dave. Extending his hand, he announced, "*Ramon Miranda, a sus ordenes.*"

"Bill Robinson," he replied after hoping from the stool, stretching out his hand and gulping down the food in his mouth.

"An American, I presume."

"Yes, yes, I am, in fact," Dave replied cautiously.

"Welcome to Cortesia," Miranda said with a bow and a grand, sweeping gesture with both arms.

Dave, taken aback, tilted his head slightly to one side, a mannerism he had picked up from his lover.

"I wasn't aware that we Americans were so . . . uh so popular here," he finally managed to get out of his mouth.

"In truth, you are not, *Senor*," He answered, lowering his voice. "But you must understand, I studied in your country. And I am aware that all Americans do not think alike on such matters as are currently . . . pressing. It is true, I believe, that the Leader of the Opposition Party does not look favorably upon the military adventures of the seated government. The election draws near in the United States. Perhaps the Governor will soon be President, and we will not have to contend with these . . . these threats and shells."

"That is possible," Dave replied, bowing slightly as is the custom in Spanish-speaking countries. "And it is, I would add, much to be desired."

"Ah . . . good, good," the Cortesian exclaimed, placing his hands on his chest in a gesture of self-satisfaction at having made a correct judgment of another in such a complex situation.

"Ah, ah," he stammered, "where are my manners? *Senor Robinson*, allow me to present you to my Sister Consuela."

Dave nodded to the lady, and she delicately extended her hand to him.

Thus was fulfilled the requirement of Spanish tradition that a man and a woman be properly introduced before they can converse.

"*Mucho gusto,*" Dave said perfunctorily.

"You are here *en negocios?*" the young woman with dark, red-tipped hair began warily, nervously.

"Yes, you see, I'm in mining. I'm looking for minerals."

"And for what minerals are you . . . wanting, *Senor?*"

"Oh . . . well, any. That is to say, I'm looking for anything of value . . . mineral-wise that is."

"Interesting work, I would assume."

"At times," Dave replied noncommittally.

Dave noted that Ramon had left their side at some point. He appeared to prefer darts to their fumbling conversation.

The bartender winked knowingly as Dave and Consuela left the cantina after having eaten together.

They walked down the street toward the home of Consuela, Ramon and their parents.

When they got to the house, Consuela leaned up against the stucco wall by the door.

"Good evening, *Senorita Miranda*," Dave said politely, stepping back to leave.

The young woman eyed him quizzically.

"Are you so busy as this, or do you have a *novia*?"

"I guess both," Dave answered.

CHAPTER **23**

# "YOU CAN'T BOMB PEOPLE BECAUSE THEY'RE NOT GOING TO VOTE THE WAY YOU WANT THEM TO"

D ave left Consuela's home and walked down the dirt road heading northeast out of town. He strolled casually, giving the appearance of an after supper walk with no purpose.

After traveling about a quarter of a mile down the road, an army truck, soldiers crowded into the back, went rumbling by. He made it a point to wave, just a guy out for a late night walk, nothing whatever to hide.

There it was ahead, just as the map had shown it. It was a bend in the road. It swept broadly to Dave's right. He knew that the middle of that curve lay less than a mile from the border.

He glanced nervously about, knowing that to be caught around this particular spot was sure to provoke suspicion. He inched his way through the dense undergrowth and into the jungle.

The rattle of a big truck echoed down the lonely lane. Its lights bounced just inches from his face. There being no possibility of appearing casual at this point, he dove into the bushes.

Flat on his face with the vines seeming to be grabbing for his arms and legs, he waited and listened. The truck sounded like it was slowing. There was the squeal of brakes. "Oh, ohhh," he thought to himself. Had he been discovered?

There was a series of clicking sounds. Were they readying weapons? Something stuck into his right leg. He hoped it was just a thorn. Then there was a familiar aroma. It was coffee. The soldiers had just chosen this place to take their coffee break. What a place! A small bug crept over Dave's outstretched arm. This was going to be the world's longest coffee break!

As he lay there, he felt relieved, uncomfortable but relieved. They were obviously completely unaware of his presence, or they would have conducted their search for him before breaking out the coffee. He spent the time lying there wondering what obstacles he might face at the border itself. Might there be a fence? Would there be a cleared path like at the U.S.-Canadian border? Would the border be patrolled on foot? Cortesia had never been important enough for such information to have been collected, so he had no idea what he would be facing.

"OK, you guys," came a loud voice in Spanish, "break's over. Time to get back to work."

"What work, Sarge? We're just running up and down the road."

"Yeah, Sarge," came another young voice, "There's not an American within a hundred miles of here."

"Well, first of all, you wise guys, like they say, 'somebody's got to do it.' And there just happens, for your information, to be an American in town. We're going to go check on him right now. We're going to make sure he's having a nice time here in Cortesia. So get back in the DAMN truck!"

"Ohhhh," Dave thought to himself lying in the bushes, "they're not going to find me where I ought to be if they happen to look hard enough." Of course, his thinking continued in a rambling, pressured manner, he would be absolutely safe on the other side of the border. Surlandia was staunchly pro-American. And, in reality, getting back to Cortesia was not all that important to his mission. After all, he had been pretty much cut off from any useful military information. Oh, he had "written home" about a few troop movements he had observed, some precautions in the Capital. But they were nothing out of the ordinary, just standard procedures for a country that believes it's going to be invaded.

As he thought of never going back, his heart seemed to sink in his chest. He closed his eyes, trying to shake off without moving and thus rustling the vegetation which surrounded him, a sudden wave of sadness. That would, he feared, mean the end of Elena and him. Relations between the U.S. and Cortesia had grown so bad that it would be a long, long time before he could just "drop in" on La Navidad.

There was a sudden increase in the amount of light. The army vehicle had turned its headlights back on. After the light disappeared, Dave moved cautiously, hoping that nothing had slithered up and taken hold of some part of him. He began

THE INQUISITIVE YANQUI                    251

to stand up without difficulty, so he had apparently escaped whatever might lurk in that thick jungle.

He stopped his rise in the half-standing position. The combination of the moonlight and having kept his eyes shut during most of the coffee break made it seem about as light as day. A furtive glance up and down the road revealed that the truck was long gone. He was all alone again. "Well," he thought to himself," time to get moving again."

It was slow going through the thick undergrowth. He kept looking for a clearing or a fence that would indicate the actual border. Nothing. At that late hour, the jungle was alive with movement. The bushes rustled and the limbs of trees swayed as creatures made their way from place to place, hunting, gathering or whatever it was they were about. Birds squawked and cackled at each other, first from one direction, then the apparent "answer" from another. All this was against the hum of a background chorus of bugs. He strained his ears, trying to call upon his old training, listening for something different, something that might indicate another human presence, a rhythmic "clump-clump" sound to the movement, a cough, anything metallic. How ironic it was, Dave thought to himself, that of all the animals in this pest-infected jungle the one he most feared was his own species!

He trekked on, ever slower and more carefully as he thought he was approaching the border. On and on. He had a mission. It was just that at times he wasn't completely sure exactly what that mission was. He went on slowly for what seemed hours and miles, miles and hours. Movement was tortuous through this dense vegetation.

Upon reflecting, his current terror of his fellow man was not just ironic, but perhaps silly as well. After all, there were snakes in this region that could kill you instantly. There were bugs like that too, at least so he had been told. And he didn't really believe the Cortesians would execute him. His perceptions were distorted by the game he was playing. Yes, that's what it was, a game. How in the world had he gotten mixed up in a game like this?

The undergrowth got even thicker, indicating that it had been exposed to increased levels of sunlight. He could see the moonlight glinting through fewer and fewer trees up ahead. There it was, the border. Slowly, carefully, cautiously, he advanced. No unusual sounds. He inched ahead. There was bare ground. It was a road.

He glanced up and down. No one. No sounds of activity. Looking more closely, he noted that the dirt road was well traveled. There were the droppings of large animals, so it was used by farmers. Clearly, this wasn't just a military access road to the border. This was the road shown on the map as being in Surlandia. For the first time in almost seven months, he was outside Cortesia. And he had answered his question about what was at the border—nothing. That would be useful for future reference, he thought, the result of years of training.

After a rest behind some trees, in which he may have dozed off, he rose. "Now, let's see," his thoughts went. "I was headed east through the Briar Patch. Santa Evita is north, so I go this away."

Dave walked to the center of Surlandia Highway 5, turned left and began a brisk stroll into town. As he struck a comfortable pace, he began a consideration of how he was going to get his message through. There were, he thought, two routes, the private and the governmental. The private route would involve seeking out a civilian residence and, quite literally, phoning home from the site of the family's hospitality. The advantage to the civilian alternative was that it just might leave unimpaired his anonymity and freedom of action. That way, Dave figured, he might even make it back to Cortesia to resume his "second life," no questions asked. Of course, the fact that that loud, damned sergeant was going to check on his "comfort" may well have put the proverbial fly in that ointment. The governmental route would sure make things a lot easier. He could simply walk up to some Surlandian functionary and identify himself as an American agent. They would check out his pass codes, and the communication facilities of this already bought little banana republic would be completely at his disposal. But then, he would become a pawn to be shuffled about by the two countries. It had happened to him more than once before. Perhaps, he thought further, he could have what was, under the circumstances, the best of both worlds. He could try the private thing, and, failing that, government agents could be, if not likable, at least sufferable, but then . . .

The clamorous rattling of yet another military vehicle let him know at once that the decision had been made for him. Our hero had been focusing on his own thoughts and the gentle sunrise, not on the road ahead. He had been seen. It was far too late to avoid detection. He had, he recognized, placed himself in the autocratic hands of the Government of Surlandia.

Dave just kept walking.

The heavy truck ground to a halt about twenty yards ahead. Two machinegun-armed soldiers hopped out, one from each side. They advanced toward him, their weapons in the carry-arms position. He stopped, holding his arms outstretched to demonstrate that he himself carried no weapon.

"Halt, *Senor*," the soldier to his left cried out, despite the fact that he had already halted.

The thin, cadaverous corporal stopped a few feet in front of Dave. "We will require some identification," he said.

"Will a New York driver's license do?" Dave asked, giving the Surlandian a rather apologetic look.

"Well, then, I guess we'd better see it . . . slowly."

The other soldier walked around to Dave's back to watch him withdraw his wallet, slowly.

"What in the name of Jesus are you doing out here?" the corporal spurted out as he examined the license.

"I'm a spy," he answered simply.

"A spy? A spy!"

"Oh, not on you. On them," he announced, allowing himself to gesture grandly in the direction from whence he had come.

The corporal cast his gaze up to the sky. He had a bemused, puzzled look on his face. He appeared to be seeking some guidance as to how to deal with this slightly nutty *gringo* who had appeared from out of nowhere.

"I think you'd better come with me, *Senor*," he said matter-of-factly after his period of contemplation.

"I kinda figured you'd say that."

The soldiers in the back of the truck kept wary eyes on Dave as they jostled their way to their destination, wherever and whatever that might be.

Dave was taken to a small military checkpoint. There he explained to the young captain in charge that, quite simply, he was a U.S. agent who was gathering information in Cortesia and that he had sneaked across the border in order to communicate back to Washington an urgent message. He further explained that he did not wish to risk sending the message from Cortesia because he feared it would be intercepted. Surlandia, he went on, was such a good friend of the United States that he felt safe in coming to them. He told them that it was quite possible to check his story out.

He later had a chance to repeat his story to a colonel who had come from somewhere. The colonel listened to him skeptically. But he did take Dave's driver's license, in the name of William Robinson, and the sheet of paper on which he had written a list of phone numbers and codes while he had been held in another room. Dave sat in a wooden, straight-backed chair under the watchful eyes of armed guards and waited.

The colonel returned a few minutes later wearing a broad smile on his face. "Your documents are in order, *Senor.* You are who you say you are."

Dave was relieved to hear this. There had been times of late when he himself had wondered who he was.

"In what way may we serve you, *Senor?*" the officer asked solicitously.

"I need to use your telephone."

"Our telephone?"

"Yeah, just any telephone I can call the States on."

The colonel pointed to the old-fashioned black phone on the desk and grinned.

As the soldiers left the room to give him privacy, he looked up at the colonel and said, "Don't worry, I'll reverse the charges."

"Reverse the charges? . . . Oh, oh, reverse the charges. Ha, ha. American humor, *Dios mio*"

Alone at last he picked up the telephone and, just like in the old days, dialed "O." "I would like, please, to make a collect call to the United States—anyone at Eastern Mining— Area code 212-279-6339. My name is William Robinson."

A phone rang on a desk in the corner of the third floor of an intelligence agency building in Washington. The secretary at the desk was a bit startled. That particular phone rarely rang, "Eastern Mining" having no actual business to conduct. Glancing at the sheet of paper mounted on the table in front of the instrument, she assured herself that she knew the proper way to answer.

"Eastern Mining. This is Cathy. How may I help you?" she said into the mouthpiece, trying to be upbeat and professional at the same time. The name "William Robinson" being on the list, she accepted the call.

"Hi, Cathy," Dave began as though the two actually knew each other. "Is the boss in from the golf course?"

"You must be living right, Bill. He just walked in. I'll ask him to pick up the line. Hold on, please."

She pressed down the intercom button and said, "William Robinson on the Eastern Mining line."

This message was piped into a large room containing rows of file cabinets and bookshelves. One of the men pouring over documents at the massive table in the center of the room rose and walked toward a phone-equipped cubicle. He was the Latin American Duty Officer for that day. He stopped in route at one of the cabinets and, without even the need for searching, withdrew a file marked CORTESIA/92-001.

"This is Frank Weatherby," he announced while flipping through the file in search of recent entries.

"Hello," Dave responded flatly.

"Well, how ya doin', Guy? Bet it's a lot hotter down there than up here!"

"Look, John, I don't have time for that crap. You people have just got to understand that you're off on the wrong track in a big, big way . . ."

"What the . . ."

"These people in Cortesia don't represent any threat to the United States. They're trying to . . ."

"Are you mad, Man? They're probably monitoring every call to the States, if they have any sense at all."

"I'm not even in Cortesia. I got over the border into Surlandia. So they won't hear any of this. Maybe they should! Look, you guys act like they're a bunch of hoodlums spreading Communist terrorism. There's every sign that you're even going to invade them! They just want to be left alone. They want to hold free and open elections. You've just got to understand . . ."

"Our information is that a supporter of Cuba might well win your 'free and open' election," John interrupted, biting his words.

"Good God, Man! You can't bomb people because they're not going to vote the way you want them to!"

"Look, you can't tell US what we can and can't do, damnit! As a matter of fact, we're not so impressed with you up here, Buster. We're worried about your stability. In fact, someone in the agency questions your loyalty."

"Molly."

"If you must know. In any case, I'm going to recommend that you be reviewed for possible suspension and disciplinary action. Where the hell are you?"

"Uh . . . at the border crossing at Santa Evita."

"We'll be back in touch. Stay right where you are, and . . . try not to start any more revolutions!"

Dave stared for a few seconds at the phone he still held in his hand. He began thinking of Elena. He was overwhelmed by a need to be with her.

He sat for a while thinking and considering, finally planning.

CHAPTER **24**

# "HOW CAN I?
THAT'S WHERE I AM"

H e stuck his head out the door of the office he had
phoned from, looking somewhat frantically up and
down the hall. Greatly to his relief, the colonel was still in the
building. He was just down the hall, apparently trading jokes
with the border guards.

Dave rushed up to the gold decorated officer. "I must," 
he said, allowing himself an air of importance, "return to La
Navidad at once! My Government will be most appreciative
for any help you can extend to me, Sir."

The colonel appeared perplexed. "Well, how, *Senor*," he
inquired, "did you get yourself on this side of the border?"

"I just sneaked across."

"Can you not then just 'sneak' back?"

"Actually, it's not that simple. You see, I left a vehicle and
some personal effects. And they were looking for me. So you
see . . ."

"Ah, this will require a bit of, how you say, subtlety," the colonel exhaled.

"Yes, a bit of subtlety."

"Hmmm," he paused. "I shall have to consult with what you would call your 'G-2,' no? *Un momento*"

Returning to the office, the mustachioed officer picked up the old black phone and, after having reached the appropriate duty officer, explained in passionate Spanish the situation.

Putting the phone down, he announced, "*Senor*, this is a rather complex situation. Given the present international situation, we cannot, of course, merely escort you back across the border."

"I understand that, of course."

"They are checking into the various possibilities for getting you back into Cortesia. They will inform us as soon as they have a proposal."

"Thank you."

Dave's anxiety level grew as he sat watching the phone. He hoped that they would hear from their "G-2" before Washington had a chance to call and possibly get in the way of his return to Elena.

He thought his heart was going to jump out of his chest when the phone did finally ring. "Whew," he thought to himself with relief as the colonel conversed with the caller in Spanish. It obviously wasn't someone calling from Washington. They wouldn't stoop to speak anything but English.

"We have a plan, *Senor*," the colonel finally announced.

"Let me guess. I go back by water."

"Precisely so."

"Thinking about it," Dave commented, "It's the only way I could figure."

The American spy was taken to a nearby dirt airstrip. He was flown in a single engine propeller plane to the Surlandian port city just east of the border with Cortesia. They were met at the airport there by an Army jeep which conveyed Dave to the port itself.

In the Harbor Master's shack, Dave was introduced to Raul, who appeared to be a typical fisherman. And he was a typical fisherman. It was merely that every now and then he took on a little assignment for the Army.

The lieutenant who had escorted Dave from the airport shook his hand in taking leave of him and pronounced, "Good luck, Sir."

Dave eyed the telephone on the Harbor Master's desk as he would a poisonous snake. He tried to hide his intense desire to get away from it.

"Well, we'd better get going, Raul," Dave stated in an upbeat, "let's get the show on the road" manner.

"You Americans are always in a hurry."

"My mission, you see."

As the two men strode down the planks to the dock, Dave asked his new host, "By-the-way, Raul, does your boat happen to have a radio?"

"Just a transistor radio for receiving weather reports. We cannot talk to others, if that's what you mean. I asked the Army for one, but they said no, Raul, your boat must stay a simple fishing boat. That way, you see, when they search it, which they have done, they will find nothing to show them that Raul isn't just another fisherman, no?"

Dave smiled, apparently in appreciation of Raul's commentary on the lack of a radio, but in actuality out of relief that he would, hopefully, soon be completely out of contact. With any luck, he would be with Elena again soon.

After they stepped aboard, Raul threw Dave a small cap, one like the fishermen in that part of the world wear. "Here," he said, "this will make you look more like Raul."

"*Gracias*," Dave acknowledged.

The little boat chugged out of the harbor and turned right, west along the coast. Raul waved at other boaters they passed. He appeared to be a very well-known figure. He gave Dave some simple instructions on how to spread out the nets on the deck. Dave probably didn't actually accomplish anything, but it did make him appear busy, like a real fisherman.

Less than five miles up the coast, Raul announced, "We are now in the waters of Cortesia."

"Good," Dave said with a smile of contentment, a minor victory having been won. "Very good, indeed."

"*Bueno*," the Harbor Master said, after picking up the ringing phone on his battered desk. He listened, a puzzled look on his face.

"No, Colonel, they have departed already."

"No, Colonel, Raul has no radio on his boat."

"I can send one of our Harbor Patrol speedboats out. If they have not yet left our waters, perhaps we can intercept them."

The Harbor Master, ever conscious of his status of being on the brink of retirement, shook his head as he strode as fast as he could to the Harbor Patrol building. They were, he thought to himself, so anxious to get the *gringo* spy into Cortesia. Now they want him back! "No wonder the world is such a mess," he concluded silently to himself.

Raul's boat moved slowly west. The sea was calm, and they were coming to the end of a beautiful, sunny day. Dave reflected on the fact that he had begun this day crouching in some jungle vines in the distant mountains. Spying, it seems, is a good, if not ideal, way to do some sightseeing.

Dave's heart leapt again in his chest as he glanced up from his "work" and spotted a Cortesian Coastal Patrol boat's deck officer looking their way through binoculars. He sure hoped he made a convincing fisherman!

The implications and possibilities raced through his mind. At the worst, he decided, he would be detained in Cortesia. They would surely, his thinking went on, allow him to get word to Elena, one of their own Government Officials. Eventually, he would get back to her, which he now fully admitted to himself was his real and only goal.

Throughout all this mental activity, he attempted to keep his hands and back in as much of a work mode as possible, for the sake of appearances. Apparently, he and Raul were pretty convincing as the military craft veered away, concluding, it would seem, that their time was better devoted elsewhere. Still on the original plan, he decided, as his body returned to its usual only slightly tense state.

As dusk settled over the sea, the captain of the little boat made an announcement. "The fishing banks end here. To go farther down the coast would bring us . . . attention. There is a small village in the cove over there. They know Raul very well there."

Having tied the boat up at the creaky wharf, the two men walked into the bar and eatery, which was the central feature of the village. Dave celebrated his return to Cortesian soil with a mug of local beer and a chicken taco.

After eating hurriedly, Dave shook hands in gratitude and goodbye with Raul.

"How far are we from La Navidad?" he inquired of the barkeep.

"About a hundred and thirty kilometers."

"*Gracias, Senor.*"

Dave walked quietly out of the bar and up the cliff to the two-lane asphalt highway to the Capital. It had been a long time since he had hitchhiked, but that was exactly what he was going to do this evening.

He stuck out his thumb, figuring that that gesture was universal. Suddenly remembering that he was probably "wanted," having left his maps and Elena's vehicle in the mountain village and all, he moved his position several hundred feet down the road. From there he could duck into a grove of trees should an authority figure, such a police car or a military vehicle, make its appearance around the bend.

Thoughts raced through his brain. He sure wasn't "home" yet. When, if and when he decided, he got picked up he would try as best he could to hide his less than perfect *espanol*. Perhaps he could act retarded. Or mute? Really didn't sound too promising.

A big truck rounded the curve, bumping and rattling noisily as it went. It sounded so much like the military vehicle that had carried him around Surlandia that Dave was about to head for the bushes. But he paused long enough to observe what a state of disrepair the truck was in. Obviously, it was instantly apparent to him, it was not operated by the Cortesian Army.

The ancient truck ground to a halt. The driver, clad in a dirty shirt, apparently long ago used for dress, stuck his head out of the cab and looked down at Dave. He doffed his sailor's cap to the local. Dave looked dark enough at this point to be a local himself, and it seemed that his visage bore no danger. The trucker threw his thumb toward the back of the old vehicle. Dave bowed gratefully, like a peasant. Luck was with him. Not only had he obtained a lift, hopefully to but at least toward the City, but he would also be spared the task of trying to hide his accent.

Through the night they hurtled at what Dave thought a recklessly high speed, given the darkness and road conditions, as well as the fact that livestock frequently ambled onto these rural thoroughfares. He wasn't complaining, though. He was getting where he wanted to go, and fast.

He could see more and more homes through the slats of the truck's sides. They were obviously getting close to the City.

The truck slowed, not much, but it did reduce its speed a little bit in respect for the fact that the Eastern Coastal Highway had given way to the streets of La Navidad. The driver continued to hug the coast by going down Harbor Street. When Dave began seeing buildings and fountains he had passed so many times on his "walks" to gather information in La Navidad, he rapped on the back of the cab. The breaks squealed. The truck did come to a halt, but not for long, just long enough for him to hop down. The old truck was so tall that the impact of his jump was such that he had to pitch himself forward on his hands to break his fall. As he scrambled to his feet, he could hear the truck chugging on down the street. He waved to the farmer, but he had no idea whether this gesture of gratitude had actually been observed or not.

Two different feelings competed within him as he regained an upright position. They were excitement and, yes, fatigue. It had been a long, long day in the spy business! He set himself with a sigh to the task ahead and began plodding up the steep hill to Elena's apartment.

A wave of anxiety swept over him after he had gone a block or so. He had been gone less than two days, and yet a lot can change in forty-eight hours. Would Elena still want him? Would she be cross with him for having disappeared as he had done? No, he reassured himself, she would understand. He could explain. He had to believe that things would be for them just as they had been, perhaps better in that he could now be completely honest with her.

He trudged on.

He could see in the moonlight that the entrances to the public buildings had been sandbagged. Guns had been placed behind the defensive perimeters that had been constructed with the sandbags. Soldiers patrolled the streets. It reminded him of the movies he had seen about London during the Blitz. His tiredness made him giddy enough to almost expect to see Mr. Churchill come around the next corner in his "siren suit," black cane in hand. He pulled his cap further down toward his eyes, hoping to avoid recognition, should anyone care, and he pushed himself forward, up the hill.

At last he was at her door. He removed the key from his pocket, the one he had run his fingers over so many times during the last two days in his efforts to make himself feel better when he had missed Elena, when he feared that "they" would stop him from returning to her, and inserted it into the lock. Breathlessly, he watched as the door swung open.

Everything within looked the same.

He walked softly through the sitting room and stood at the open door of the bedroom.

Elena's hair hung over one corner of the twisted sheet, glistening in the moonlight.

He sat on the edge of the bed and after an appreciative, almost reverent pause, he stroked her bare shoulder.

She moaned and then seemed to shake herself. "Ah . . . Oh, Dave," she said in relief, pulling his hand to her chest. "I was so worried," she said as she threw her arms around him.

"I was a bit worried myself," he replied with characteristic understatement.

Suddenly, she put her hands on his shoulders and pushed herself back a bit from him. Her eyes widened as she announced, "Oh, Dear, they're looking for you."

"Who?"

"Everyone—our Security Force, and there's an urgent message for you from the States they gave me." She pointed to a note written on a police incident report on her bedside table.

Dave recognized the number he was to call as that of "Eastern Mining."

"They're not happy with me," he said by way of explanation. "I guess no one is."

"I am, if it matters," she said, moving a hand to the back of his neck.

Dave bowed his head slightly while trying to control his emotions. He mumbled, "It matters very much."

Elena tilted her head in that way of hers. *"Mira,"* she began softly, "you once asked me to go away with you. Might you consider staying here with me? I could call Roberto. He realizes you've never attempted or intended to harm us. I'm sure . . . ," she allowed her voice to trail off as she looked at him intently with her soft brown eyes.

"He looked back at her lovingly and then up toward the ceiling. "I'd better return the call," he finally said in a voice full of fatigue.

They kissed desperately as the call went through. Elena's eyes were searching and moist.

He was connected with Frank Weatherby again, but he had a different voice on this occasion. There were the preliminaries about hating to be the bearer of bad news, etc., but "Frank's" basic message was that his mother was seriously ill. That didn't upset Dave at all. Had his mother really been sick, an entirely different set of codes would have been used to tell him. When he failed to ask the questions which would have brought forward his instructions, the voice on the other end, obviously annoyed, blurted out, "You'd better come home."

Dave looked into Elena's face. His hands trembled slightly. After a few seconds hesitation, he spoke slowly into the mouthpiece. "How can I? That's where I am."

He put the handset back on its cradle and handed the entire telephone to Elena. Softly, he said, "Please call Roberto for me."

# THE END